SPIRITS, PIES, AND ALIBIS

ALSO BY NICOLE ST CLAIRE

Don't miss the entire Witches of Pinecroft Cove series of paranormal cozy mysteries!

Spirits, Pies, and Alibis

Covens, Cakes, and Big Mistakes*

Magic, Lead, and Gingerbread*

*Coming soon

Visit NicoleStClaire.com to discover more titles coming soon!

SPIRITS, PIES, AND ALIBIS

THE WITCHES OF PINECROFT COVE BOOK ONE

NICOLE ST CLAIRE

Apple Blossom Press
Bolton, MA

Spirits, Pies, and Alibis
The Witches of Pinecroft Cove Book One
Copyright © 2019 Nicole St Claire

Developmental Editing by Em Stevens
Edited by Kelly Hashway
Proofread by Paula Proofreader
Cover Design by: Victoria Cooper

Find out more: www.NicoleStClaire.com
Contact the author: Nicole@NicoleStClaire.com

ISBN: 9781078368735

Apple Blossom Press
PO Box 547
Bolton MA 01740

CHAPTER ONE

It was the first day of summer, and the air along the Southern Maine sea coast was as thick and fishy-smelling as a bowl of New England clam chowder. As I pulled into the parking lot of the ferry terminal and followed the bright red painted stripe on the pavement to the waiting area for the service to Summerhaven Island, I held out hope for a cool ocean breeze to come along and make the temperature bearable. My hopes were quickly dashed. People used to tell me I lived a charmed life, but recently it was like I'd been enrolled in a crash course for crushed dreams. If I hadn't known better, I would have sworn I was under a curse.

I reached across to the passenger seat and picked up the letter my great-aunt Gwen had sent. Yes, a real letter. Pretty retro, right? And as letters went, this one was even more old school than most. It had been written in scrawling cursive with real ink from a fountain pen. The stationery was heavy and bore the logo of the Pinecroft Inn, a house that had been in my mother's family for generations and which my great-aunt had recently turned into a bed and breakfast.

Dear Tamsyn, the letter began, *I know it's been a few years since we've been in touch.*

A few? Try fifteen. I know because that was the last time I'd stepped foot on the island. That summer had started with the death of my grandmother, and by the end of it, my mother had vanished, and I'd been shipped off to Ohio for my father and stepmother to raise. I'd basically spent the worst summer of my life in Pinecroft Cove and had certainly been in no hurry to return.

I'd like to invite you to spend the summer with me, the letter continued, *learning the ins and outs of running a bed and breakfast. If it goes well, you may even decide you'd like to stay.*

Here's the funny thing. Under any other circumstances, if I'd received a letter like this from a great-aunt I could barely remember, who hadn't sent so much as a birthday card my entire life, I probably would have laughed and tossed it into the trash. Drop everything and travel halfway across the country to help her run her inn? Talk about presumptuous. After all, I was a successful woman with a college degree and a solid career as an accountant. I worked my butt off for my company and was pretty sure I had a promotion on the horizon. Plus, I'd just poured most of my savings into the first and last months' rent and security deposit for a great apartment I was about to move into with my boyfriend, Greg. What did I need with some crazy old aunt and her bed and breakfast in Maine? My life was just about perfect.

Only, this is the part where it gets weird. Like, really weird. Remember what I said earlier about feeling cursed? This was why. The very same morning that letter arrived, I walked into my office to find out my company was up and moving to Los Angeles. Just like that, I was out of a job. They didn't even give me the option to relocate. I'd say being laid off was the biggest shock of my life, except *that* particular distinction goes to what happened a few hours later when I called to share the bad news about my job with Greg.

See, Greg's an artist, but the real money in the art world goes to the gallery owners, which is why I'd spent a year helping him figure out how to get in on the action. Well, when I called, I let him know we were going to need to pull the trigger on the opening a little sooner than planned. That's when he told me the gallery had never been his idea, and that he'd decided to move into that fantastic apartment, which I'd paid for, with some other woman. A woman, who supported his dreams. I told him dreams don't pay the bills. He said I'd never understood that he was a real artist and then promised to pay me back all the money

I'd spent on the place, just as soon as one of the paintings he had on display at the local coffeehouse sold.

Yeah, I know. I'm not holding my breath.

In one day, after years of working to build the perfect life, I found myself single, unemployed, and about to be homeless, with every possession I owned stuffed in boxes all around me and no idea what I was going to do. Suddenly, Aunt Gwen's letter was like an answer to a prayer. I packed up Miss Josephine and headed out the next week.

Miss Josephine's a car, not a cat, just in case there was any confusion. I've never been the sort to want pets. Never really wanted an ancient brown station wagon, either. Yes, brown. That was exactly how old my hand-me-down Volvo was. It was manufactured back in the day when brown was a color people honestly thought cars should come in. Before I was born, my father drove her off the lot with just seven miles on her odometer. He never so much as missed an oil change, as he took immense pleasure in reminding me after he'd offered me the car, and I'd responded by asking him how he could possibly think I would want to drive such an ugly old thing. I was saving up for a new car, I'd told him, something befitting a soon-to-be junior partner at the second-largest accounting firm in Cleveland. But I'd changed my tune quickly enough when I lost my job and realized the appeal of a vehicle that hadn't required a car payment since the Reagan administration.

When the twenty-first of June rolled around, I'd hit the road early and was already a couple hours outside the city by the time the sun came up. As luck would have it, the sunrise coincided almost to the second with when the air-conditioner stopped working. And remember that part about being cursed? Perhaps it wouldn't surprise you to know the meteorologist on the radio said it was the hottest start to a summer in over a decade. What with the open windows and the humidity, not to mention the eight-hundred-mile drive I made in a single day. By the time I hit the Maine border, any hair that hadn't plastered itself to my neck had turned into a halo of bright red frizz around my head. I was exhausted and more than a little cranky, but with my final destination only an hour away, just a fifteen-mile trip across Penobscot Bay, I held out hope that it would be clear sailing from here.

Once again, I'm aware that when it comes to holding out hope for things, I don't have a great track record.

I looked back down at the letter in my hand, focusing on the instructions I'd been given in the last paragraph. *The ferry to the island can be busy this time of year,* she'd warned me, *but if you park in line overnight after the final ferry departs, you should be able to get one of the unreserved spots the next morning.*

Despite my aunt's crowd warning, the parking lot appeared deserted. A seagull cawed from the top of a post, and a shaggy black cat prowled the rocky shoreline, probably searching for an unsuspecting critter to have for dinner. The last ferry of the day was still at the dock but almost ready to go, or at least I thought it was, as I could see a worker in a brightly-colored vest who had just started to close the safety gate. Confident I had followed all the directions I'd been given, down to the last letter, I switched off Miss Josephine's engine, leaned back in my seat, and shut my eyes. Exhaustion had turned every muscle in my body into a lead weight, and I was certain I would sleep soundly until morning.

Aunt Gwen's letter hadn't been specific about what I should do with my time between dropping off the car in the evening and setting sail on the dawn ferry. She'd probably assumed I would call a taxi and find a nearby motel for the night, maybe grab a bite to eat at a local restaurant for good measure. That would have been a fine plan, except that, unlike my aunt, I happened to know what my checking account balance was. Let's just say it wasn't pretty. Miss Josephine and I would be fine in the parking lot until morning. As for dinner, I had a granola bar in my backpack to tide me over, the crunchy type that I always thought was more filling because it took longer to chew.

My eyes had only been closed a minute when a tapping on the windshield sent them flying open again. I sat up straight, overcome with a sense of guilt even though I was pretty sure I hadn't done anything wrong. A man stood beside the driver's side window, his neon-yellow vest identifying him as the same ferry worker who had been closing the gate a moment before.

"Uh, excuse me, miss?" he said, his lilting accent pegging him as a lifetime Mainer.

"Am I not allowed to park here?" I asked, not sure what I would do if the answer was no. I grabbed Aunt Gwen's letter and held it up for him to see. "I was told it would be okay, that I should park in the line overnight and wait for the first ferry in the morning."

"You're okay to park," the man told me. "It's just I thought you might want to know you've got some smoke coming out of the tailpipe of your car. Saw it when you turned into the lot."

That thread I'd been hanging on to hold me upright until I reached the island snapped at the news, and my whole body slumped like a marionette with cut strings. "You've got to be kidding me. My father's mechanic just gave Miss Josephine a perfect bill of health three days ago."

"Well, she's an old one," he pointed out diplomatically. "Things can change quickly."

"Peas and rice!" I exclaimed, and yes, I did actually say it in those words. I'd made a bet with my friend Bailey when we were in college that I could go the longest without swearing. At six years, eight months, and thirteen days, I'd more than proven my point, but my make-believe cuss words were second nature now. "Please tell me there's a mechanic over there, because

I can't afford to stick around on the mainland to have her fixed."

"Larry Sloane's your guy. He's got a shop out by Cabot Field, and his prices are fair."

"Thanks," I said, trying not to worry too much over the fact that just because prices were fair didn't mean they were low. Worst-case scenario, I'd be doing a lot of walking this summer.

"You're headed to the Pinecroft Inn?" As the man pointed to the letterhead, there was a shift in his expression that I couldn't quite read, and it put me on edge.

"My great-aunt runs the place, and I'm going to help her for the summer?" For some reason, though it was one hundred percent true, my statement came out as a question. My self-confidence always plummeted when I felt nervous, a trait that drove me nuts.

To my relief, he broke into a grin. "Why, you must be Tamsyn!"

I blinked. "That's me. How did you—?"

"Miss Gwyneth's been talking all week about her niece visiting, although I could've sworn she said you'd be gettin' in tomorrow."

"I am arriving tomorrow. That is, I'm just parking here tonight so I can get a spot for my car on the first ferry in the morning."

"Did you not call ahead for one of the reserved spots?"

I shook my head. "I tried, but I was told they're completely booked until the middle of July."

"Ayuh, that'll happen. Summerhaven's become a real popular tourist destination these past few years, since the condos went in." He glanced back at the ferry, which had yet to depart from the dock, possibly because he hadn't actually finished shutting the gate and raising the ramp. "Tell you what. Give me a minute. I think I can squeeze you on."

"What, on this one? Tonight?" I flashed him a grateful smile. I might have been resigned to sleeping in the parking lot, but I hadn't exactly been looking forward to it. After weeks of rotten luck, finally something was going my way. "That's really kind of you."

He waved his hand dismissively, but I could've sworn the man's cheeks turned three shades of pink. "I wouldn't do it for just anyone, but Miss Gwyneth makes the best blueberry pie I've ever tasted, with those little berries that grow wild on the island. Maybe if you just let her know that Walter at the pier helped you out…"

"You got it, Walter. I'll make sure she's got a whole blueberry pie with your name on it, even if I have to beg."

Walter hurried back to the ferry, and I watched as one by one, the last row of cars backed off the boat, traveled partway down the ramp, then pulled back onto the deck in a tighter configuration. Sure enough, by the time the last car was in place, there was room for one more. He waved me on board.

"Thank you again," I called through the open window as I slowed to a crawl and maneuvered Miss Josephine into the narrow spot. "That was like magic, how you made the space appear." A funny look crossed his face when I said the word *magic*, but it was gone in an instant.

After fourteen hours of driving, my legs ached with the need to stretch. I eased myself out of the car as soon as the boat was underway, pulling my phone from my pocket so I could give Aunt Gwen a call and let her know I would arrive ahead of schedule. As I turned toward the stairs that led to the upper deck, I found myself staring into the glinting, green eyes of a black cat, the same one I'd seen prowling around on shore, who was perched on top of the metal railing. My gut twisted as the ferry lurched into action with a bumping jolt that threatened to send the ragged creature right over the edge and into the water.

"Hey there, fella," I cooed as I inched toward the edge of the deck. "What are you doing here?"

The cat watched me with unblinking eyes, then lifted a paw and began to groom it with his pink tongue as if he weren't one careless move or oversized wave away from certain death.

"Why don't we get you somewhere safer?" I soothed, though as I've already mentioned, I'm not a cat person, so it probably wasn't very convincing. He lifted himself onto all four paws and arched his back. You don't have to be a cat lover to have a heart, and mine nearly stopped as one of his rear paws slipped. "Easy, buddy. You need to get down from there right now."

Without warning, his other leg slipped and now the cat dangled from the railing with nothing between him and the sea to break his fall while his back claws desperately sought purchase in the metal mesh that made up the ferry wall. He let out a plaintive mewl, and I cried out as I lunged, reaching toward him with both arms. At the same moment, he must have achieved a good grip with his claws, as he catapulted from the railing and came hurtling toward my head.

My arms flew up for protection, and the phone I'd forgotten I was holding slipped from my grasp and landed with a plop in a large puddle of salt water on the deck. The cat scampered beneath one of the cars and disappeared from sight. As I dropped to one knee to retrieve my waterlogged phone, I felt the waistband of my skirt come loose as the top button popped off and disappeared over the side of the deck. When I flipped the dripping phone over in my palm, the screen had gone dark, and it sported a spiderweb of cracks in the glass.

That rotten luck I'd been so sure was coming to an end? Turns out I was mistaken.

CHAPTER TWO

*A*s I made my way to the passenger cabin on the upper deck, I tried to remember how many years of bad luck having a black cat cross your path was worth. Seven? Thirteen? And then there was the phone. I mean, technically it wasn't a mirror, but I did often use the selfie function to check my hair and makeup, and the way things were going, it wouldn't surprise me if the universe decided to count the cracked screen against me. Even if it didn't, the stupid thing was still broken, and I couldn't afford to fix it.

What I needed at that moment was a strong cup of tea. At least I knew where I could get one. Every summer when I was growing up, after we'd made the drive up from Boston, where my mom and I lived, she would order an Earl Grey tea as soon as we boarded the ferry. Then we'd sit at a table by a window to watch the waves. I could almost taste the bergamot oil on my tongue after all these years, and the strength of the memory surprised me. Most of that period of my life was lost in shadows and mist. Once I'd settled into life in Cleveland with Dad, selective amnesia had been my best defense against the pain of unanswered questions surrounding her disappearance. I'd been determined to move on, not to let the mystery of her fate haunt me. For years, I'd assumed my efforts had succeeded, but my return to the island would be the ultimate test.

To my disappointment, I entered the cabin to discover the snack bar and tables were gone, replaced by two rows of wide seats covered in heavy, green vinyl upholstery and separated by a narrow aisle. The space looked remarkably similar to a 1950s' school bus and exuded about the same level of comfort, though thankfully it had a slightly better smell. I grabbed a seat near the window, second row from the back, and though the cabin was nearly full, I was lucky enough to find a spot where both seats were empty so I could stretch out. It would have been nicer if the view of the water wasn't mostly obscured by a thick layer of salt from the constant sea spray, but the last rays of evening sunshine that filtered through the grit were warm and soothing on my face as I rested my head against the glass.

Behind me sat two elderly women who, if their wire pushcarts overloaded with plastic bags were any indication, had spent a day shopping on the mainland.

They sported nearly identical hairstyles, that permed helmet shape that results from visiting the hair salon once a week for a wash and set. They may have been sisters, or perhaps best friends. The only discernible difference between the two of them was that one had snow-white hair while the other's was a surprising shade of lavender. I wondered if it was an intentional choice or the result of a salon-day calamity.

Exhaustion overtaking me once more, my breathing slowed, and my eyelids drifted shut. As if on cue, the two ladies chose that moment to start chatting. Based on their volume, I'd guess at least one of them was a little hard of hearing, but there was definitely nothing wrong with their lungs.

"Can you believe all these folks on the ferry today, Ellie?" one of them asked.

"I'll tell you, June, it seems to get more crowded every summer," the other replied. "It's those darned condos Doug Strong keeps building. Brings in the riffraff. It's no wonder Sheriff Grady's looking so haggard."

"Now, you know Joe Grady don't look so rough 'cause of workin'. He's been up all hours of the night having dinner, and going out dancing, and who knows what else with Sheila Briggs."

"You don't say! How'd you hear that?"

I stifled a laugh. There was no mistaking how jealous Ellie sounded that June had scooped her on the gossip. I had little doubt there was a constant battle between them to see who could get her nose deepest into other people's business. Of course, from what I recalled, the island was rife with gossips and snoops, as small towns often are.

"Oh, I have my sources. As for the condos, I don't think they're so bad. I mean, they're ugly as sin, but you can't deny they bring in good money," June argued. "Deirdre's shop was just about to close a few years back, and now she's hired two new workers just to keep up."

"Maybe so, but does that make up for how Doug treated Minnie?" I had no idea who Minnie was, nor Doug, but this sounded like it had the makings of a soap opera, and I'll admit, since it looked like I wasn't going to get that nap I'd been hoping for, I wouldn't have minded hearing more. Sadly, it seemed June already knew the details, as she responded with a disapproving grunt, and Ellie didn't elaborate.

"You seen Dr. Caldwell for that pain in your knee yet?"

I think it was June who asked this, although their island accents were equally thick, and I found it hard to distinguish one from the other.

"I've got a follow-up appointment on Monday."

"Oh, a follow-up?" The way she said it, I definitely detected teasing. "Since when do you spend money on follow-ups?"

"You can't be too careful with your joints!"

Whether it was June or Ellie, she was definitely getting defensive.

"No, not when your doctor looks like a young George Clooney."

I snorted loudly over this observation then tried to cover the sound by pretending to cough. I remembered Dr. Caldwell, and he wasn't exactly what I would describe as young and handsome. I mean, he might be what you'd call distinguished looking, but he'd already been graying at the temples fifteen years back. Then again, Ellie and June were probably close to eighty, so perhaps their perception of youth was relative.

Dr. Caldwell had a son, Noah. He'd been a couple years older than me, a soulful, angsty teen with a tragically geeky haircut and thick glasses. When I was thirteen, he wrote me a poem and tried to slip it into my pocket while waiting in line for ice cream, only some other boy had grabbed it and read it out loud so everyone could hear. The poem had described my hair as the color of carrots and then rhymed it with something about parrots, and long story short, I was instantly renamed Polly the Parrot Girl for the rest of the summer. If anyone ever wondered why I never wanted to move to the island, that story pretty much sums it up. I doubted Noah had stuck around long, either. I pictured him now with a hipster beard and flannel shirt, reading poetry on open mic night in one of those coffee shops where Greg tried to sell his paintings.

At this point, the ladies launched into a comparison of their assorted aches and pains, and I couldn't help noticing that my own bottom was still sore from so much sitting, so I stood and wandered outside to the observation deck. The wind was fierce, but after the intense heat I'd experienced for most of the trip, I was grateful to finally feel cool. Directly below me was the car deck, and my eye was immediately drawn front and center to a 1920s' roadster whose chrome trim glistened in the sun. I wasn't an expert on cars, but what I did know was *that* one was a beauty. Its body was painted a deep shade of green, and its soft convertible top was a rich dove gray. Why hadn't my father's taste in old cars run a little closer to that?

I could count about fifteen vehicles from where I stood, plus one full-sized parcel delivery truck. Until that moment, it had never occurred to me to question how deliveries were made to the island. Whatever I might have imagined, it would definitely not have been sticking a delivery truck on a boat; that's for sure. I watched, fascinated, as the driver wandered around the deck in his distinctive tan uniform, delivering packages from car to car. Each time he stopped, he would chat with the person inside for a while, and though they were too far down for me to hear, it was obvious they were all well acquainted.

Sometimes he would get to a car that was empty, the driver having left as I had to ride on one of the decks above. When that happened, the delivery man

would place the package inside the vehicle before
moving on, clearly confident that he knew the vehicle's
owner. It drove home just how small and close-knit
the island community was and made me wonder, with
a slight stab of panic, exactly how I was going to fit in
and if anyone would remember me. I might be a full-
grown adult now, but if anyone called me Polly and
asked if I wanted a cracker, I'd be lying if I said there
wasn't a good chance I would melt with embarrassment on the spot.

The sun hung low in the sky as the ferry
approached the Summerhaven dock. It was one of the
island's quirks that the sun set over the ocean, which
is a real rarity on the East Coast. I watched it from the
observation deck, a spot of glowing orange on the
horizon giving way to peaceful shades of purple and
gray overhead. It was dusk as I maneuvered Miss
Josephine up the ramp, the last car to leave the ferry.
When I'd crossed onto solid land, I pulled over and
tried once more to boot up my phone, but it was no
use. My early arrival would come as a complete
surprise to Aunt Gwen. I hoped she wasn't already
in bed.

As I drove along Main Street through Summerhaven's nineteenth-century downtown, it looked
unchanged from how I'd last seen it, yet somehow
nicer, too. The vaudeville-era theater had a newly-
restored neon billboard twinkling out front, the
carousel horse outside the old-fashioned soda fountain

had been freshly painted, and dozens of quaint shops and cafés had opened where, on my last visit, there had been only empty storefronts. People walked dogs across the lush green grass that carpeted the town square, and inside a whitewashed gazebo, a jazz band was setting up for a summer concert in the park. My busybody seat mates from the ferry had been right about one thing: quiet old Summerhaven appeared to be enjoying a significant renaissance.

The road forked just beyond the main drag. To the right, I saw a whole section of cookie-cutter buildings I'd never seen before. The street was packed with young people and families. Banners sponsored by beer companies that announced trivia nights and wet T-shirt contests rippled in the evening breeze. This was party central, for sure. I saw a large sign for the Strong Corporation, announcing new condos and vacation units for sale and lease. A scrawl of rude graffiti covered the logo, which was jarring. It seemed out of place on an island that in every other way looked like a picture-perfect movie set.

I made a note to come back another time to explore this new section of town before heading off in the opposite direction. My aunt's place was to the left. The crowds of vacationers thinned rapidly as the winding road hugged the edge of a jagged cliff overlooking the sea. It was the path that led to the exclusive neighborhood of Pinecroft Cove, where the money lived.

As the sun sank below the horizon, my view of the

road rapidly became obscured in inky darkness. Pinecroft Cove was one of those neighborhoods where an overzealous residents association, made up mostly of women with strong opinions and too much time on their hands, had for decades been passing ordinances against anything they considered an eyesore. This included streetlights. They claimed the darkness added historical ambience, but if you asked me, it just made things unnecessarily hard to see. Fortunately, the turnoff for my aunt's driveway was relatively easy to find. Since converting the old house to a bed and breakfast, she'd installed a tastefully carved wooden sign with gold lettering, illuminated by a single, no doubt committee-approved, low-wattage bulb.

As I made the turn, I heard the familiar crunch of the crushed-shell driveway beneath my tires. I slowed the car to a crawl as I rounded the sharp turns, then hit the brakes abruptly as a black shadow darted in front of the car. I couldn't tell for certain, but I thought I saw a flash of cat eyes before it was out of range of my headlights. What was it with me and cats all of a sudden?

Hands shaking on the steering wheel, I eased Miss Josephine the last few yards until the house came into view. Confusion washed over me. Beyond the tall trees at the end of the drive stood the same house I remembered from my childhood summers, with its gray cedar shingles, wide gambrel roof, and that wraparound porch where I had spent many a lazy afternoon curled up in a rocking chair with a good book. But in the middle of the expansive front lawn stood at least a dozen figures dancing around a roaring bonfire.

The women were clad in flowing white garments so sheer that the glow from the leaping flames revealed much more of the bodies underneath than perhaps the dancers had intended, giving the jarring impression that they wore nothing at all. Floral wreaths encircled their heads like crowns. Though none were young, they chanted and swayed with an almost childlike abandon.

One woman stood apart from the rest, beating a steady rhythm on a drum that hung around her neck. She was short in stature, her figure plump with rounded hips and belly. Her faded red hair was loose around her shoulders, framing her age-creased face in a frizzy haze. I touched a hand to my own head and knew mine looked the same. That family resemblance alone was enough to confirm it. Whoever these women were, my great-aunt Gwen was leading them.

CHAPTER THREE

"*T*amsyn, is that you?" Aunt Gwen froze mid-drumbeat and squinted into the night as the slamming of the car door alerted her to my presence.

"Yes, it's me. I'm sorry I didn't call to tell you I'd be early," I replied. "I had a phone issue."

"Oh, that's all right." Aunt Gwen hurried over to my car and welcomed me with a warm hug, which I returned in stunned silence. If she had a good explanation for why she was dancing around in front of the house like a crazy lady, wearing nothing but a flimsy cotton nightgown, she wasn't quick to share it.

"Walter at the ferry dock was able to squeeze me on at the last minute," I explained as I wrestled a suitcase from the back seat of the car.

"How very kind of him. I'll be sure to send him a pie in the morning."

"As a matter of fact, I kinda promised him one.

Blueberry." I shot her a suspicious glance once I finally I caught up, and the space between my shoulder blades tingled. "Did you read my mind?"

She took one of my lighter bags and, ignoring my protests, carried it right past the congregation of women, who were milling around and apparently not at all concerned that the lawn was on fire, all without her so much as acknowledging they were there. My aunt was much more sprightly than I'd expected, and I had to quicken my pace as she led me up the porch steps and through the front door.

Instead of answering my question about the mind reading, she remarked on the unpleasantly warm air that evening and inquired as to whether I'd encountered much traffic between Cleveland and here. She didn't seem to expect a response to her steady stream of chatter, which was good because I was in too much shock to give one. What bizarre ritual had I just witnessed? Just the word made the skin on the back of my neck prickle, conjuring up images of every horror movie I'd ever seen. If I'd arrived a few minutes later, would they have been sacrificing a goat? On the one hand, the thought seemed crazy, but on the other hand, it's not like I'd stumbled into the middle of a knitting circle. Whatever they'd been up to, odds were it was something creepy.

I entered the house in a daze, but not without noticing as we passed through the living room that the antique cream-upholstered sofa and armchairs were

still in the exact arrangement as they'd been fifteen
years before. I recognized the lace tablecloth on the
round coffee table as the one my grandmother had
crocheted. It sat atop the crimson-and-blue Persian rug
she and my grandfather had purchased on their honey-
moon. The woodwork gleamed with a soft sheen, and
the familiar smell of lemon and wax permeated the air.
The overwhelming sense of returning home surprised
me. I hadn't thought of this house in that way for
years.

After climbing the wide curving staircase to the
second floor, Aunt Gwen opened the door that
concealed the much narrower stairs that led to a small
bedroom that had been carved out of the third-floor
attic. Like the rest of the house, this room, too, had
been frozen in time. As I paused in the doorway to
catch my breath, I took in the room's familiar whitewashed dresser and nightstand, with their matching
blue-and-white fringed scarves on top. The twin-size
wrought iron bed, also painted white, where I had
always slept as a little girl, occupied the same space I'd
expected it to be, and the bright floral quilt my grandmother had stitched by hand still covered its top. For a
second time that night, an unexpectedly sweet sense of
nostalgia washed over me.

The closest we got to discussing the strange gathering I'd witnessed in the yard came when, after
wishing me goodnight, Aunt Gwen paused at the door
and gave me a thoughtful look. "We'll have a good,

long talk in the morning," she assured me. Oh yeah. She could count on it.

A million questions ran through my mind, but I had no energy to process them. Instead, I washed up as quickly as I could in the small adjoining bathroom, then stripped off my rumpled clothing, threw on a clean T-shirt and a pair of lightweight cotton pajama bottoms with a drawstring waist, and crawled into bed. In a matter of seconds, I plunged into a deep, dark sleep, devoid of dreams.

The next time I opened my eyes, I was immediately aware of two things. First, bright sunshine was streaming through the open window, along with a light morning breeze that brought with it a whiff of the wild roses that grew in the woods. Second, sometime during the night, a twenty-pound weight had been deposited on my chest as I slept. I cracked one eye open. A pair of green eyes stared back at me, unblinking, surrounded by a profusion of black fur. I struggled to sit up, but the enormous cat on my torso held me down.

"Hey!" I groused as I shook my shoulders from side to side. "Go on, now."

The cat let out a mournful bawl, and as recognition washed over me, I stared in disbelief.

"Wait. I know you." There was no doubt in my mind that it was the same cat from the ferry, the one whose daredevil antics made me break my phone. "You're my aunt Gwen's cat? How can that even be?"

He cried out again, mocking me, and didn't move an inch even as I gave the covers a jiggle.

"Listen, cat," I warned. He shook his head like a lion shaking its mane, and the fur billowed out wildly all around him. The twinkle of a brass name tag that hung from a collar around his neck caught my eye. I squinted at the letters engraved on it. "Gus. Is that your name?" He meowed loudly, which I took as a yes.

I gathered all my strength and propelled myself upward. Gus rolled off my chest and landed at the foot of the bed. He promptly began licking his hind leg as if that was exactly what he'd had in mind to do at that precise moment all along. "Let's get this straight," I informed him as I rose and smoothed the covers back into place. "This may be your house, but it's my bed, and I don't like to share. Especially not with a flea-bitten thing like you." The look he gave me as I left the room made it perfectly clear he had understood everything I said and simply had no intention of listening to a single word of it.

As I wandered across the second-floor landing, all the bedroom doors were shut, with the exception of the one that belonged to Aunt Gwen. The mouthwatering scent of cinnamon that permeated the air, along with the clattering of pots and pans, told me I'd find her in the kitchen, so I headed directly there by way of the back stairs. By the time I hit the first floor, the smell of my aunt's famous sweet-potato waffles was so thick in the air I could taste them when I breathed in.

"Good morning, Tamsyn," my aunt greeted me, turning from her spot at the stove. The whorl of red curls had been tamed into a bun, and a large apron covered her generous hips. She held something aloft in her right hand, and I had the oddest impression of sparkles emanating from it. For a moment, I could have sworn she was holding a magic wand, but it turned out to be an ordinary wooden spoon.

"Morning," I mumbled. Clearly, what I'd witnessed the night before was getting the better of my imagination.

Aunt Gwen smiled. "Waffles?"

"Yes, please," I answered, although there was hardly a need to since she'd already started to prepare my plate. I followed her to the dining room and took a seat at the long table. After tucking a cloth napkin into the T-shirt I'd worn to bed the previous night, I grabbed the jug of real maple syrup from the table and gave it a liberal pour.

Aunt Gwen sat beside me, angling her chair to face me. "Well?" she asked as I took my first bite.

"Mmm, so good," I assured her, my mouth too full to say more.

"It's a family recipe, you know."

I nodded. My grandmother had made the same waffles all through my childhood, and my mother sometimes, too. When it came to the women in my family, I was the only one the cooking bug had failed to bite. My stepmother used to like to say I was the only person she'd ever known who could burn water. Contrary to how it sounds, my stepmother was not an evil woman. We actually got along pretty well. I'm just legitimately that terrible of a cook.

"Speaking of recipes, Tamsyn, there's something I wanted to talk to you about."

I swallowed my bite of waffle and washed it down with a sip from the mug of tea that my aunt had somehow not only managed to set beside me when I wasn't looking, but had prepared exactly the way I liked, with milk but no sugar. "Recipes can wait. I want to know what was going on when I arrived last night."

Aunt Gwen laughed, which annoyed me just a little. I think I'd meant for my words to come out as a stern demand, but it turns out sternness is hard to muster when you have syrup dribbling down your chin.

"It all goes together," she assured me, though I didn't see how that could be. What did family recipes have to do with a houseful of wacky women setting fire to the grass? "Tell me, dear, have you ever had strange things happen to you, things you couldn't explain?"

"Strange things?" I snorted. "You mean like showing up at my grandmother's old house to find her sister and a bunch of strangers prancing around with torches, half-naked in the woods?"

"Young lady." Aunt Gwen managed to produce all the sternness I had lacked. "We were fully clothed."

"Trust me. From where I was standing, I saw plenty."

"Well, there were definitely no torches. It was a bonfire, to celebrate the solstice. You see"—she paused to take a deep breath—"I'm a witch."

"Cool."

She slumped a little, as if my response had stolen her thunder. "My dear, I don't think you understand. I'm trying to tell you I'm a witch."

"Uh-huh." I mean, what did she expect me to say? I'd kinda guessed that something witchy was afoot with the fire and the flowers and the prancing around to a drum. Besides, it was the twenty-first century. Even living in Ohio, it's not like I'd never met a Wiccan before. "That's awesome, Aunt Gwen. I'm really happy you've found a religion that works for you."

"You still don't get it." She twisted her lower lip and aimed a puff of air at some wisps of faded red hair that had fallen into her eyes. "Your mother was a witch. Your grandmother was a witch. *Our* mother before us was a witch... Are you starting to notice a pattern here?"

"I...thought Grandma was Episcopalian." As responses go, I'll admit it was lame, but now that she'd gone and brought the whole family into it, I was even more confused than I'd been the night before.

Aunt Gwen had the decency to chuckle before dropping the bombshell news. "Tamsyn, dear, *you* are also a witch. I don't mean it in a New Age kind of a way. Not that I have anything against that, mind you, but this is something a little different. The Bassett family is one of the last guardians of magic in Pinecroft Cove."

"But," I scoffed, "there's no such thing as magic."

Aunt Gwen rose and walked to the kitchen, and for a moment, I feared I had offended her. I hadn't intended to. Even though what she was saying was clearly nutty and hopefully her idea of a joke, I should have been more sensitive. I considered going after her to apologize, but before I was out of my seat, she'd returned. In her arms, she carried a massive book, and when she plopped it on the table beside me, dust rose from its pages.

"Do you know what this is?" she asked.

"The family recipe book," I replied. I'd seen my grandmother cook from it many times as a kid, and even if I'd forgotten what it was, the word *recipes* was embossed across the battered leather cover in flaking gold script.

"Not just a recipe book," she said solemnly. "This is a grimoire."

I frowned. "A grim what?"

"A book of magic, Tamsyn—our secret kitchen magic—which has been passed down from the Bassett family women for centuries. You see, the Bassetts are kitchen witches. This means we work our spells in the kitchen."

"No offense, Aunt Gwen," I said, eyeing the pleather binding skeptically, "but that book doesn't look much older than the seventies, and I'm talking *nineteen* seventies."

"Hmph." She fixed me with another one of her stern looks. "Even magical books need to be rebound from time to time. It doesn't mean the contents aren't mystical and ancient. As are these."

She placed two wooden spoons on the table beside the book. The handles were carved with an unusual design. I reached out to pick one up for a closer look, but her hand was on top of mine, lightning fast, holding it back. I frowned. "What? I just wanted to see."

"Not without proper instruction, my dear."

"I'm twenty-eight years old. I think I know how a spoon works."

"They're more than spoons, and until you've had some training, you mustn't touch them. I wouldn't want you to get hurt or cause anything to explode."

I drew my hand away, not sure how a spoon could make something explode but also not wanting to ask. My front teeth dug into my lower lip as it struck me that my great-aunt was one hundred percent serious about all of this. My heart sank. Had she suffered a stroke recently or possibly dementia? I was going to need to call Dr. Caldwell to find out. In the meantime,

I weighed whether it would be better to humor her or nip this craziness in the bud, but the look on her face was so sincere I didn't have the heart to tell her flat out that she was off her rocker. "Let's suppose for a moment that I believe you. What does this mean for me? You said I needed to be trained. Are you going to send me off to some sort of wizarding school?"

"Don't be ridiculous. This isn't a movie." She rolled her eyes, and I half hoped the next minute she would laugh the whole thing off as a practical joke. "You'll do your studies right here, of course, with the other members of your coven."

"My...what, now?" I knew what the word meant, and a new understanding began to dawn. "Is *that* who all those dancing women were, your coven?"

Aunt Gwen smiled. "That was more like a convention. Our guests have traveled here from all over New England to celebrate the solstice. No, a coven is more personal. That's the small group of witches you spend your time with and really get to know. You need at least three witches to form a proper coven. As a Bassett, that usually means teaming up with the Wolcotts and Hollings."

I knew the names well. Sue Ellen Wolcott and Bess Hollings had been my grandmother's closest friends ever since they were little girls. "You mean you think Aunt Sue Ellen and Aunt Bess are—"

"Witches. Yes, dear." She gave an indulgent nod, and suddenly, I felt like the slow kid in class who finally got an answer right. "Their granddaughters, Sybil and Cassandra, are just about the same age as you."

I thought for a moment, sifting through my hazy childhood memories of the summers I'd spent on the island. "I remember Sybil. We used to play together. I don't think I knew a Cassandra, though."

"No, she's a few years younger than you, so you might not have met. Anyway, both she and Sybil started showing undeniable signs of having the gift a few years back."

"Signs? What kind of signs?" Even through my considerable doubt, I gave a surreptitious glance to my bare forearms, as if the sign she was talking about might be visible, like a birthmark. I had three little moles on one shoulder that sort of formed a triangle. Could that be it?

Aunt Gwen placed a hand on my arm, as if she knew what I was thinking. "It's nothing you can see. Remember how I asked you before if you've experienced strange things, like knowing something before it happened?"

I shook my head. "But I never have."

"You've never picked up the phone before it rang or thought of a friend and a minute later they were standing at your door?"

"Never."

"That's impossible."

"Trust me, Aunt Gwen. A week ago, I was fired

from my job, and my boyfriend broke up with me. On the same day. If I was going to be seeing the future, you'd think that would have been a good time to start."

"A week ago?" For some unknown reason, Aunt Gwen's eyes sparkled.

"Yeah…" I paused, suspicion niggling at the back of my mind. "The exact same day your letter arrived. You didn't put some sort of hex on me to make that happen, did you?"

"Of course not." To her credit, her indignation seemed genuine. "We never do harm with our magic. But as it happens, I had a strong feeling the day I sent the letter that it was the right time to invite you."

"I'm sorry to disappoint you."

Aunt Gwen blinked. "Disappoint me how?"

"By not being a witch, like you'd thought."

To my great surprise, she laughed. "Oh, don't you worry. You're definitely a witch."

"But…" Even if I were willing to grant, for Aunt Gwen's sake, that witches were real, there was one thing I still knew for certain, and that was I was not one. How could I convince her of this? "You said the Bassetts are kitchen witches, right?"

"That's right." She gave the recipe book—excuse me, *grimoire*—a loving pat. "We work our spells in the kitchen, using food to create our magic."

There was one bite left of sweet potato waffle on my plate, and I popped it into my mouth. "I won't argue that you make a magical waffle, Aunt Gwen. But that's your proof, right there. I'm a lousy cook."

"No Bassett woman has ever been a lousy cook."

"Technically, I'm a Proctor. So maybe that's the issue."

"No, you're not. You're a Bassett." She picked up my plate and carried it to the kitchen. I followed behind her, still clutching my half-finished tea. "I was there when you were born, don't forget. I saw your mother fill out the birth certificate myself. Bassett women are *always* Bassetts. We never change our names for anyone."

"Maybe so," I argued, "but when I went to live with my father, he sorta changed it for me. Tamsyn Proctor. It says it right on my driver's license."

"That will never do," Aunt Gwen informed me with a sniff as she set the syrup-covered plate down in the sink. I hoped she would elaborate, but instead, she turned her head, shifting her attention to the makeshift pajamas I'd thrown on the night before, looking me up and down with an expression that said my taste in clothing, like my last name, was another thing that wouldn't do. "You did bring a nice dress, didn't you? There's a party at Doug Strong's house tonight, and we're expected to attend."

"Expected? But I just got here." The last word ended in a yawn, as if to highlight how tired I still was from my travels. A party sounded like sheer torture.

"Everyone from Pinecroft Cove was invited. It would be rude not to attend."

"I don't even know Doug Strong," I countered, though as soon as I said it, I realized I did know his name. I'd overheard it on the ferry. "Isn't he that real estate guy, the one with the condos?"

"Yes, that's him. He lives directly across the cove, at Cliffside Manor."

"Cliffside Manor?" As much as I had no desire to socialize, I'll admit, the mention of the massive estate that lay directly across the water from our house piqued my interest. I could see its roofline from the third-floor bedroom window, but as far back as I could remember, the old mansion had always been empty. The chance to see inside was tempting, but... "I still don't see why I have to go. It's not like I'm friends with him. We're not even acquaintances."

"No, but I believe you know his nephew Noah."

"Noah Caldwell?" My cheeks prickled with the remembered mortification of the Polly the Parrot incident. "Haven't seen him in years."

"Well, you'll see him tonight." There was a certain twinkle in her eyes that made me think she'd misunderstood the reason for my scarlet cheeks.

My hand shook as I set my mug on the counter. Just how many of the people I'd known as a child were still around, and what exactly was I getting myself into by returning? "I'm surprised he's still here. He always swore he was going to leave this island and never look back."

"He's Dr. Caldwell now, the island doctor. He took over the practice when his father retired."

Noah Caldwell, writer of angsty poetry, with his crooked bowl-cut hair and Coke-bottle glasses, had become a doctor? I swear to you, the lightest breeze would have knocked me over on the spot. "He used to have the biggest crush on me," I admitted, without giving any thought to the consequences.

"Did he? He's the most eligible bachelor on Summerhaven Island, you know." My aunt had one of those cat-who-caught-the-canary smirks on her face when she said it, which made me realize she'd missed the epic eye roll that had accompanied my statement. I recognized the look immediately as the one older relatives get when they stumble upon a matchmaking opportunity for an unsuspecting young person, and it didn't take a witch's mind-reading powers to figure out what she was thinking. Heaven help me.

CHAPTER FOUR

*I*n as many minutes as it took to eat a waffle, I'd been told I was descended from a long line of witches, I was expected to go to a party that night at a millionaire's mansion, and the awkward kid who'd had a crush on me but was now a handsome doctor would be there, along with the two other members of the coven I was supposed to join. Was it any wonder the moment I'd put my dishes in the dishwasher, I went to my bedroom to hide?

I did a belly flop onto my bed before realizing that the quilt was covered in a thin layer of long black cat fur that flew into the air upon impact and tickled my nose. If it hadn't been for that, I might have started to believe Gus was a figment of my overactive imagination. I mean, come on, a black cat who keeps showing up and causing trouble right when you find out you're supposed to be a witch? Talk about a cliché. Next thing

I knew, he was going to start talking or something. I swept the corners of the room with my eyes, but the little devil was nowhere to be seen.

I stretched out and pretended to read, but mostly I just tried not to think about all the craziness I'd had dumped on me. The only thing that kept me from losing it completely was that I was absolutely certain witchcraft was make-believe. Even so, I was rattled, and for good reason. My summer on the island was supposed to be a much-needed chance to relax and regroup. Instead, I was facing the very real possibility that I would have to have my elderly aunt committed. Was I getting in over my head?

After a while, I heard the doors on the second floor opening and closing as the rest of the guests in the house began to stir. If I'd had any plans to venture back downstairs, they were quickly put aside. All things considered, the last thing I needed at the moment was to end up in the middle of a witch convention.

Aunt Gwen seemed to understand because she left me alone until lunchtime, at which point there was a tap on my door. When I opened it, she stood outside my room, holding out a plate.

"Thought you might be getting hungry," she said. "It's ham and Swiss."

"My favorite." Of course, it was. She had no reason to know that, yet she did, like she was some kind of witch or something. It must have been a lucky guess.

"Oh, Tamsyn," she said, stopping after she'd made it a few steps down the stairs. "Could you be a dear and check the attic for some extra blankets when you get a chance?"

"Blankets?" I laughed. The heat wave was still going strong, and I had a sheen of sweat on my neck and brow to prove it. "You've got to be kidding."

"Storm's coming."

"Not according to the forecast." I grabbed my phone from my pocket to double-check my trusty weather app but was met with the broken screen.

"What happened to your phone?" she asked, holding out her hand.

"A mishap on the ferry." I handed her the phone with a shrug. "It fell in a puddle, and now it won't work."

"I'll see what I can do to fix it."

"How?" I asked, my insides growing jittery. What was she planning to do, cast a spell?

"Rice."

I frowned. "Magical rice?"

She raised an eyebrow. "No, Uncle Ben's. You put the phone in a bag of uncooked rice, and it pulls the moisture out."

I cringed and felt the heat rise in my face. I should have known what she'd meant by rice. What was wrong with me today? There was nothing I hated more than saying something dumb.

"Don't forget the blankets," she said as she headed down the stairs. "We're going to need them."

I wasn't sure about the temperature dropping, but the way she spoke about it with such certainty did send a chill down my spine. A case of the willies wasn't quite as good as a blast of cold air-conditioning, but it was a close second. And let's just say that venturing into the attic of a house that had been gathering junk since the 1890s did nothing to minimize my day's creepiness factor.

The attic door was just down from my bedroom, at the end of the hall. Now, as spooky attics went, I would say the one at the old Bassett house might score around a six out of ten. On the one hand, it was filled to the brim with all your basic Hollywood horror movie props: dusty steamer trunks, wicker baby carriages, and at least one dress form that, if you saw it out of the corner of your eye, looked like a floating body with no head. On the other hand, the space had a light, and it wasn't one of those bare lightbulbs with a dangling cord hanging from it, but a proper switch that controlled an overhead lamp. Plus, all the newer items that had been stored there, including the blankets I'd been sent to find, were in clear plastic bins close to the door. There's nothing scary about that. Also, there were none of those disturbing porcelain dolls that look like they've been possessed by a demon. You know the ones I mean. So, no, I wouldn't opt to sleep in the attic overnight, but I wasn't breaking into a cold sweat just by being there, either. Not quite.

It took no more than a few seconds to spot the bin I needed. Aunt Gwen must have been feeling particularly well organized when she'd stored them, because each one was clearly labeled on all four sides and the top as well. I could have left right then, except after I'd pushed the blankets into the hallway, but before I'd turned off the light, I heard a sound like a rolling or a scraping coming from the far end of the cavernous space.

Yes, I know. This is the part where, if I had been watching it in a movie, I would've started yelling at myself to run. I even thought that exact thing at the time as I stood there and weighed what to do next. Of course, I didn't run. I did what all the dumb heroines do and took a few steps in the direction of the noise. So next time you watch one of those films and smugly think you'd be smarter, trust me, you wouldn't be.

Immediately, I detected the scent of roses, like what I'd smelled that morning in my bedroom, but stronger and more concentrated. It struck me as odd since it was an enclosed area with no open windows, and I couldn't imagine where it was coming from. I went deeper into the space, and it was when I was about halfway to the other end that it occurred to me once more what a terrible idea this was. I'd heard scraping and rolling in an attic? Forget ghosts and chainsaw killers. There was about a ninety-percent chance I was going to stumble upon a mouse. Or a rat. I shuddered and turned toward the door, but a black shadow stopped me in my path. My heart pumped like mad as my blood turned to ice water in my veins.

"Meow," said the shadow.

"Gus?" I gave a shaky laugh as two shining green eyes peeked out from behind a trunk. "You nearly gave me a heart attack, you bad cat." Remember when I said I had no interest in owning a cat? Now you know why.

I walked toward him, moving to scoop him up and carry him out, but he was too quick for me and ran toward the door. Instead of following, I went to investigate the trunk where he'd been hiding and quickly discovered the source of the rose scent. The trunk lid was open, and an old perfume bottle had been knocked over. The last few drops of its highly fragrant contents had dribbled down the side of the trunk. If I had to blame someone for this accident, my money was on Gus.

I removed the upset bottle, set it on the floor, and peered into the trunk. It was filled with clothing, and with mild curiosity, I pulled out the top piece. It was a gold silk dress, sleeveless like something you'd wear to a fancy evening party, with intricate beading. While I didn't know much about vintage styles, it looked like something a flapper might have worn, and it was very high quality even to my untrained eye. I longed to pull out the rest and see what they looked like, but I hesitated. Some of the fabrics looked delicate, and I was uncertain if touching them would be harmful. With a sigh, I pulled my hand back and closed the lid of the trunk to keep the dust off. I would have to ask Aunt Gwen later if she knew anything about them.

As my eyes were drawn along the oily trail the perfume had left, my gaze came to rest on the spot where the bottle's glass stopper had fallen onto the rough pine floor. Next to the stopper, and partially obscured beneath the trunk, was a short length of dull silver metal. At first, I thought it might be a coin or religious medal, but when I grabbed it and gave it a gentle tug, several additional links emerged, and I realized I was holding a bracelet. It was dirty, but the overall design was beautiful, and I could just make out some engraving on a few of the links. Intrigued, I fastened it around my wrist for safe keeping before I made my way back to the hallway. I grabbed the blankets and then went straight downstairs, partially with the thought of delivering the bin to my aunt as she had requested but also with the intention of cleaning up my newly discovered treasure.

When I met Aunt Gwen in the kitchen, she was adding a final glass of thick red liquid to a serving tray. I regarded her with squinty-eyed suspicion. "What do you have there?"

"Secret potion," my aunt replied with a wink.

"Really?" My pulse ticked higher, and my throat

constricted. Potions? I was so not ready for the conversation to turn in that direction again so soon.

"My world-renowned hair of the dog potion." I must still have looked half terrified because Aunt Gwen laughed and added, "Bloody Marys. Some of the ladies over imbibed last night and are having a hard time getting going today, so I whipped up a little something to help out." As if to strengthen her case for them being nothing but harmless cocktails, she grabbed a handful of celery stalks and plunked one in each glass.

"Ah, right." I let out a breath, which I hadn't realized I'd been holding. If I was going to survive this stay with my aunt, I was going to need to develop a much better sense of humor about all things witchy and magical—and quick. "Do you have any silver polish?"

"There's baking soda in the pantry, or I might have something stronger in one of the cupboards. What are you trying to clean?"

I held out the wrist with the bracelet on it for her to see. "I found it up in the attic. Do you know anything about it?"

After examining it for a moment, Aunt Gwen shook her head. "I've never seen it before. How about you take those drinks out to our guests while I look for something that might work."

"Uh," I replied. It was the best I could manage. The moment I'd looked at the tray of Bloody Marys, a lump formed in my throat. It hadn't occurred to me before to wonder how that particular cocktail got its name. Now I knew. It looked like blood. I swallowed uncomfortably. I'd just been tasked with delivering goblets of blood to a room full of witches. Was this really my life?

No feeling sorry for yourself, Tamsyn, I chided myself silently. *Your life may be in shambles, but you have a job to do at the inn, and you need to do your best at it.* I straightened my shoulders and picked up the silver tray, trying to keep my hands from shaking as I walked through the dining room toward the living room, where they had assembled. Did all the women in there really believe they could turn people into frogs by waving magic wands? And, if so, was I going to need to get a psych consult for the whole house?

As I entered the room, I honestly was not sure what I expected a gathering of self-proclaimed witches to look like in their downtime. Like, when they weren't dressed specially for a ritual, what did they wear to relax in? I pictured a room filled with old crones in pointy hats and shiny black shoes with big brass buckles. Maybe green skin, too. What I got was the most ordinary collection of middle-aged women I could've imagined. I'll admit, it was kind of a letdown.

Contrary to my imagination, not a single one of them had a wart on her nose, a broomstick at her side, or a cat on her lap. Gone were the white robes, floral wreaths, and flowing hair from the night before.

Instead, the women wore yoga pants and T-shirts with slogans on them that proclaimed their interest in topics that mostly ranged from books to wine, or a combination of the two. Their graying hair was caught up in messy buns. Those who weren't napping were reading, except for a few who were knitting. They wore reading glasses. Reading glasses! If they had any true magical powers at all, wouldn't they at least fix their eyesight?

Deflated but no longer the least bit intimidated, I cleared my throat. "Would anyone like a drink?"

There were grateful murmurings all around, and I began to circle the room, holding out the tray. As each guest took a glass, I kept one eye on a woman who sat in the corner, playing a game of solitaire. She was very much unlike the rest. This woman appeared to be older than the other guests by about a decade, though her long, pure silver hair was somewhat at odds with her more youthful-looking skin. I found myself unable to say for certain whether she was barely sixty or well over eighty years of age. One thing I did know was that, dressed from head to toe in black linen, this witch looked the part.

When everyone else had been served, I approached her with the final drink balanced on the tray in front of me. "Would you like a Bloody Mary?"

She plunked down a couple of cards before looking up, and as I studied them, I realized this wasn't a regular pack of playing cards. The backs had an intri-

cate design of moon and stars, and the faces had
pictures of things like cups and swords instead of the
more typical hearts or spades.

I took the cocktail from the tray and held it out to
her. "Last one."

As she reached out, the hand brushed against the
silver bracelet on my wrist. Her face settled into a deep
frown. "That doesn't belong to you."

I swallowed, unnerved. "I found it in the attic a few
minutes ago."

"Sit down, and I'll read your cards."

I shook my head. "No, I don't really think—"

"You don't want to see your future?"

I squeezed my eyes shut, suddenly remembering
the sight of all these women in their see-through
nighties. I'd seen my future then, all right, and it
wasn't pretty.

"The tarot is a powerful tool, child," she prodded.

"I'm sure it is, but it's really not my thing."

She shrugged and took a sip of her drink. "Suit
yourself. May I take a closer look at that bracelet?"

I eyed her nervously but eventually stuck out my
hand. "I guess so."

She ran her index finger over each tarnished link. "I
see the letter L and an airplane."

"See them, you mean the engraving?" I took my
hand back and squinted at the bracelet but couldn't
make out anything. For a silver-haired woman, she

sure had good eyesight. No reading glasses for her, so maybe she had a touch of real magic after all.

"That's not exactly the type of seeing I meant. Here." She pulled a card from the velvet bag on the table and handed it to me. It had the same design on the back that her tarot cards did. At first I thought she was giving me one of them, but when I flipped it over, I saw that the name Madame Alexandria was written across the top in fancy script, and there was a phone number and address for a shop on the mainland.

"A business card?"

"I know you think you don't need me," she said, and I tried not to laugh out loud. Didn't think I needed her, huh? It hardly took a psychic to pick up on that. "Keep it anyway, and call when it's time."

"Yeah. Sure." I shoved the card in my pocket, hoping it would humor her long enough for me to get away before the interaction became any weirder than it already was.

"Promise me, Tamsyn."

I nodded then spun around and headed as quickly as I could for the stairs. She only looked like a witch, I reminded myself as I dashed across the second-floor landing and took the stairs to my bedroom two at a time. I knew this was true, because witches and magic weren't real. They weren't real. They weren't. Even so, I couldn't shake the coldness that had overtaken me when she'd looked me in the eyes and said my name as if she could see into my soul.

CHAPTER FIVE

$\mathcal{I}$t was late in the afternoon when my aunt called upstairs to remind me of the party at Cliffside Manor. Just what I needed, a daunting event where dozens of virtual strangers would be sure to ask, "So, what do you do for a living?" Yeah, my unemployed self was really looking forward to that social gem. But, having already tried once, I knew I couldn't back out of going, so I rummaged through one of the suitcases I'd brought up the night before and found what I hoped would be a suitable outfit for the occasion. It was a wraparound dress with spaghetti straps, in white knit jersey with navy blue stripes that gave it a nautical appearance. It wasn't fancy, but it was the best I could do on short notice.

When I entered the living room, my aunt's quick review of my ensemble earned an approving nod. "You'll want a sweater," she told me.

"It's almost ninety degrees," I said with a laugh and followed her to her car without heeding her advice.

The evening was in full swing as Aunt Gwen and I made our way past Cliffside's intricate wrought iron gate and up the tree-lined avenue to the front door, which stood open wide to receive guests. The sound of laughter, clinking glasses, and a live jazz band drifted through the open doors of a house that could have come straight from the pages of *Architectural Digest*. I'd seen it from a distance but had never been inside. As far as I knew, the house had been unoccupied for decades, but apparently, Douglas Strong had staked his claim and restored it to its former glory.

Compared to other parts of the island, houses in Pinecroft Cove had a reputation for being large and stately. Most of them had sprung up during the Gilded Age, built as summer cottages for wealthy New Yorkers who were always trying to outdo one another. How my own family had ended up living in one, I have no idea, because we were never part of the upper crust. But compared to its neighbors, Cliffside Manor was in a league of its own. It had been modeled after a chateau in France and hovered at the edge of the island's jagged tip like an imperial presence lording it over the rest of us, surrounded on three sides by the sea. I could see the chateau's high mansard roof and towering turrets from my bedroom window, and the beam from the lighthouse that sat on the edge of the estate could be seen as far away as the mainland on a clear night.

As I entered the house for the very first time, I stopped dead in the massive foyer, my mouth agape. To my right, a marble staircase swept in a graceful curve, like something Cinderella would lose a shoe on while running down it at the stroke of midnight. The steps were wide enough that five adults could easily walk down them side by side, and they were cushioned with a thick carpet that looked like red velvet. Ahead of me, at least a hundred people filled the great hall, a room made completely of marble and carved throughout with sea serpents and mermaids. In the center of the room was a fireplace large enough to stand in, and hanging above it in a place of honor was a life-size painting of a distinguished-looking man with sandy-blond hair that had grayed slightly at the temples. His suit and tie were modern in style, so this was not a portrait of a long-dead ancestor, and I assumed it must be our host, Douglas Strong.

I clutched Aunt Gwen's arm as we made our way into the crowded room, and she gave my hand a pat, seemingly unfazed by our surroundings. I wasn't sure if that was because she'd visited before, or just that it was a lot harder to be intimidated by things when you honestly believed yourself to be a witch.

Moments after we'd entered, we were greeted by a man with the type of preppy good looks that were usually confined to the glossy pages of a *Vineyard Vines* catalog. His blond hair had been tousled to exactly the correct degree to project a carefully calculated sense of casualness, and he wore immaculately pressed khaki trousers, boat shoes without socks, and a button-down shirt that anywhere else on the planet would be described as pink but for some reason in certain northeast social circles was known instead as Nantucket red. Though he bore a passing resemblance to the portrait above the mantel, he seemed much too young to be our host, probably just a few years older than me at most, yet he strode toward us with the air of a man who owned the place.

"Welcome, ladies," he said, flashing a distractingly white smile and oozing charm in a way that immediately put me on guard. I'd only just met him, but already I could tell he had all the sincerity of a used-car salesman who was behind on his quota. He held out his hand to me. "I'm Curtis Strong."

"Hi, I'm Ta—"

"No way, it's Polly Parrot!" He said it loudly enough that several heads swiveled to look in our direction. A couple hands went up to wave, and I could've sworn I heard someone from across the room yell *Polly wanna cracker?* If I'd been worried the islanders had forgotten that incident, I could rest assured they had not. "Haven't seen you around for a while, Polly."

"It's Tamsyn. Tamsyn Bassett." I corrected him through gritted teeth, too focused on masking my annoyance to realize I hadn't gone by that last name in fifteen years.

"Oh, I know. I just got such a kick out of teasing my cousin over all that poetry of his. Man, he had it bad for you back then." As Curtis uttered a hearty laugh, I realized he didn't just remember the defining embarrassment of my childhood; he'd been the one who coined the phrase. "We really should catch up now that you're back."

"Yeah, sure," I agreed, my heart not in it at all.

"Maybe drinks on the balcony later on, just the two of us? You should see the sunset." It was obvious he wasn't actually interested in me, just turning on the charm out of habit, and I had a feeling he'd said this to every halfway attractive woman under the age of forty who'd come through the door that night. But as I fumbled for a polite way to decline, his eyes narrowed and his face darkened. "Excuse me for a moment."

He stormed across the room to where a woman in a bright red cocktail dress was draping herself over an unsuspecting and very uncomfortable-looking gentleman. She straightened up a bit as Curtis got closer, and though I couldn't see her face, her body language signaled repentance. From the scolding look Curtis gave her, he wouldn't be so easily placated. I kind of felt sorry for the woman, whomever she might be.

However, his departure was a lucky break for me, and I let out a massive sigh of pure relief. "Was he smarmy or what? I thought I'd never get rid of him. And who on earth is that floozy in the red dress?"

I said all this to Aunt Gwen, who was standing beside me, only when I turned, it wasn't Aunt Gwen there after all. It was a tall man with thick, dark hair, soulful brown eyes, and a strong lantern jaw brushed with just a trace of shadowy stubble. He wore a button-down shirt of pastel plaid, left open at the collar, and a lightweight linen jacket. Turns out those busybodies from the ferry had been right about the young Dr. Caldwell after all. If I hadn't known better, I would have sworn I was staring at a carbon copy of a young George Clooney.

"Curtis can be an acquired taste. The floozy is his mother, Audrey, although she's less floozy and more boozy tonight. I haven't seen her this drunk in a while. Uncle Doug usually keeps her in line, but he hasn't arrived yet." He looked me squarely in the eyes as he spoke, and the corners of his mouth twitched. Although he managed to keep his outward composure, I knew deep down he was laughing, and I was pretty sure it was less *with* me than *at* me. "Tamsyn. You haven't changed a bit."

"Hello, Noah," I said, or at least I tried to, only when I reached his name, I swallowed the second syllable and my throat closed up in one of those choking coughing fits where your face turns purple and you're pretty sure you're going to die. *Hadn't changed a bit?* It was impossible to argue, as suddenly, I was displaying all the grace and sophistication of a thirteen-year-old girl.

His lips stopped twitching, and his look of concern was genuine. "Come on. Let's get you a drink."

He took me by the arm and led me out an open set of French doors and onto an expansive flagstone patio. A bar had been set up on the far side of it, overlooking a stunning ocean view with the tall, black-and-white-striped Cliffside Light in the distance.

"There's Sybil," he said, pointing toward a petite woman whose platinum hair was styled in a short bob. "You were friends, right? Looks like she's coming over. Wait here with her, and I'll get you a drink."

In my memory, Sybil Wolcott was a freckled kid with braces, whose bright yellow hair was always tinged green at the tips from mornings spent taking swimming lessons at the country club pool. The Wolcotts were fancy like that. Sybil and her mother had lived in Manhattan most of the year and were the type for whom things like country club memberships and art gallery openings came second nature. She wore a brightly colored jumble of silk scarves and shiny baubles over her fashionable black sheath dress, and any one of them probably cost more than I'd earned in a week back in the good old days when I was gainfully employed. I could tell in an instant that Sybil had grown into exactly the self-possessed beauty she'd been raised to be, and my insides churned at how she would react when she found out what a failure I'd become.

"Tamsyn! I would have recognized you anywhere." Much to my surprise, Sybil held out both arms and, before I could protest, had folded me into a tight embrace. I laughed with relief. She might have turned into a glamorous socialite, but underneath it all, I could sense she was the same old Sybil I'd had so much fun with years ago. For the first time since my arrival, I felt genuine happiness at being back in Pinecroft Cove. Maybe starting over here wasn't such a far-fetched goal after all.

"It's the hair you recognized, isn't it?" I joked when she finally let me go, holding up a stray lock of fiery red that was a Bassett family trait.

"I would've killed for that hair when we were kids. Still would." She grabbed my hand, flipping it back and forth to get a better view of my wrist. "And this gorgeous antique bracelet. Where did you get it?"

I flushed with pleasure at her compliment of my new treasure, remembering as I did that she'd always had a knack for saying something that instantly made you feel better about yourself, even on the worst days. "Up in Aunt Gwen's attic. It still needs a good cleaning, but it is pretty, isn't it?"

"It's beautiful. If you want, I can give you some tips on how to clean it properly. Say, was there anything else like this up in that attic?"

"Tons. There are dozens of steamer trunks and

boxes up there with old clothes and all sorts of stuff.
Aunt Gwen said I can go through them if I want."

"Old clothes?" Sybil's entire body seemed to perk
up. "You mean, like vintage?"

"I assume so. I don't know much about that kind of
thing. Do you?"

Sybil laughed. "You could say that. I'm opening up
a vintage clothing boutique on Main Street later this
summer."

"You mean here, on the island? Full-time?" The
news surprised me. Neither Sybil nor her mother had
ever struck me as the type to consider living on the
island year-round.

"Between you and me, I'm tired of Manhattan and
being so close to my mother's drama. Believe me, I'm
looking forward to island life, not to mention our little
magical… Wait, I assume your aunt has told you?"

"Uh, well…" My mind went blank. She couldn't
possibly be referring to the witch thing, could she? I'd
accepted the fact that old Aunt Gwen was batty, and
the guests at the inn, too, but if Sybil was buying into
all the hocus-pocus talk, I really didn't know what to
make of it.

As I fumbled for an answer, Sybil's eyes slid away
from me and toward the patio doors. Her face lit up,
and she waved her hand vigorously at someone
behind me. "Hey! Over here!" She looked back at me
apologetically. "We can discuss that more later, but
listen, if it's not too much trouble, maybe you'd let

me have a look at the clothes in that attic of yours sometime?"

"Yeah, of course," I agreed, just as happy to leave the coven discussion for another time, like maybe the Tuesday after never.

"Excellent!" She waved again. "Cassandra!"

My body stiffened at the name, and I whipped around to see who this other member of our so-called coven might be. I saw a young woman of medium build and bronze skin, whose curly black hair cascaded down her back almost as far as her waist. Her style of dress was best described as boho, with a long flowing skirt and peasant blouse. I knew without needing an introduction that this was Cassandra Hollings. If I'd had to choose which of us out of the three looked most likely to be a witch, it was Cassandra. She even wore a silver pentacle charm on a ribbon around her neck. Beside her was my aunt Gwen.

"Cassandra," Aunt Gwen said, "this is my niece, Tamsyn."

Cassandra gave my aunt an inquiring look. "Have you filled her in on everything?"

"Yes. She's fully up to speed," my aunt assured her. I wasn't so sure her assessment was correct. Hearing what she'd had to say and accepting it as truth were two very different things. I wasn't exactly certain where I'd gotten with the issue, but I was pretty sure I wasn't anywhere close to moving full speed ahead. I glanced at the bar, where the bartender was handing

Noah a plastic cup with a lime garnish. It could either be plain water, or possibly a gin and tonic. All things considered, my vote was for the latter.

I could tell by looking at her that Cassandra was a few years younger than I was, but the impression of youth was intensified as she hopped up and down with the type of glee one rarely finds outside a group of kindergarteners who've just been shown an all-you-can-eat candy buffet. "Isn't this so exciting, girls?" She looked from Sybil to me then grasped our hands.

Teetering off-balance, I reached out and placed my free hand on Sybil's shoulder to steady myself. The moment I closed the circle, a jolt like an electric current traveled up both of my arms. I gasped. "Did you feel that?" I asked. Both of their faces registered surprise, but before either of them could answer, the deep rumble of rolling thunder sounded above our heads, like a freight train charging across the rapidly darkening sky. It was accompanied by a blast of icy wind that instantly drove away the stifling heat.

My stomach tightened in a knot. Cassandra's eyes were wide, and Sybil's mouth had dropped open, but Aunt Gwen beamed with satisfaction. "Here comes the storm."

There was a crack of lightning, and then the skies burst open, and heavy drops of cold rain poured from above. One second, the water was streaming down my face, and I shut my eyes to keep it out, but then I felt a warmth descend around my head and shoulders, along with a hint of scrumptious bay rum aftershave, as a hand pressed gently between my shoulder blades, guiding me. When I opened my eyes again, I was out of the rain and standing inside the mansion's great hall, with Noah standing beside me and his jacket wrapped around my shoulders. The temperature had plummeted, and another blast of wind through the French doors sent a shiver coursing through me. Noah grabbed the doors and slammed them shut, locking them in place.

Lightning struck again, a jagged bolt that ripped through the sky. A loud boom followed immediately after, shaking the ground. The lights inside the mansion flickered once. Then the room was plunged into darkness. Nervous murmurs echoed throughout the space, and someone cried out in alarm only to be quickly hushed by others before full-out panic could ensue. Outside, the rain fell in sheets, the only illumination coming from the intermittent flashes of lightning and the rhythmic sweep of Cliffside Light as it circled on its path across the edge of the wide backyard before returning to sea. As I watched its movement, almost trancelike, I saw a man standing on the grass, drenched in rain but seemingly unbothered by it. He was too far away to see clearly, but I would have sworn it was the man from the portrait above the fireplace— Douglas Strong. Then the light moved on, and the yard was dark. When it returned, the man was gone. I had no idea what to make of it.

I huddled in the dark with Sybil and Cassandra. Noah had wandered off, to where I wasn't sure. My pulse beat like a hummingbird's wings until finally the lights came on again. When they did, Noah was standing at the front door. Two men in police uniforms stood there, too, dripping from the deluge. Curtis and Audrey stood nearby, and when one of the officers addressed her, Audrey shrieked and crumpled to a heap on the floor. The room grew completely still, and then the whispers began, like a swarm of bees buzzing through the crowd, until finally I could hear what was being said.

"His plane went down in the bay," the voices said. "Douglas Strong is dead."

CHAPTER SIX

"More pies?" I stared in astonishment as my aunt dumped another basket of blueberries into the large pot on the stove. And yes, it took every ounce of restraint for me not to call it a cauldron because that's what it looked like, a cauldron filled with a sweet, syrupy mass of bubbling, boiling fruit. "Don't get me wrong. I love pie. But didn't we make two dozen pies yesterday?"

It had been a simple cooking lesson, not a magic lesson, as Aunt Gwen had been quick to assure me. Just pies. "What could be easier than that?" she'd wanted to know. I mean, I could think of several things that were easier. Those brownies that get microwaved in a mug, for instance. I hardly ever messed up those. But pie? I seriously thought pies emerged from factories, fully formed. After a few tedious hours of rolling out crusts, cutting perfect circles, and weaving strips into lattice across the tops, I'd gone to bed early, utterly drained. Now she wanted me to make more?

"The funeral's tomorrow, and half the island will be there. Grieving people like to eat," she replied without looking up from her work. "Besides, a few of the pies needed to be replaced."

"Oh no." She'd said it in an offhanded way, but immediately I knew I was to blame. "I warned you I wasn't good in the kitchen. What did I do wrong?"

"Oh, it was nothing, dear. Simple mistake. Salt and sugar look so similar even I have a hard time telling them apart sometimes."

Yeah, right. I watched as my aunt moved with almost choreographed precision, filling the cauldron— I mean the pot—with all the necessary ingredients without even stopping to measure. By now, I'd had a chance to sample the finished product, and Walter at the ferry had been right. Her blueberry pie was the best in the world. She didn't need to follow a recipe. She knew with all the instinct and skill of a master artisan exactly what was needed to make each batch perfect. Was it magic? I wasn't sure, but it was some- thing special.

"Do you need some help?" It was only polite to ask, but I tensed, praying the answer would be no. I didn't want to risk another disaster.

"As a matter of fact, I have a whole load of pies boxed up and ready to deliver to Cliffside, if you wouldn't mind running them over."

Smart woman. The best way to guarantee this batch of replacement pies came out perfectly was to get me as far away from them as possible. There were just a few problems. I had yet to get my car to the mechanic. Plus, every time I closed my eyes, I saw Douglas Strong's face, and the thought of returning to Cliffside turned my insides cold. I decided to address the first issue only and keep the other strictly to myself.

"I'd like to, but I'm not sure Miss Josephine can manage it."

"Why don't you load them into my car, then?"

"I can do that," I told her, with slightly more confidence than I felt considering the damage I'd already caused. But seriously, how hard could it be to deliver a carload of baked goods? *You've got this, Tamsyn.*

As I drove slowly down the long driveway to Cliffside Manor, my tension grew, though I did my best to tamp it down. It had been almost a week since the party that had ended so tragically, and the first difference that struck me was that this time there were no other cars or people in sight. I parked close to the massive front door, which—unlike last time—was shut tight as if to discourage visitors of any kind. Aunt Gwen had given me one of those collapsible wagons, the type you can keep in your car, and I unfolded it now and began loading it with boxes. She'd really outdone herself. In addition to her famous blueberry pies, she'd made peach, cherry, and apple. There was enough to feed the entire island for a week.

I pulled the pie-laden wagon as far as the front steps, leaving it at the bottom while I went the rest of the way up to the door and rang the bell. I could hear the chime echo inside, a low and forlorn sound, and even though I knew they were expecting the delivery, I immediately regretted intruding on their private grief. A foreboding feeling settled over me, and I almost turned around to leave, but just at that moment, I heard someone approaching the door. Aunt Gwen had explained that Curtis and his mother, Audrey, lived in the big house, which they had shared with the recently departed Douglas Strong. Hoping to avoid an awkward moment, I'd prepared myself to say a few kind words to whichever one of them would open it. As it turned out, it was neither of them.

"Oh, Noah. It's you." Belatedly, I snapped my mouth shut. It had dropped open as soon as I saw him standing in the doorway. I had no idea why. It's not like I had been the one with the teenage crush, but for some reason I couldn't seem to stop staring even once my mouth was closed. So much for avoiding those pesky awkward moments.

"Tamsyn, it's nice to see you again," he said, not looking the least bit flustered. How was that even possible? When we were teenagers, he'd been nothing *but* flustered. Now he was the cool one, whereas I...

"I brought pies," I blurted out, sounding mentally

deranged. I tried to laugh it off, but the sound that emerged from my mouth was like nothing I'd ever heard a human make before, some sort of snort-cackle that left the impression I must be the love child of a goose and a potbellied pig.

He blinked, his politeness covering whatever horror he surely must have felt at my animal-like outburst. "Oh, right. Audrey mentioned your aunt was sending some over. Do you need some help?"

I looked at the wagon, trying to figure out how I could get it up the three large granite steps on my own, but it was no use. I nodded meekly. "Yes, please."

We each took one end of the wagon and lifted it easily into the foyer. Without pausing to ask, Noah took hold of the handle and began to pull it across the marble floor. I followed behind him, forcing myself not to notice how nicely his jeans fit and, instead, quizzing myself as to why, after fifteen years of never giving the man a second thought, being around Noah Caldwell suddenly had this bizarre effect on me. My pulse was racing, and I felt like a tongue-tied teenager. Were love potions a real thing? Because if they were, I was beginning to suspect Aunt Gwen had slipped one in my tea.

When we reached the kitchen, Noah began to unload the boxes onto the huge butcher-block island that dominated the middle of the room. It was the biggest kitchen I had ever seen outside of a restaurant, but unlike Aunt Gwen's cozy mess of a workspace back at the inn, this one had an almost antiseptic, clinical feel to it. The stainless-steel appliances gleamed as if they had never been used, and I had a hard time picturing anyone cooking a meal here.

"I'm sorry about your uncle," I said as it suddenly occurred to me that I'd been so thrown off when he was the one to answer the door that I hadn't actually shared any of the polite condolences I'd planned. "Were you two close?"

"He was a good guy. I'm going to miss him." A mistiness settled across Noah's deep-brown eyes, making them sparkle. I quickly reminded myself it was in very poor taste to think how attractive it made him look. "Although Curtis was his favorite nephew, of course."

"Oh, I'm sure that's not true," I assured him, with absolutely no proof to offer since I'd never met the man. It just seemed like the thing to say.

"No, it's okay. Uncle Doug was like a father to Curt, ever since his dad died when he was in college. Uncle Doug really took him under his wing after that, gave him a job, invited both him and Audrey to live here. He was grooming Curt to take over his real estate development business someday. It made sense. Curtis shares the Strong name."

"Why's that important?" First the Bassetts, now the Strongs. Seriously, what was it about the people on this island and their weird obsession with last names?

"Uncle Doug was really big on preserving the Strong family legacy. It was his passion, really,

genealogy and family history. He was convinced the
Strongs were related to the Davenports, who built this
mansion back in the eighteen hundreds. It's why he
bought it. He'd even ordered a bunch of those DNA
kits recently for all of us, to see if he could prove it."
Noah closed his eyes, and I got the impression he was
holding back tears.

"I'm really sorry. How are Curtis and his mother
handling all of this?" As if prompted by the question,
the deep boom of a man's voice, uttering a steady
stream of curse words, bellowed from an adjacent
room.

"About how you'd expect," Noah replied. "Audrey
won't come out of her bedroom, and between you and
me, I think she's been drinking regularly now that
Uncle Doug isn't here to stop her. Curtis has been on
the phone all morning with the investigators,
demanding answers. I keep telling him it's too early
and to let them do their jobs, but…"

A door slammed, and footsteps echoed down the
hall, coming closer. The next minute, Curtis Strong
entered the kitchen. His hair was disheveled, but
unlike the last time I'd seen him, it was clearly not an
intentional choice, and his deeply creased clothing just
added to his overall unkempt appearance. He barely
glanced my way, plowing straight ahead to where his
cousin stood.

"I've had it with this island!" he fumed. "Sheriff
Grady should be fired."

"You can't fire a sheriff," Noah responded with a measure of calm that was equal in intensity to Curtis's rage. "It's an elected position."

"Then I'll pay someone to run against him! He's got it in for the Strongs because we're not year-rounders like he is."

"Curt, why don't you take a minute, calm down, maybe say hello to Tamsyn, and then tell me what's going on?"

It wasn't until Noah said my name that Curtis really seemed to notice my presence. He gave me a nod, and I answered the gesture with an awkward wave. I hadn't entirely forgotten that I disliked him, but now was hardly the time to hold it against him.

"I was dropping off some pies for your mom," I told him, just in case the four dozen boxes next to me stamped with "Homemade Pie" on all four sides in bright red lettering hadn't clued him in. "How's she doing?"

Curtis sighed and raked a hand through his mop of hair. "She can barely get out of bed. If she catches wind of our local idiot sheriff's latest theory, I don't know what'll happen."

Noah cleared his throat. "I've gotten to know Joe Grady pretty well the past few years, and he's not such a bad guy. Sure, he sometimes trash talks the summer folks in the bar with the rest of the locals in the off-season, but I've never seen him let that type of thing get in the way of doing his job." Noah turned his attention toward me. "Since I'm the only full-time doctor on the island, I assist the state medical examiner's office when the need arises. I've worked with the sheriff's office on investigations a number of times." He placed a calming hand on his cousin's shoulder. "What's he done that has you so upset?"

Curtis's jaw clenched, and his nostrils flared. "He had the nerve to suggest that Uncle Doug's crash was no accident."

"Not an accident?" A deep crease formed in Noah's brow. "They think someone wanted to kill him?"

Curtis shook his head. "They wanted to know about his mental state, asked all sorts of questions about whether he'd seemed troubled or depressed."

"You don't mean suicide?" Noah asked.

"That's exactly what they were getting at," Curtis said, "and I'll say again now what I told Grady on the phone. There's no way Uncle Doug killed himself. I'm heading into town to settle this with Grady face-to-face." Curtis strode out of the kitchen, and a few seconds later the whole house reverberated with the sound of the heavy front door being slammed. A car engine revved shortly after that, followed by the squeal of tires as Curtis carried through on his threat.

"I'm sorry you had to see him like that," Noah said when the sound of the car's engine had faded into the distance.

"It's my fault for intruding at a time like this. It's no wonder he's upset. His mom, too." I thought of

Audrey on the night of the party, crumpling to the floor in her bright red dress when the sheriff delivered the news. "I hope it's not rude of me to ask, but I couldn't help but wonder whether your uncle and Curtis's mom—were they involved?"

Noah frowned and shook his head. "Like, romantically?"

"She seems to be devastated by his death."

"No, they weren't a couple, but they were close. Plus, she took over her husband, my uncle Jeremy's, position on the Strong Corporation board of directors after he died. Speaking of that"—he hesitated, as if weighing whether to continue—"is it true that you're an accountant?"

I nodded, uncertain where this was going. "Yeah, until recently, anyway. Why?"

"Well, my mother's on the Strong Corp. board, too. She was Uncle Doug's sister, and I told you how he was about family. She and my dad moved to Portland last year on account of some health issues she's been having, and I have a whole box of Strong Corp. financial reports and records that I've been keeping for her until she's better able to deal with them. I've been meaning to go through them and never did. Now that this has happened, and considering the questions the sheriff's asking about Uncle Doug's mental state, it occurs to me maybe I should give those a closer look and know for myself what's been going on in the family business."

"I could take a look at them if you want," I offered, though I wasn't sure why I said it, as forensic accounting was hardly my specialty. "That is, if you don't mind getting help from an accountant who just got fired."

"That would be great," Noah said with a smile, completely ignoring the final part about me getting fired, which I'd muttered under my breath. "I've got the box back at my place, but I can drop by with it sometime this week."

"Sure," I replied. From all the butterflies in my stomach, you'd think I had just said yes to a date. What was wrong with me? Noah had never had this effect on me before. Sure, he was mega-handsome now instead of being a dork with a terrible haircut, but was I really that shallow? Judging by the way my heart was beating in my throat, apparently I was. "I'd be happy to help."

"Thanks." Noah checked his watch. "I'd better get back to the clinic. I have patients coming in this afternoon. Can I show you out?"

I followed him back to the front door, the collapsed wagon tucked under Noah's arm. We passed the French doors that led to the patio, and a sudden chill crept up my spine as I took in the hulking blackbird that now sat on the exact spot on the lawn where I had seen Douglas Strong standing in the pouring rain. Was it a crow? A raven? I was no bird expert. It was spooky, and that's all that mattered. Though I tried to put it out of my mind, I couldn't shake the uneasy feeling that settled over me until I'd reached the other end of Pinecroft Cove.

I hadn't told a soul about what I thought I'd seen that night. I knew it sounded crazy, and in the upheaval that followed Sheriff Grady's official announcement confirming the small plane carrying Douglas Strong had gone down in Penobscot Bay, I began to question whether I'd seen anything at all, even though I could recall every detail the minute I closed my eyes. But after returning from my second visit to Cliffside Manor, it was all I could think about that night. I guess I shouldn't have been surprised when the troubling dreams began.

The first several times I woke up, it was with the image fresh in my head of Douglas Strong standing on the lawn as I'd seen him that night. Rain ran down his face, drenching his clothing. He stared straight at me, unblinking and seemingly unfazed by the downpour. Each time, just as he would open his mouth to speak, I woke up, heart racing, in my bed.

The last dream, the one I had right before waking up for good at dawn, was altogether different.

I FOUND MYSELF IN THE MIDDLE OF THE living room, and while I recognized it as being the Pinecroft Inn, it was different, too. A bright green wallpaper with large pink roses covered the walls. I stood on top of a piano stool. The clicking of high heels rang in my ears but grew fainter with each step as whoever was wearing them retreated down the hall. The cloying scent of an expensive rose perfume burned my nostrils.

There was a young woman in the room with me, her chestnut hair styled in the type of Marcel wave that was popular in the 1920s. She kneeled by the stool, her mouth filled with pins. As I looked down, I saw I was wearing a gold silk dress, a sleeveless party dress with intricate beading. Every so often, the young woman would place a pin in the hem.

"Thank goodness she's gone," I said, and the relief I felt flowed through every inch of my body like it was my lifeblood.

"Who's that, miss?" the woman asked, her teeth never losing their firm grip on the pins as she spoke.

"My mother."

She nodded but didn't join in my criticism, changing the subject instead. "These are the finest dresses I've ever seen, if you don't mind my saying."

"They're just dresses."

"They're fit for royalty."

"She'd be so glad to hear you say it. She's invited Lord Rochester to visit this summer from England."

"Must be a real swell, then, I'll bet."

"I suppose, but swells aren't really my type."

"Oh, but they're mine," she said with a giggle.

"He's rich and handsome?"

"Rich, yes. I wouldn't know about the handsome. I've never laid eyes on him. Even so, she insists I shall marry him in the fall."

"Jeepers creepers, what a pickle!"

Laughter bubbled up inside me at her sincere assessment of my situation, and I found myself in sudden, desperate need of a friend. "Say, wanna sneak outside for a ciggy?"

She hesitated, but I could see the temptation in her eyes. "I don't know. It wouldn't be proper."

"I don't give a fig about proper," I told her, hiking up the pinned hem of my dress as I hopped off the stool.

I padded toward the door in my stocking-clad feet. When I paused by the front door, I looked in the mirror, and the face I saw wasn't exactly the one I'd been expecting. My skin was its usual pale, almost ghostly white, my eyes the same brilliant blue, and my hair its familiar shade of Bassett red, but it was styled in a similar fashion as what the other woman wore. There were subtle differences in the shape of my lips and chin that gave me the sensation of looking at a stranger, and I felt a tingling of electricity course through me as I realized that perhaps I wasn't me after all. I dismissed the thought quickly, as it made me uneasy.

I opened the front door and slipped out onto the porch, with the seamstress following a few steps behind. I pulled a cigarette and lighter from my garter. The cigarette appeared to be hand rolled, and the lighter wasn't a modern plastic one but an old-fashioned type made of metal that was heavy in my hand. Though I've never been a smoker, somehow I sparked the flint like an expert, and the glow of the flame glinted off one of the links of the silver bracelet on my wrist. I placed the cigarette between my lips and took a long drag. The action seemed as natural on the one hand as it did completely foreign to me on the other, like I was two people inhabiting the same body, with all the memories and knowledge of both. "Say, do you know of any places on the island where a girl can get a drink?"

My new friend took the cigarette from me and gave it a few puffs as she thought. "Depends. Do you like music?"

"What type?"

"Jazz, of course."

"Now, that's the berries!" I replied, knowing it meant something good even though that, like many of the other words I'd been using, was slang I'd never heard before.

She flashed a conspiratorial smile. "Then you're in luck. My brother Freddy plays piano at a speakeasy down by the docks. If you can sneak out Saturday night, I'll take you there."

Then she pulled out a pin and stabbed it into my left breast.

THIS TIME WHEN I WOKE, IT WASN'T WITH A
vague sense of dread, but with a heavy weight on my
chest and a sharp pain concentrated just above my left
nipple. I gasped for air and got a mouthful of fur
instead.

"Meow."

"Gus!" I gave the covers a shake and heard a loud
thump as the cat jumped to the floor. "Good riddance,
demon cat."

I stretched and closed my eyes, but my mind was
racing as I tried to remember the details of the dream,
only to have them slip away bit by bit before I could
grasp their significance. With a sigh, I flipped my wrist
over, searching for the time on my watch. Instead, I
saw the silver bracelet, exactly as I had seen it in the
dream. The only difference was that now, it was dulled
from stubborn tarnish that none of my efforts at
cleaning it could remove. With no hope left of getting
more sleep, I swung my legs out of bed and vowed to
search out Sybil's shop as soon as I could to pump her
for the promised jewelry-cleaning advice. I brewed a
mug of tea and took it into the living room. The walls
were the familiar shade of breezy white I was used to
seeing, but as I sipped my tea and stared at the sturdy
oak piano with its old-fashioned wooden stool, I
couldn't shake my overwhelming sense of déjà vu.

CHAPTER SEVEN

The Monday after the funeral was gloriously sunny and the perfect day to get out and explore. While my aunt's rice trick had brought my phone limping back to operational status, cracked screen notwithstanding, Miss Josephine was still out of commission, so I borrowed a bicycle from the stash my aunt kept for guests. It was a three-speed style with white-rim tires, a leather seat, and a woven basket on the handlebars. I made my way downtown, walking along the brick sidewalk of Main Street as I pushed the bike, looking at each storefront until I found the one I wanted. The shop's name, Rags to Riches, was painted across the window, but the naked mannequins on the other side of the glass were a sure indicator it wasn't open for business just yet. A sign on the door said *Closed*, but when I tried the latch, it was unlocked, and a bell jingled as I walked inside.

As I took in the tongue-in-cheek chic interior, with its oversized gilt mirrors on the walls and several leopard-print chairs shaped like high-heeled shoes near the dressing rooms, I could feel Sybil's personality shining through. Though we hadn't kept in touch since we were young, her presence on the island made my spirits soar. I'd had friends back in Cleveland, of course, but never the type of close relationships that stuck through thick and thin. I was still very much on the fence about the whole coven thing, but the prospect of having a best friend or two to lean on at this point in my life was very appealing. With any luck, I hoped Sybil and Cassandra might turn out to be just that, even if the supernatural aspects of our arrangement filled me with doubt.

"Tamsyn, you found the shop." Sybil emerged from the back room, wearing a pink, full-skirted 1950s' party dress in a martini-glass print. She couldn't have chosen a better outfit to match her store. Beaming with pride, she gestured around the nearly finished space. "What do you think?"

"I love it," I told her with a grin. "When do you open?"

"Couple of weeks. Any news on those trunks in your attic?"

As I recalled the contents of the trunks, an image from my dream flashed through my brain, a vivid memory of the silky feel of the gold, sleeveless dress against my skin as I wore it in my dream, and I could feel the smile fading from my face. Sybil must have seen it, too, because she clasped her hands together in front of her chest with a worried look. "Oh no! Don't tell me Aunt Gwen changed her mind about them."

"No, it isn't that. It's just..." I paused, not sure if I should continue. Did I really want to start down this path? I sensed that if I did, there would be no turning back, yet I needed answers, or I feared I might eventually drive myself insane with questioning. "If I tell you something strange, will you promise not to think I've lost my mind?"

"Of course. What is it?"

"I had this vivid dream last Saturday night, where I was wearing one of the dresses I found in the attic and the bracelet, too. It was like I was myself, but not exactly, and I was in Aunt Gwen's house, only it was a long time ago." I bit my lip, knowing I wasn't explaining it right. "The whole next day, I felt so odd, like I was having memories that weren't my own."

Instead of laughing at me as I had feared, Sybil ran a finger along her chin, deep in thought. "Like a past life?"

"No, of course not. I don't believe in that kind of thing. Do you?" It was only after I said it that I realized this was a woman who just might believe she was an honest-to-goodness witch. Why wouldn't she believe in past lives, and who knows what else? "Can I ask you something?"

"Sure."

"Aunt Gwen's been trying to convince me since I got here that...well, you know. And the way you were talking at the party got me wondering, do you really believe in all of this magical stuff?"

"I've grown up around it my whole life, so of course, I do." She said it like it was the most natural thing in the world. "Don't you?"

I shrugged. "It sounds ridiculous, but then again, I was raised by a father and stepmother who were about as practical as they come. It's a good thing I didn't move there until I was a teenager, because I'm pretty sure even Santa and the tooth fairy wouldn't have been in either one of their repertoires. Look, I understand that some people think of spells as part of their religion, like prayer, or meditation, or something. I can respect that. But I think Aunt Gwen actually believes she can turn people into toads."

"No, she doesn't," Sybil assured me with a hearty laugh.

I laughed as well. "That's a relief."

"Transformation isn't her specialty. She's a kitchen witch. She works magic through food."

My laughter trailed away as I realized it wasn't the belief in witchcraft that Sybil was dismissing, just the example of a spell I'd given. Toads aside, it was clear there were other spells she believed my aunt Gwen could perform with ease.

"But that's..." I thought of the waffles she'd made me for breakfast again that morning. Just one bite of them and my entire outlook could improve in a way I'd never experienced with any type of food before. It was hard to argue that my aunt's cooking wasn't in some way magical. It opened up the possibility that maybe there was some part of all this I could accept on some level, as long as I didn't have to buy into all the abracadabra mumbo jumbo that went along with it. "So, is that the kind of magic you and Cassandra are supposed to be able to do, too?"

"No, we all have different gifts. That's why we'll make a good coven."

"Uh-huh." The shakiness of my voice reflected the effect the word "coven" had just had on my insides.

"You see, the Wolcotts are what's called glamour witches. It means we use our magic to alter the perception of the people around us so they see things the way we want them to be seen."

I gave her shiny bob a sharp look. "Is that why your hair is always so smooth and perfect?"

"No, that's the styling gel I get from my hairdresser. Talk about magic. But it's the reason a customer might buy a dress here, and every time she puts it on, she feels more confident and beautiful than she does in anything else in her closet."

"You sell enchanted dresses?"

Sybil laughed. "Something like that."

"Interesting," I replied, still not sure whether to believe her completely or not. "And Cassandra?"

"Let's just say Cass is still trying to find her specific

gifts, but the Hollings generally work in healing potions and divination."

"Still trying to find her gifts?"

"She's had a few mishaps with her potions."

"That sounds familiar." It's not like I wished failure on my fellow coven mate, but I'd be lying if I said knowing she was struggling like me didn't raise my spirits a bit. "Did you know I used salt instead of sugar in the pies for Doug Strong's funeral the other day? Aunt Gwen had to remake the whole batch."

"It doesn't mean you're not a witch." Sybil's tone was reassuring, but the words were anything but since being a witch was the last thing I wanted. I was supposed to be an accountant. I was pretty certain the two occupations were mutually exclusive. "Remember that jolt of energy when the three of us formed a circle?"

"It was in the middle of a thunderstorm," I argued. "Maybe that was just the static electricity making our hair stand up on end. I'm a normal person. How can I possibly be a witch?"

She tilted her head to one side and gave me a searching look, as if there was something I wasn't getting and she was trying to figure out why. "Do you know the history of Pinecroft Cove?"

I shrugged. "Sure, I guess. The Davenport family bought up half the island in the late eighteen hundreds and invited their friends. It became a summer colony for rich New Yorkers, like Newport and Bar Harbor."

"All of that is true, but I'm talking about the history before that."

"Not sure. Lobster village?" I guessed.

"The lobstermen have been here a long time, too, but I was referring to our ancestors, the early settlers of Pinecroft Cove."

I frowned. "I thought your family was from Manhattan. Isn't that how you got here?"

"Goodness, no." Sybil rolled her eyes. "That's just my mother who decided to move us to the city. The Wolcotts settled in Pinecroft Cove as far back as the rest of the magical families had."

"The rest of the magical families?" I swallowed a lump in my throat. "You mean, like, werewolves and vampires and leprechauns?"

"Get real, Tamsyn. Werewolves and leprechauns are fictional."

"Phew," I said with a nervous laugh but then paused as I realized she hadn't included vampires in her list. "Wait, does that mean—you know what? Never mind. I don't think I want to know."

"Mostly the community was made up of healers, psychics, and mediums. Anyone with a gift was welcome. Most of the original settlers moved here around the time of the witch hysteria that swept through New England in the seventeenth century."

"Are you talking about the Salem witch trials?" Growing up with my dad, I hadn't learned much about my mother's family history, but I never would've guessed they'd been around that long.

"Salem, and a lot of other towns, too. The irony, of course, is that none of the people who were executed in Massachusetts were actually witches, but contrary to the people who say that's because there's no such thing, there were plenty of us living in the area at the time. At least a dozen families packed up, headed north, and eventually made it out to Summerhaven Island. There are only three families left now, exactly enough to form a coven, so it's up to us to preserve magic in Pinecroft Cove for another generation."

"I had no idea." I struggled with how to process all this new information. When Aunt Gwen said it, it had been easy to dismiss, but for some reason when it was coming from Sybil, I found myself starting to believe. "So, what about the dreams I've been having?"

Sybil arched an eyebrow. "You've had more than one?"

I scuffed my foot along the tile and looked away. I hadn't meant to mention that part, but there was no way out of it now. "There might have been another one," I mumbled.

"Tell me."

"It was Doug Strong. I saw him in my dreams, over and over, the night before the funeral. He was standing on the lawn at Cliffside Manor, drenched in rain. He kept trying to say something to me, but as soon as he would open his mouth, I'd wake up."

She nodded. "Interesting. I could look up the meanings of some of the symbols in a book of dreams, if you'd like."

I took a deep breath. "There's something else. It wasn't the first time I saw him like that; only the first time wasn't a dream. It was the night of the party, during the storm when the lights went out. One minute, he was standing in the rain outside on the lawn. The next minute, he was gone. It was just after that the sheriff came and told everyone about the crash."

"A premonition, then. Or a ghost." Far from acting like she was humoring a nutcase, I could tell Sybil was dead serious, and the hairs on my arm stood up on end. "We should call Cass. I think it's time we convene the coven for real."

I swallowed hard but nodded in agreement. Did I believe I was a witch? Not necessarily. But I knew something strange was going on. Whatever it was, I felt better knowing I wouldn't have to face it alone. Before heading back home, I took off the antique bracelet and left it with Sybil, who said she'd shine it up for me, good as new. She also promised to send me a text as soon as she'd gotten in touch with Cass. Since the bag of Uncle Ben's had brought my phone back from the grave, I gave her my number, though I'll admit to being a little disappointed the coven didn't have a secret means of communication. I'd been hoping for a bat signal.

It was midafternoon when I arrived back home. The inn was empty, and a cardboard box was sitting on the porch. It was one of those sturdy banker boxes with a lid that you use to store files. Sure enough, when I opened it, I saw it was filled to the brim with financial records, each featuring the Strong Corp. logo across the top. I shook my head. Only an islander would leave an entire box of personal information sitting unattended on the porch. Noah must have brought them by while I was out. The flutter in my tummy as I pictured him climbing the porch steps to deliver the box reminded me I needed to quiz Aunt Gwen about the efficacy of love potions and whether she'd brewed any lately.

I carried the box to my bedroom and set it on the small writing desk under the window, tossing the lid upside down onto my bed. No sooner had it landed than Gus appeared seemingly from nowhere. He hopped onto the cardboard, spun around a few times, then curled into a ball and offered me a clear view of all of his teeth as he gave a most self-satisfied yawn.

"Just make yourself comfortable, buddy," I told him. "I live to serve."

The documents inside the box were loose and didn't appear to have been organized in any way, so the first thing I did was pull them out one by one, placing them in piles on the floor to sort. There were board reports and financial statements but also random letters and papers mixed in. About thirty minutes into the project, I pulled out a thick report, and a scrap of lined paper that had been wedged between the pages came loose and fluttered to the floor. When I retrieved it and read the handwritten words that had been scrawled across it, my body temperature plummeted like I'd wandered into a deep freezer.

DS, you're a cheat and a liar. You deserve to die.

"Gus," I said, as I read the note again, "I don't think Douglas Strong's death was a suicide after all."

Gus rolled over onto his back, exposing his belly for me to rub, which I did with trembling hands. To be honest, the words shouldn't have impacted me as much as they did. I didn't know the victim after all. But he was Noah's uncle, and besides that, it was hard not to care what happened to a person when his ghost kept popping up in your dreams. At the very least, I needed to make sure the proper authorities were aware of the threat.

"Do you know what this means?" I asked, continuing to address Gus, although I don't know why since he never answered back, which frankly dashed all my expectations of how being a witch with a black cat was supposed to go. "Someone wanted Douglas Strong dead."

Gus stretched his front legs, spreading his toes wide so all the fur between them stood out in little clumps. He blinked at me before closing his eyes and going back to sleep, completely unimpressed with anything I'd said.

"Fine." I shook my head at the lazy little beast. "Take a nap. I'm going to find Noah."

Though I didn't have his phone number, I assumed that at not quite three o'clock on a Monday afternoon, Noah would most likely be at the health clinic. I hopped on my bicycle and pedaled my way downtown for the second time that day. The island clinic was a squat brick building with a sign out front that listed half a dozen doctors, although I happened to know Noah was the only one who was there full-time. The others were specialists with practices on the mainland and only came to visit on set days throughout the month. Though the summer population of Summerhaven was over ten thousand, most of the time the island had only a few thousand residents and didn't need more than one doctor.

When I arrived, the waiting room was empty except for the receptionist, a middle-aged woman with her graying brown hair pulled back into a bun. She looked up as I entered, an expression of mild surprise on her face, mixed with a hint of annoyance.

"Can I help you?" she asked, discreetly closing the paperback book in front of her, which I guessed was the source of the annoyance. I was cutting in on her reading time.

"I need to see Noah."

She glanced at the large, round clock on the wall.

"Do you have an appointment with Dr. Caldwell? We close in fifteen minutes."

"Oh, I'm not here for an appointment. It's more of a personal visit. My name's Tamsyn Proct—"

"Yes, I know who you are, Miss Bassett," she said, cutting me off. Technically, she'd gotten the last name wrong, but I was kind of getting used to being called Bassett, and besides that, her aggressive attitude told me it was pointless to argue.

Now granted, there were only so many people on the island, and my family was the only one whose members naturally sported fire-engine-red hair, but her hostile tone went beyond simply knowing who I was. Was it personal? It occurred to me that she might remember the whole poetry-reading debacle of my youth and hated me for it. I smiled weakly. "Could you let him know I'm here to see him?"

She gave me a quick look up and down as if assessing exactly how much damage I could do. "I'll see if he's available," she informed me, after apparently deciding my presence wouldn't sully the good doctor's reputation.

I took a seat on one of the wooden chairs in the small waiting room. As she picked up the phone, I pondered just how quickly rumors spread in a town of this size. I was pretty sure that by breakfast, half the locals would have heard how I'd dropped by looking for Noah. I wondered what else would be added to the story.

"He said to go on back," she informed me before turning her attention once more to her book.

Noah was waiting in the exam room at the end of the hall. He wore a casual pair of khakis and a navy-blue polo shirt, topped by a white lab coat. A stethoscope hung around his neck. It took all my concentration to remember I'd come there for a reason other than to just admire what a fine-looking doctor he'd turned out to be. I wondered again how Aunt Gwen might have gone about slipping me a love potion. Had she hidden it in my maple syrup?

"Tamsyn, are you feeling okay?" His gentle look of concern almost made me wish for a second that I could say no, just because I was so certain he would take good care of me if I were sick. This really needed to stop.

"I'm fine," I assured him. I reached into my pocket and pulled out the scrap of paper with the note. "I came to show you something I found in that box you brought over."

He came closer and took it from me, holding it out to read. "What is this?"

"I'm not exactly sure," I replied, fighting to focus on the matter at hand and not at the intoxicating scent of aftershave I'd come to associate with him, "but it looks like proof your uncle's death wasn't an accident or a suicide after all."

"And you found it in the box of papers?"

"Yes. I started sorting them, and when I got about

halfway down, this was wedged inside one of the reports."

He turned it over to examine the other side. "And there was no envelope or anything?"

I shook my head. "It was just loose, but do you see that crease in the middle and the way there's a streak across the back like it got wet? I was thinking it looks like someone might have folded it up and put it underneath the windshield wiper on his car."

"Could be. But there's no signature."

"No. Even so, I thought maybe I should bring it to Sheriff Grady and see what he has to say."

"I'll go with you." He took off his coat and hung it on a hook behind the door. I followed him out of the exam room, and when we passed the receptionist's desk, he called out, "Marian, I'm heading out for the day."

I saw the telltale glint in her eyes as she watched us walk out together. Yep, the story of Dr. Caldwell leaving work early with Polly the Parrot would be the talk of the island by sundown.

The sheriff's office was housed in a plain cement building near the docks, just a few minutes by foot from the clinic. We walked there together, exchanging the usual pleasantries. I'm not sure what kind of reception I would have received on my own, but as soon as the officer at the front desk saw Noah, we were treated with the utmost respect and immediately ushered into Sheriff Grady's office. We'd barely settled into our seats when we were joined by Sheriff Grady himself.

He was younger than I'd expected, maybe in his mid-thirties at most, with the type of athletic build that was a prerequisite for looking even halfway decent in the brown polyester uniforms I was fairly certain the island had originally purchased sometime in the Nixon administration. His skin was tanned from time spent outside, and his dark hair was trimmed short in a practical, almost military cut.

"Dr. Caldwell," he said, extending his hand.

"Sheriff," Noah replied, giving his hand a firm shake. The greeting struck me as oddly formal, given that the two had worked together many times and were roughly the same age, but I supposed it was typical of their professions to show one another respect.

"What brings you here today?" the sheriff asked, his face a little pinched. He pulled the chair out from behind his desk and sat down. "I've already told Curtis everything I know about your uncle's crash, and I won't get another update from the head of the NTSB investigation until later in the week."

"I understand. I'm not here looking for information. Actually, I'm thinking I might have found a lead. That is," Noah added, looking my way, "Tamsyn found it, but I think it's worth a closer look."

Noah handed over the threatening note, but Sheriff Grady barely gave it a glance before tossing it onto his desk. He lifted his hands in a sort of shrug. "What do you want me to do with this?"

I cleared my throat. "I thought it might be proof the crash wasn't an accident or—"

"Oh, did you?" he interrupted, leaning forward in his seat and giving me a hard stare.

I stiffened immediately at his confrontational tone, but I willed myself not to shrink backward into my chair. "Or suicide," I finished.

Grady scowled. "Where'd you hear that rumor?"

Despite the seriousness of the situation, I had to bite the inside of my cheek to keep from laughing. Was he serious? Whether or not Douglas Strong had taken a nosedive into Penobscot Bay on purpose had been the primary topic of debate at his funeral the day before, which at least half the island had attended. It was hardly top secret that suicide was the prevailing theory.

"If someone was threatening Mr. Strong before his death, don't you think it's proof—?"

"I think it's proof, Miss Bassett, that you've watched a few too many murder mysteries. We may be in Maine, but this ain't Cabot Cove." He rose from his desk, shoved the scrap of paper into my hand, then moved toward the door, looking smug. "I know all you summer folks come from away, thinking we're just a bunch of hicks on this island, but we're not. Investigations like this are delicate operations and should be left to trained professionals."

"Well, thanks for your time," Noah mumbled, standing and taking a step toward the door, which now stood wide. Reluctantly, I rose and followed.

"Thank you for stopping by," he said to Noah with a level of respect in his tone that faded as he turned his attention to me. "Do tell your aunt for me that her blueberry pie yesterday was as delicious as always."

I'm not sure what kind of reception I was hoping for from the sheriff's office, but it certainly wasn't that. By the time Noah and I stood on the sidewalk outside, I was fuming. "The nerve! He didn't even catalog the note as evidence, or take a formal statement, or anything." The man's condescending arrogance made me bristle, as if all I should care about was keeping to the kitchen and making pies. *Little does he know I'm descended from a long line of kitchen witches,* I thought with every bit as much smugness as the sheriff had possessed, *so he'd just better watch out if I do.* Worst kitchen witch ever or not, if he made me angry enough, I just might find a way to turn him into a toad after all.

"I'm sure Grady knows more about it than we do." Noah pressed his lips together until they formed a thin, pale line across his face. I could tell he wasn't pleased but was trying to make the best of it. "I appreciate your help, though, Tamsyn. If you don't mind continuing to go through the records... I mean, after this, I understand—"

"Of course, I'll still take a look," I assured him.

And that wasn't the only thing I planned to look into, that was for certain. Every time I closed my eyes, I could see Douglas Strong standing in the rain, trying to speak. There was more to his death, that much I knew. If the authorities weren't going to take me seriously, I would just have to find the truth myself. I took a deep breath and squared my shoulders. That would show Sheriff Grady. I was going to solve the mystery of Douglas Strong's death, somehow. There had to be a way, and if I couldn't do it alone, I'd get Sybil and Cassandra to help. Whatever had caused the crash, I would figure it out, even if it took embracing my destiny and becoming a full-fledged witch to succeed.

CHAPTER EIGHT

*W*hen Sybil told me we were meeting at Cass's family's tearoom, I have to be honest, my imagination ran away with me. I pictured a dark, mystical sort of place, with magical potion ingredients like eye of newt and dragon scales kept in bottles and jars or maybe one of those big apothecary cabinets with all the tiny drawers. I assumed there would be a beaded curtain, behind which nervous-looking clients would furtively slip in order to get their palms read. What I didn't expect was to walk into a room that looked like it was set for an afternoon tea in Wonderland.

Each of the shop's four walls was painted in their own shade of pastel blue, pink, yellow, or green. There were a dozen or more small, round tables, each draped with a different floral-print tablecloth. Lace doilies covered every visible surface, and I had the impression the Hollings had somehow managed to collect one of every variety of china tea pot or cup and saucer pattern that had ever been created. It was a Tuesday around noon, and every seat was filled with people dressed in their Sunday best, eating delicate sandwiches and pastries from three-tiered serving trays.

I waited near the front door for a minute before Cassandra entered the room, wearing another of the long, flowing skirts and peasant blouses that seemed to be her signature style. Her long black hair was braided in a single rope down her back. When she saw me, she smiled and walked quickly toward where I stood.

"Hi, Tamsyn!" She greeted me with a quick hug. "Sybil's already here. We're meeting in the back room."

Aha. So, there *was* a back room after all.

But it, too, was not as I had imagined it. As it turned out, the private room where we met was the one usually reserved for birthday parties, which is how I found myself attending my first official coven meeting while seated on a massive throne with the words "Birthday Princess" painted in golden script above my head. Again, not exactly how I'd pictured the day going. The one thing that did match my imagination was the Ouija board that had been placed on top of the velvet-draped table. When Cass and I entered the room, Sybil was just setting the heart-shaped pointer on the board.

"Have you ever used a spirit board, Tamsyn?" Sybil asked once I was seated on my throne.

I shrugged. "Sure. I think there was something like this at Becky Johnson's birthday party when I was in the seventh grade. I distinctly remember one of the other girls pushing the pointy thing toward the word *no* when Becky asked if Matt Blake would ask her to the middle-school dance."

Sybil and Cass both laughed, though I wasn't certain why. Everyone knew Ouija boards were a bunch of hooey. No matter how much everyone swore they wouldn't, someone was always going to push the marker to make the board say what they wanted to hear.

"You've never used a spirit board with real witches, then," Sybil said knowingly.

"Obviously not," I muttered.

"Do you have the note?" Sybil asked.

I took the crumpled note from my pocket and put it on the table. I started to place my fingers on the wooden pointer, but to my surprise, Cass put her hand out, stopping me.

"Not like that," she said. "We don't touch the planchette."

No touching the planchette? I couldn't help but wonder what the whole point of this exercise was. Were we just going to sit and stare at the board? I was about to ask when a sulfurous smell tickled my nose and caught me up short, tying my stomach into a knot. The thick white pillar candle Sybil had been holding was suddenly lit, but there was no sign of a match. My skepticism waned, replaced by a mounting apprehension. What would I do if it turned out all this was real?

As if nothing out of the ordinary had happened, Sybil set the candle in a brass holder beside the board. Then she and Cass joined hands, and each reached out to take hold of mine, too. Just as it had happened the night of the party, the moment our fingers touched and the circle was closed, a current of electricity moved through my arms. I jumped and tried to pull my hands away, but my friends tightened their grips. After a few moments, the sharp tingling I'd initially felt settled into a more manageable hum, and my muscles relaxed, though my pulse continued to throb as if I'd just run up a flight of stairs.

"Now what?" I whispered.

"Now we center ourselves."

Center ourselves? I thought. *Definitely hooey.* I sighed heavily, my frustration getting the better of me. "I'm sorry, but that's the type of nonsense people always say to do, and I have no idea how to do it."

"Start by taking a few deep breaths," Sybil instructed me.

"Clear your mind of any distractions," Cass added. "Then think about the question we want answered."

I nodded, and despite my grave misgivings, I respected them both enough that I gave it a shot. Having failed miserably at both yoga and meditation in the past, I didn't have high hopes, but shockingly, I could almost feel the stillness entering my body as I drew my first breath.

"I think it's working," I said with much surprise as I pushed the air out of my lungs. "What should we ask first?"

"Let's start," Sybil said, "by finding out if Doug Strong's death was a murder, a suicide, or an accident."

I nodded. "So, I just ask that? Spirit board, was Doug Strong's death a murder, an accident, or a suicide?"

"No, no," Cass corrected. "It's best if you start with a yes or no question. Asking it to spell out too many long messages can take all day. And you can just address it as *spirits*, not spirit board. It's more polite."

"Oh, sorry," I said, directing my apology at the rectangle of cardboard on the table and then feeling about as ridiculous as one might expect when I realized I was addressing an inanimate object. Still, the others were counting on me so I had to go through with the ritual as best as I could. I took a deep breath and spoke loudly. "Spirits, was Doug Strong murdered?"

"Good job," Sybil assured me.

I stared at the board, but nothing was happening. This was hardly a surprise since the three of us were just sitting there, holding hands, and not touching the board or the planchette at all. "Now what?"

"Now, we wait," Cass informed me.

That's it? I nearly yelled, only managing to keep my cool because I was so relaxed from all the breathing in and out that my body could have been made of limp spaghetti. Instead of throwing a fit, I kept my mouth shut and stared intently at the wooden planchette, breathing to the point I feared I might hyperventilate.

The first time the heart-shaped scrap of wood moved on its own, I thought I had imagined it. My head was dizzy from the breathing, and the movement was so slight that it could easily have been attributed to my eyes playing a trick on me. I blinked a few times and had just decided that the movement had been in my mind when it moved again, and not just a little. Without a single one of us touching it, the planchette slid shakily across the board all on its own, coming to rest on the word yes. I was no longer breathing at all. "Did you see that?" I whispered.

Sybil nodded. "Spirits, tell us who sent the note."

After a few tense seconds, the planchette jerked and chugged across the board until it landed on the letter L. I gasped. Without thinking, I pulled my hands back, breaking the circle. The candle's flame flickered and went out.

"Tamsyn," Cass said with a groan, "do you know how much energy it's going to take to get started again?"

"I'm sorry, but I just remembered something that happened the afternoon of Doug Strong's party, when the inn was filled with all of those, uh, witches." I stopped and swallowed. Even considering my present company, and the fact that I'd just watched a wooden pointer move itself across a spirit board unaccompanied, I still couldn't shake the belief that talking about witches as though they were real was ludicrous.

"Yes, the witches from the mainland. They visit every year for the solstice," Cass said as if it weren't at all unusual to talk about a supernatural convention descending on the island on an annual basis, which I supposed for her it wasn't. "What happened?"

"There was an older woman," I continued, "Madame Alexandria. She offered to do a reading for me. I said no, but then she just went ahead and told me anyway that she saw the letter L and an airplane. I hadn't really thought about it until now, but here's the letter L again. That has to be the killer, don't you think?"

Sybil nodded excitedly. "I think you might be right."

"All we need are the rest of the letters in the name." I reached one hand out to each side to form the circle again, but Cass and Sybil both shook their heads.

"It's no good," Cass explained. "We've used too much energy already. There's no way we'll be able to make a connection again so soon."

"I'm afraid she's right," Sybil agreed, yawning, and now that I thought about it, I could feel my own exhaustion creeping up on me. "Let's meet up tomorrow and try this again."

With nothing left to do but wait, I headed back to the inn. What I really needed was a nap, but when I got to my bedroom, I was greeted by one very naughty black cat wallowing in the middle of the Strong Corp. financial papers, plus the new documents Noah had given me, which all had been knocked off the desk, mixed around, and spread in a thin layer across the floor.

"Oh, Gus," I groaned. As I took a step in his direction, Gus saw fit to hightail it out of the room before the door shut and locked him in with my wrath. As I reached down to gather the papers in a pile, my eye was drawn to a yellow slip that was badly rumpled from having been directly underneath the massive feline. It was a carbon copy of a handwritten invoice from a mechanic who had done some work on Douglas Strong's plane. It was dated June 19, just three days before the crash. To my eye, there was no mistaking the similarities between the writing on this invoice and what was on the threatening note I'd found the day before.

The mechanic's name was one I'd heard before: Larry Sloane.

The letter L and an airplane. Bingo.

I raced down the stairs to the kitchen at double speed, finding Aunt Gwen where she always seemed to be, cooking something delectable.

"Tamsyn, ready for that lesson on how to bake lemon pound cake?"

"Another time, if that's all right," I replied. "If I needed to find some information on a local resident, where would I start?"

Her eyes narrowed. "What kind of information, exactly? This doesn't have anything to do with you and Noah Caldwell, does it?" From the way she said it, and the mischievous gleam in her eye, it was impossible not to catch her meaning.

"Noah and I? But we aren't... That is, I've been helping him sort through some of the Strong Corp. accounts. Purely professional."

"Oh." Her disappointment was palpable. But had she asked because the gossip had already come home to roost, or because she'd been trying to cast a spell on me?

"Aunt Gwen..." I was about to ask her straight out if she'd been slipping me a love potion, but I changed my mind. Finding out about Larry Sloane was more important. "The research?"

"Who are you trying to find information about?"

I hesitated, not sure I wanted to admit to all the snooping I was doing. "I need to get my car fixed, and I wanted to check out a local guy that was recommended to me, Larry Sloane."

"Oh, I know Larry. He's very good."

Of course, she knew Larry. He was probably the only mechanic on the island. Why hadn't I thought of that before mentioning his name? "Yeah, but I want some customer review kind of things."

She thought for a moment. "Your best bet is checking with Sue Ellen Wolcott."

"Sybil's grandmother?"

My aunt nodded. "She volunteers over at the library, managing the town archives for the historical society. Plus, she knows everything about everyone."

Great. In a town full of busybodies, my aunt just happened to be best friends with the queen bee.

It was almost four o'clock when I chained my bicycle to the rack outside the library. Technically, I probably didn't need to lock it up since I was floating on an island with almost no crime, but it's how I was raised. The library was empty when I arrived, and it took little effort to locate Sue Ellen Wolcott behind the archives desk. She had dark brown hair that was either kept that way with the help of a hairstylist or possibly by magic—now that I was privy to some of Pinecroft Cove's better-kept secrets. Though she was well into her seventies, she was stylish and radiated vitality, and I was beginning to understand what Sybil meant by glamour magic.

"Um, Auntie Sue?" It's what I'd always called her as a child, but I hadn't seen her in years, so I tripped over the greeting. Was that really what I should call her? I wasn't sure. Still, Miss Wolcott seemed too formal, but addressing a woman from my grandmother's generation by her first name alone felt equally wrong. Apparently, Noah wasn't the only element from my past that made me doubt myself. Since returning to the island, I'd discovered a new way to feel less certain of myself every day. Yay, me.

"Tamsyn!" Auntie Sue beamed and didn't seem to notice my awkwardness at all, which put me at ease immediately. Her eyes crinkled when she smiled, but in a way that somehow didn't make you think of her age. More glamour magic, for sure. "How can I help you?"

"Well, this might sound strange, but Aunt Gwen tells me you know everything that goes on in town. I was hoping you could tell me if there was ever any bad blood between Douglas Strong and his mechanic, Larry Sloane."

Auntie Sue's perfectly manicured eyebrows shot up in obvious surprise. "As a matter of fact, there was something a couple years back. Hold on, and I'll see if I can find it in the archive."

Being a millennial, I guess I was expecting some sort of digital archive, so I was more than a little surprised when she came back a few minutes later carrying several thick binders filled with actual paper news clippings. She rifled through the pages until she came to the one she was looking for.

"Here we go," Auntie Sue said, opening the book flat so I could see. "It's not always so easy to find things, but I was just organizing this part of the archive a few weeks ago, and this was quite the topic of conversation on the island in its day. Five years back, Doug Strong was buying up land near the waterfront to build his first set of condos on the island. It just so happened that it had been a couple of terrible years in a row for the lobstermen, and a number of them were looking to sell. He managed to buy up a whole row of houses, except for one, which was owned by Minnie Sloane."

Minnie Sloane. I was sure I'd heard the name before, but I couldn't remember where. "She refused to sell?"

"She made a counteroffer, for double what he'd paid the others. I guess she figured, being the last one, he'd make it worth her while. Plus, Minnie's husband had a small pension from the coast guard, so they weren't in as bad of shape financially as some of the others were. Who could blame her for holding out for as much as she could get, right?"

"Makes sense. Did he take the offer?"

"Well, a funny thing happened. All of a sudden, some investigators from the EPA came by, and Minnie found out she had toxic chemicals in her soil from the boats her husband stored there. The state was going to make her pay a fortune to clean it all up. So, Doug bought the property for the original price he'd offered and promised to take care of the cleanup out of his own pocket."

I frowned. "That sounds pretty generous under the circumstances. Why the bad blood?"

"Well, folks around here were split on that. Some

agreed the offer was generous. Minnie tried to be greedy as far as they saw it and then had some bad luck, and Doug came to her rescue, making sure she made out the same in the end as all her neighbors had. But others found the timing a little too convenient and swore that Douglas Strong had orchestrated the EPA investigation himself, maybe even paying some people off along the way to get the results he wanted. After all, a lot of people store boats on their properties, so why was hers the only one that was contaminated?"

I nodded slowly. It was the type of thing that was easy to imagine a real estate developer doing, especially one who had friends in high places. "Was there any proof he'd done it?"

"Not a shred. But I recall Larry was pretty vocal at the time about it all being a setup."

She flipped the page to another article, and I saw a large photo of a Strong Corp. sign covered in graffiti beneath a headline that read "Vandalism Spree Continues to Plague Downtown Summerhaven." The similarities between the graffiti and the handwriting on the invoice and note were impossible to dismiss. My pulse ticked faster as I recalled the graffiti-covered sign near the new condos, and I stood quickly, eager to go check it out in person. If Larry held a big enough grudge against Doug Strong after five years to still be defacing his signs, and he had access to the plane, who knew what else he might have been capable of doing?

"Tamsyn, there are some articles in the back you

might be interested in. About…well, about your mother."

My insides froze. My mother was a topic that had not yet been broached since I'd arrived on the island. It shouldn't have surprised me that someone would bring it up eventually, but I felt blindsided. "What about her, exactly?"

"The investigation into her disappearance, dear. News coverage, eyewitness statements. You were so young at the time and then going off to Ohio so soon after it happened. I wasn't sure how many of the details you'd ever been given."

I fiddled with a sharp edge on my thumbnail as I focused my gaze on the edge of the desk. I dreaded seeing the pity in Auntie Sue's eyes. "She took the boat out on the cove and never came back. There were squalls reported that day, so she probably drowned, though her body was never found, so who knows? But, I think I've got the gist of it."

"There's a bit more than that, Tamsyn."

"Dad and Nancy never thought I needed to know more, and I kind of agree. It was so long ago. What's the point?"

"But you're a grown woman now, and she was your mother. Don't you think—?"

"Thank you, Auntie Sue, but another time. I really have to go."

I sprinted toward the exit, pretending it was the excitement of the discovery that drove me to hurry, not my desire to put distance between myself and the articles about my mother's disappearance. I was almost to the main door when I stopped, my attention drawn to a photograph on the wall that I hadn't noticed before. It was the portrait of a young woman. Its faded sepia tones suggested it was an original print, while the woman's hairstyle and clothing appeared to be from sometime in the very early twentieth century. No name or date accompanied the photo, though there was a discolored spot on the wall where it looked like a plaque of some sort used to be. I found myself rooted to the spot, my eyes unable to look away from the woman's face, which felt hauntingly familiar. I had no idea who she was, but she could have been my long-lost twin.

CHAPTER NINE

The next morning, I rose before dawn with the intention of finding out as much as I could about Larry Sloane. I crept down the back stairs to steal a quick breakfast before anyone else was up, but as soon as I got a glimpse of the kitchen, it was clear I had miscalculated. The old farmhouse table on the far end of the room had been cleared of its usual collection of odds and ends, and on its scratched and well-worn surface sat a massive book with an unmistakable leather binding. The grimoire. Beside it were two wooden spoons, the very same ones I had been warned might make things explode, plus measuring spoons, bowls, and other assorted supplies. I hovered at the edge of the stairwell, keeping my distance.

"There you are," Aunt Gwen said in greeting as she entered the kitchen through the dining room door, exuding all the chipper good cheer of a true morning person. A fresh floral apron was already tied in place around her plump midsection, and her hair had been pinned into her usual no-nonsense bun on top of her head. "Let's get started."

"What's all this?" I asked, shrinking into the gloomy shadow behind me as if it weren't too late to hide.

"It's time to begin your studies."

"Maybe another day—" I started to argue, but she cut me off, taking me by the arm and leading me to the table.

"It's time," she repeated, more forcefully. "Bess Hollings told me all about the coven meeting, and even if she hadn't, I felt the ripples of it myself."

"What do you mean you felt it?"

"Any time magic is used, it creates a force that radiates out, like ripples in a pond when you throw a stone in the water. If you're close enough, you can feel it. If you're a witch, of course," she added with a laugh.

"I had no idea," I mumbled, not sure how I felt about this revelation. Not only did I still need to come to terms with the fact that I was a witch, but if I ever learned to use magic—and, staring at the cooking implements on the table in front of me, that was a big *if*—every other witch around me would know about it. My world got weirder every time Aunt Gwen opened her mouth.

"That's what I'm here for, to teach you everything

you need to know about being a kitchen witch." She picked up one of the wooden spoons and used it to gesture to the other. "Go ahead."

I eyed it warily and shook my head. "I don't think so. You said things could explode."

"Not just by picking it up, dear."

Oh sure, like that was supposed to be obvious. Tentatively, I brushed the spoon with one finger. It felt like…a wooden spoon. No sparks. No electrical current traveling up my arm. No puff of smoke. I curled my fingers around the handle and picked it up, breathing easier. "Now what? Do I wave it at the table, and all of the ingredients will magically combine to form a cake?"

Aunt Gwen fixed me with a look like I'd grown a second head out of my shoulder. "You have quite a vivid imagination."

Right. You're about to give me a magic lesson from a grimoire masquerading as a 1970s' cookbook, and I'm the weirdo in the family?

I watched as she opened the giant book to a batter-splattered page and then set out the ingredients it called for: sugar, cornstarch, salt, cinnamon. I groaned as she lifted a basket of freshly picked wild blueberries from the floor and plunked it onto the table.

"Not pie again."

"Just the filling," she said knowingly. "That's where the magic is."

"Only in the filling? You mean all that pie crust I rolled out for Doug Strong's funeral was a waste?"

"Of course not. You can't make pie without a crust."

"But you can buy crust already made from the grocery store!" I knew, because up until recently, I thought that was simply how it came.

"Well, I..." she spluttered. Frankly, the expression on her face would have been more appropriate if I'd just suggested making the filling out of kittens as opposed to simply using conveniently packaged frozen pastry product to make a pie like everyone else on the planet did. "Put the berries in the pot."

I picked up the basket and carried it to the stove. The cauldron-shaped pot was in its spot, and I dumped the berries in, spilling a few on the floor in the process.

"Carefully," she chided. If magical cooking school was like regular school, I was cruising for a detention. "Now, before you add each of the ingredients, I want you to close your eyes and focus your intentions. Stir three times, clockwise, with the spoon, then repeat."

"Um." I looked from the pot to the spoon, then to my aunt. "What's an intention?"

"That's the spell you're working or the purpose for the magic. For example," she continued when my facial expression revealed I was completely lost, "with something like this blueberry pie, you might infuse it with happiness. You would think of things that make you happy, usually three things because three is a powerful number, and you would meditate on them as you stir, until you can feel the magic flowing into the pot."

My mouth dropped open as understanding dawned. "That's why everyone ate so much pie at the funeral. You filled it with happiness!"

"Happiness, comfort, fond memories. Pie is a very good choice for funerals. And holidays." She shrugged as she reached past me to turn on the burner. "Makes a good breakfast, too."

My mind flitted back to the mysterious note I'd found in Doug Strong's papers, and the revelation Madame Alexandria had made about an airplane and the letter L. "What if I wanted to find out something in particular, like who had done something, for instance? Could magic help with that?"

"Kitchen magic is less suited for that type of thing, although there are some ways. I remember when I was a little girl, our mother wanted to find out which of the neighborhood children was picking the tomatoes out of her garden. She made a blueberry pie with some particularly magical berries that grow nearby and infused it with truth. When we'd all had our fill, she simply asked who was doing it, and the guilty party confessed on the spot."

Great. So, all I had to do was make enough pie for everyone on the island whose name had an L in it, and I'd find the killer in no time.

I took a pinch of cinnamon and sprinkled it over the berries, stirring clockwise in multiples of three. Nothing exploded, and I let out the breath I'd been holding. I repeated it with the sugar, my mind wandering back to the problem at hand. It was the height of summer, and that meant the island population had swelled to over ten thousand people. That was a lot of pie. But I already had a suspect in mind, so maybe all I needed to do was bake a pie and take it to Larry Sloane.

"Tamsyn! Eyes on the pot, or it will boil over."

I jumped at the sudden scolding, losing my grip on the wooden spoon in the process. Before I could stop it, the spoon slipped from my hand and fell into the pot with a plop. I jumped again at the sound of a massive boom. In an instant, the kitchen had filled with thick, black smoke.

And with that, my first magic lesson came to an abrupt end.

CONSIDERING THE EVENTS OF THE MORNING, there were now two things I could no longer deny. First, everything my aunt had told me about myself and our family lore was true. Magic was real. I was a witch. And second, given that there was likely to be half-cooked blueberry pie filling dripping from the ceiling for the foreseeable future, I was without a doubt the worst kitchen witch in the history of witchcraft.

After opening the windows to air out the smoke and mopping up as much of the sugary, blue goo as I was able to reach, there was little more I could do at the inn. Aunt Gwen did her best to remain upbeat. I truly don't know how she managed it, given what a disappointment I was turning out to be. I stuck around just long enough to make sure all the overnight guests got breakfast, washed up the dirty dishes, and then headed out on my bicycle before I could cause any more damage.

I didn't have a destination in mind but soon found myself pedaling along Island Ring Road, which, as the name suggested, made a large loop around the island. It was also the road that led to the Marian Cabot Memorial Airfield, where Douglas Strong had been headed on the night of the crash. I slowed as I approached the sign, weighing whether it would be worth stopping in to see if I could find out more about Larry Sloane.

The airfield was small, with a single runway that had at some point in its history been paved, but not very recently if the faded paint and bleached asphalt was any indication. There was a Cape Cod style house near the driveway, with white clapboard siding and green shutters. A sign on the front door identified it as the business office for Island Air Delivery Services and encouraged pilots to please check in at the front desk upon arrival. Two airplane hangars, the rounded type made of metal, stood side by side at the far end of the runway. There was one small plane visible near the hangers that may have landed recently, as someone, the pilot perhaps, was unloading boxes from it and stacking them in a pile on the ground.

I leaned my bike against the house and pondered what to do next. The hangars seemed the most likely place to start, except that I had no idea what Larry Sloane looked like, or whether he would even be working at the airfield that day. On the other hand, given the prevalence of gossip on the island, any employee at the airfield could be a source of useful information. I turned toward the business office, formulating a plan.

When I pushed the front door open, a blast of cold air hit my face, and I could hear the hum of a window air-conditioning unit. A large man with a ginger beard sat behind an old steel desk. He wore a uniform shirt with the Island Air Delivery Services logo and the name Kevin stitched on a patch above the pocket. "Can I help you?" he asked as I shut the door against the summer heat.

"I hope so. I need some information on shipping," I lied.

"Well, that's what we do," he assured me with a friendly smile that almost made me feel guilty for the ruse. "What are you wanting to ship?"

"Pies," I said. The smell of scorched blueberries

was still embedded deep within my nostrils, so naturally it was the first thing that came to mind.

"You're Miss Gwyneth's niece, aren't you, from the Pinecroft Inn?"

"Uh, yes…that's me," I stumbled in reply, still not used to living in a place where everyone knew my business. "My name's Tamsyn."

"Tamsyn, that's right. Your aunt makes the best pies I've ever had. Are you thinking of delivering them to the mainland?"

"Exactly, yes." As made-up excuses went, that one wasn't half bad. I made a mental note to bring Kevin a pie next time I was in the neighborhood. "Is that something you do here?"

"Sure. We run flights between the mainland and all the islands several times a day." He pulled out a thick ledger-style book and placed it on the desk in front of him, opening it and flipping through the pages. "Do you have an idea of how many you'd like to ship? We can price them individually, or there are discounts if you do bulk orders."

"Well, I'm not really sure," I told him, not wanting him to go through too much effort. "It's just an idea I've been playing with. I'm not ready to commit to anything yet."

"Well, I think it's a good idea," he assured me, unaware he was the one who had come up with it. "Those pies would sell like hotcakes to folks on the mainland. You could probably get orders from restaurants and grocery stores, too."

"That's…pretty brilliant, actually." One thing to be said about Kevin, he had the mind of an entrepreneur. If I hadn't just proven what an utter disaster in the kitchen I was, I would've been tempted to turn this pie delivery idea into a real business. After all, I kind of needed an income.

There was a rumbling overhead, and when I turned to look out the window, a small plane was just touching down on the runway. Unlike the delivery plane I'd seen on my way in, this one had the sleek appearance of an expensive toy.

"Summer folks," Kevin said when he saw me eyeing the plane. I could tell by the dismissive way he said it that he didn't have the highest opinion of them as a group, but that was a common enough mind-set for locals. "They always have the fancy ones. Although even that one's nothing compared to the one Doug Strong flew."

My heart started to beat faster as the conversation turned in exactly the direction I'd been hoping. "The one that went down in the bay, you mean?"

"That was a real shame. We get a lot of nice planes through here, on account of Larry being the best mechanic in all of Penobscot Bay. They fly 'em in from neighboring islands and even the mainland for him to do maintenance on. But Doug's was something special." The way he was talking, I couldn't quite tell if his regret extended to the loss of the plane's pilot, as well, or if it was just the machine that would be missed.

"Larry...Larry Sloane?" I asked, trying to play it cool. I didn't want to let on that Larry was the whole reason I was there.

"Yeah, that's right."

"And he worked on Doug Strong's plane?"

"Well, now..." Kevin paused, and I swore I could see the flicker of a troubling thought in his eyes. "It used to be that Larry was the only one Doug would trust with that plane, but he'd started bringing it to a guy on the mainland. Only, come to think of it, I swear I saw the plane in Larry's hangar not long ago."

"You're obviously an expert on planes, Kevin. Can I ask you something?" I tried to keep my tone as casual as possible. "What do you think caused Doug Strong's plane to go down?"

"You know, that's been keeping me up at night." There was a deep furrow in his brow that made me believe this was true. "It just doesn't make sense any way I look at it. Some of these billionaire types spend all their money on a plane and barely know how to fly it, but not Doug. He knew his stuff. So pilot error is pretty hard for me to swallow. Now, on the other hand, I see some planes coming through in such rough shape it's hard to believe they can stay aloft the fifteen minutes it takes to get from shore to here. But Doug's plane was fairly new, and well maintained, plus if Larry was the one doing the work on it, there's no way he would've let it fly without a clean bill of health. I just don't know."

I dropped my voice to just above a whisper. "What do you think of the speculation going around that it wasn't an accident at all?"

"Suicide, you mean?" Kevin shook his head. "I've heard that, too. I'll admit I didn't know him as well as some, but Doug didn't seem the type for that."

"Did he have enemies?"

"Show me a rich guy who don't," he answered with a laugh. "Or anyone, really."

"Good point. But I imagine building all those condos downtown made him somewhat of a controversial figure, to say the least."

"There were some troubles back when the project started. In fact, Larry and Doug had a falling out over it, but that had all been patched up some time ago."

"It had?"

"Well, sure. Otherwise, Larry wouldn't have been working on Doug's plane." That troubled look flickered across his face again, and I was certain Kevin wasn't as confident with what he'd just said as he was trying to come across. When it came to people who might've wanted Douglas Strong dead, Larry Sloane definitely remained at the top of my list.

"I'd better get going," I said, heading to the door. I'd gotten about as much information out of the conversation as I thought was likely, and more than I needed to confirm my suspicions.

"Don't forget what you came for," Kevin called out.

I blinked, having already forgotten what that was. He was holding out a slip of paper, and I took it. On it was a list of shipping prices. Oh right. The pies. "Thanks, Kevin. I'll get back to you as soon as I know more about what Aunt Gwen has in mind."

Before leaving, I walked out to the hangars just in case Larry happened to be around. The first building was empty, though the expensive plane that had landed while I was in the office had been pulled inside the hangar next to the one where I stood. At first, I didn't see any sign of the pilot, but just as I was about to step back outside the hangar, I heard muffled voices coming from nearby. Instinctively, I stepped backward where I would be hidden from view by the hangar wall.

A man in a suit stepped from the adjacent hangar into the bright noontime sun. He wore the type of expertly tailored suit that screamed money and carried a briefcase of supple leather. If this was one of the summer folks, as Kevin had called them, who was visiting the island for vacation, he hadn't dressed the part. He was talking to someone, and though I couldn't see who it was or hear what they were saying, the man appeared to be very agitated. After an intense exchange of words, the man tossed the briefcase onto the ground and strode back inside the hangar. An engine fired up, and soon the fancy plane was pulling out of the hangar, headed for the runway. When the plane was in the air, I ventured to leave, but once more, the sound of movement outside stopped me in my tracks. The unknown person with whom the man in the suit had been arguing stepped into the sunlight. As he bent to retrieve the briefcase, I saw his face, and my heart leaped into my throat. It was Curtis Strong.

I retreated as far into the hangar as I could, standing against the far wall until I heard the sound of a car starting up and rumbling along the gravel driveway back to the main road. I had no idea what Curtis was doing at the airfield or why he'd been arguing with the man in the suit. All I knew was that for some reason, I couldn't quite put my finger on, I didn't want him to know I was there. Finally, when there had been no sound or movement outside for at least a full minute, I turned to go.

As I did, my attention was caught by a bright yellow banner behind me on the wall that read *Summerhaven Flying Club Centennial 1917-2017*. Beneath it were several framed photos that appeared to picture the membership throughout the years. In the one that was dated June 1927, I found what had by now become a very familiar face, the single woman standing in a group of men beside a classic biplane. Her name was printed beneath: Lillian Bassett.

Lillian. Yet another L name. Given her last name and general appearance, we had to be related. I had never heard the name before and had no idea who she was. Then something else struck my brain with the force of a brick to the forehead. There was an airplane in the photo. *The letter L and an airplane.* What if a spirit was responsible for the crash? Or what if the vision Madame Alexandria had shared had nothing to do with Doug Strong's killer after all? I was more confused now than I'd ever been.

*a*s I retrieved a box of old clothing from the trunk of the car I had borrowed from Aunt Gwen, there was no denying I desperately needed to get Miss Josephine fixed. However, with the real possibility I was about to prove that the island's best mechanic was a murderer, I was holding off. What if Larry Sloane realized I was onto him and cut my brake line? A girl couldn't be too careful.

The near encounter with Curtis at the airfield was still on my mind, and try as I might, I simply couldn't figure out what he had been doing there, nor could I shake the lingering sense that something was amiss. I glanced toward the clinic building before crossing the street in the direction of Sybil's shop. Noah would be working there all day, I knew, but whether I would venture over to speak to him about his cousin was still up in the air.

The mannequins in the window at Rags to Riches had been dressed since my last visit, and a *Grand Opening* banner hung on the wall above the cash register. The store was not yet open for business, but I could tell the big day was just around the corner. "It looks amazing," I told Sybil as she greeted me at the door and relieved me of the heavy cardboard box I'd been carrying.

"Thanks! I can't believe opening day is a week away." She carried the box to the back counter and set it down, pulling on the top flap to see inside. "Are these the dresses from the attic?"

"A few of them. I haven't even opened most of the trunks up there yet, but these are the ones I wanted you to take a look at first."

"From the trunk where you found the bracelet?" Sybil asked, and I nodded. "Oh, speaking of that, I got it all shined up for you. Take a look."

She handed me a slim cardboard jewelry box with Rags to Riches printed on the lid. Inside was the silver bracelet, sandwiched between two layers of cotton padding. The tarnish was gone, and the engraving was now clear and easy to read.

"It looks like names," I said as I examined the writing on the links. "Frannie, Ruth, Annabel, Flo, Hannah, May, Eleanor, Daisy, and then the initials in the middle link are LB and the number twenty-eight."

"It's a friendship bracelet," Sybil explained, taking the bracelet from me and fastening it on my wrist.

"They were very popular as gifts up through World War II. Each person would buy a link and have it engraved with their name. Then they'd put them all together to make a bracelet. I think the middle link is a date, 1928, and the owner probably had the initials LB."

"LB?" My breath caught as I remembered the photo I'd found in the hangar. "Lillian Bassett."

"Who's that?"

"I'm not sure, but I've seen her in a couple of old photographs around town, both from around the nineteen twenties. Sybil..." I had to swallow the lump that had formed in my throat before continuing. "She's the one I saw in my dream. The one who looks like me."

Sybil nodded as if what I'd said made perfect sense to her. "Let's have a look in the box."

She pulled out the top dress, the gold party dress that I'd worn in my dream, and spread it out on the counter to get a look inside. After studying it for a moment, her face lit up. "Ha! I thought so. Here's the label from the designer, Jeanne Lanvin. That was a couture house in Paris. And see here, where it says *Printemps-1928*? That means it was part of the spring collection of that year." She removed another dress from the box and spread it out next to the first one. It was black and white with embroidered flowers on the bodice and skirt hem. "This one's missing its label, but the style is from about the same year, and you can tell by the quality of the embroidery that it was made in Paris."

"It's just like what I saw in the dream," I said. "The seamstress who was working on the hem seemed very impressed by the dress."

"I would imagine so, although it's a little odd." A line formed across Sybil's brow as her face settled into a frown.

"What's odd?"

"Well, usually if a lady was having dresses made in Paris, she would travel there for fittings. They'd make a dress form that was a perfect replica of her body and would have a detailed sheet of measurements to work from. When the dresses were delivered, there wouldn't be any reason to have them hemmed. Altered a little, maybe, if she'd gained or lost some weight, but assuming she was an adult, it's unlikely her height would change that much."

"Huh." I knew nothing about dresses or how rich women had shopped for them almost a hundred years ago, but when she put it that way, it did sound strange.

"I have an idea," Sybil said, scooping the gold dress off the counter. "I think you should try this on."

"Me?"

"This is the one you wore in your dream, right?"

I nodded, my palms growing slick at the thought of putting the dress on for real.

"There has to be a reason you saw it. I have a spell

in mind that I'd like to try, a way to connect you to the history of the dress and its wearer. Are you willing to give it a try?"

I drew in a shaky breath. "Okay. Let's see what happens."

After Sybil muttered an incantation over the dress, she handed it to me. I stepped into the changing room and removed the cut-off denim shorts and T-shirt I'd thrown on that morning. The air-conditioning turned my bare skin to gooseflesh on contact, and the chilliness only intensified as I slipped the smooth, silky fabric of the dress over my head. Although there were some hooks I couldn't reach, I could tell it fit as though it had been made for me. I wondered if that was part of the spell Sybil had cast on her shop or something more. The coldness surrounding me intensified.

"Wow." Sybil gave the dress an appreciative look as I emerged from behind the curtain. As I stood in front of the full-length mirror, she closed the fasteners I had missed. "It fits perfectly."

"I know. Was that your doing?"

She shook her head. "The spell I worked wouldn't affect the fit."

"How does it work, then? Because I don't feel anything happening."

"No, not yet. There's a second half of the spell that couldn't be said until you were wearing the dress. Are you ready?"

I hesitated. "What's supposed to happen?"

"I have no idea. I've never done it before."

Great. What could go wrong? But it wasn't like I had any better ideas.

"Okay, go ahead," I told her, holding my breath and shutting my eyes. I heard a whisper as Sybil quietly recited the rest of the spell, and then I felt the sensation of air circling around me, almost as if the words of the incantation were traveling around my body on a light breeze. When I opened my eyes, the shop and Sybil were gone.

The space around me had been transformed into a restaurant, with crisp, white linen on the tables. Men and women were seated all around, dressed in fashions that felt impossibly antiquated to me but would have been commonplace in the 1920s. Along Main Street, Model-T Fords vied for space alongside horse-drawn carts. It was so real that I could hear the honk of a horn and the clink of silverware against plates, and as a waiter walked past me with a tray, the pungent smell of onions tickled my nose. The next moment, it was replaced by the cloying scent of rose perfume. My head began to spin, and I shut my eyes. When I opened them again, I was back in the shop, and Sybil was staring at me with her mouth agape.

"What just happened?" I asked, my entire body trembling.

"I was going to ask you the same thing," Sybil

replied. "One minute you were standing there, and the next minute, you were gone."

"Gone?" If I'd felt cold before, it was nothing compared to the chill that overtook my bones as I repeated what she'd said. "How could I be gone?"

"I don't know." Sybil's voice shook. "I closed my eyes, and you vanished. I was about to call my grandmother for help. I looked down for a minute to find my phone, and when I looked back, there you were again, like nothing had happened."

"Something did happen," I assured her. "I closed my eyes when you started the spell, and when I opened them, I was in a restaurant, and it was like I'd stepped into the nineteen twenties."

"This used to be a restaurant," Sybil whispered. "You don't think you might've actually…"

"No way. It was just some sort of dream or illusion, like before." I wanted to believe it. I truly did, despite the fact I could still detect a hint of roses in the air. All of a sudden, I had the distinct feeling that the dress was tightening around my body, suffocating me, and I clawed at the fabric to get it away from my skin. "Get me out of this thing."

"Stop," Sybil scolded. "That's no way to treat a designer dress."

Sybil's expert fingers quickly undid the back and I darted into the changing room as soon as I felt the last hook open. Only the prospect of Sybil's extreme disapproval kept me from leaving the gown in a heap on the floor. I pinched the fabric between two fingers, holding it away from me while touching as little of it as possible. "Here, I don't think I want it anymore."

"I can't keep this. It's too valuable."

"Hang onto it for now, then, would you?" I pleaded as I booked it toward the door.

"Wait," Sybil called after me. "We still need to get the coven back together. What about tonight?"

"Uh, maybe," I mumbled, not turning around. "I'll have to see." In all honesty, though, after the weirdness I'd just experienced, I wanted to stay as far away from magic as I could, and for as long as possible. My quiet life in Cleveland had done nothing to prepare me for any of this.

OUTSIDE THE SHOP, IT WAS WARM AND humid, and for a moment I was aware of nothing else but how good it felt against my clammy skin. My insides still quivered from the strange experience I'd had, but the familiar sights and sounds of modern-day Summerhaven were immensely soothing. I shut my eyes and breathed in the salty sea air. It felt so normal, yet I couldn't bear to open my eyes quite yet, just in case when I did, I found the streets filled with antique cars again. They were still closed as I took a timid step onto the sidewalk along Main Street, only to find my path blocked and my nose pressed into something solid that carried just a hint of bay rum aftershave. I opened my eyes and saw a navy-blue polo shirt approximately three-quarters of an inch from my face.

Hurriedly, I took a step backward, my cheeks burning like I'd just lit them with a match. Why hadn't I remembered to open my eyes before walking? Such a basic thing to forget.

"Tamsyn, we really must stop running into each other like this," Noah joked.

"Very funny," I said, channeling as much annoyance as possible to cover my embarrassment. "Actually, I was meaning to look for you today."

"Well, you found me," he quipped, rubbing the spot where my nose had plowed into his chest.

I gave him my best glare. "I think I've figured out who sent your uncle that threatening note."

His joking expression quickly faded away. "You have?"

"I found an invoice from him for some work he did on your uncle's plane, and the handwriting was too similar to the note to be a coincidence. I think Larry might be the one who vandalized the Strong Corp. signs."

"Whoa." Noah held up his hands, shaking his head. "You think Larry Sloane had something to do with my uncle's crash?"

"It's a possibility."

"I don't know." That his emotions were conflicted was plain on his face. "Larry's a good guy and a brilliant mechanic. Not just planes. He can fix anything. I've had him in the clinic several times to fix equipment, and I have a hard time imagining him doing anything like that."

"Look, I'm not saying he did," I soothed, "but there was some history between them, and according to the invoice, he had access to the plane just days before the crash. Don't you think the investigators should know?"

"I guess I could mention it to Joe Grady the next time I see him."

My nose wrinkled at the mention of the sheriff's name. "I was thinking of maybe taking it directly to the NTSB. They're the ones with jurisdiction, anyway, and no offense, but Sheriff Grady just seemed…" My voice trailed off, failing to describe my impression of the island's sheriff.

Noah sighed. "I guess I can give the lead investigator a call later today. Have you managed to make heads or tails out of those financial reports I gave you?"

I sucked in my breath. With everything else that had happened, I'd completely forgotten about the reports. What better excuse, though, to wriggle my way out of a coven meeting? "I'll take a look at them tonight. I promise."

"That would be great." Noah glanced at his watch. "I'm heading across the square to meet Curtis for lunch. Would you like to join us?"

"Thanks, but no," I said, my insides tightening at the mention of his cousin. I hesitated, wanting to tell him about seeing Curtis at the airfield but uncertain how to bring it up. I could already tell he thought I was half-crazy for accusing Larry Sloane of murder based on an amateur handwriting analysis. Suggesting his cousin was up to no good based on even less evidence would definitely not tilt the scales in favor of my mental health. I decided to save it for another time. "I'd better go. Aunt Gwen's expecting me back to set up for new guests."

Technically, Aunt Gwen wasn't expecting me back, but the rest was true enough. It was the middle of July, and we were expecting a complete turnover of rooms for the arrival of a large family that would be hosting a reunion at the inn. With twenty-six new people descending upon us all at once, ranging from age two to age ninety-five, I had a feeling Aunt Gwen could use all the help she could get.

When I arrived back at the house, it was filled with the aroma of baked goods, and I could hear the clattering of metal pans coming from the kitchen. Though I poked my head in and offered to help, I knew immediately from the look on Aunt Gwen's face that she hadn't yet forgotten about how I'd made the pies explode. I backed myself out of the room as quickly as I could and spent the rest of the day washing sheets, making beds, cleaning bathrooms, and scrubbing floors. By the time the guests arrived on the last ferry, I was exhausted and aching from head to toe.

Aunt Gwen was soon in her element playing hostess, so I escaped up the back stairs to my bedroom just after the dinner dishes were done. I stretched out on my bed and tried to sleep, but every time I closed my eyes, I could see myself standing in the restaurant that had mysteriously appeared around me where Sybil's shop was supposed to be. I was tossing and turning long after I heard the doors of the bedrooms downstairs closing as the last of the guests turned in for the night. When I was still wide awake at nearly midnight, I walked down the stairs to the second floor and knocked on Aunt Gwen's bedroom door.

"What is it, Tamsyn?" Aunt Gwen asked as she opened the door a crack. I could see from her bleary-eyed expression and the darkness of the room behind her that she'd been asleep, and I felt a stab of guilt.

"I'm sorry. It's not important." I turned to go, but she stopped me.

"You seem troubled, my dear."

"I just can't seem to get to sleep," I explained, not wanting to go into the reasons why. Even for a witch, falling through a crack in the space-time continuum before lunch felt like it stretched credibility just a bit.

"I see," she said in that way she had that made me wonder exactly how much she knew. "I think I have just the solution. Follow me."

"Follow you where, exactly?" I asked, though I'm

not sure why I bothered. She was already halfway to the back stairs that led to the kitchen. "Aunt Gwen, what do you have in mind?"

"I think it's time I taught you a sleeping spell," she replied. "It's so simple, even you... That is, I'm sure you'll be asleep in no time."

In the pit of my stomach, a cold, hard lump began to form. If her intent had been to help me relax, her words had exactly the opposite effect. I was pretty sure whatever magic lesson awaited me in the kitchen, I was going to end up regretting it.

CHAPTER ELEVEN

Twenty minutes after entering the kitchen, I had managed to scald a pan of milk. I know. It sounded bad to me, too. But believe it or not, it turns out that scalding milk is not the same thing as burning milk. Basically, I just had to stir it until it started to get bubbly and remove it from the heat before it either boiled out of the pot or stuck to the bottom. Aunt Gwen's nod of approval when I succeeded felt better than winning a gold medal. Perhaps there was hope for me as a kitchen witch after all.

While I stood stirring with my magical wooden spoon, the one that still made me flinch as I set it down on the ceramic spoon rest just in case something belatedly caught fire or went up in a puff of smoke, Aunt Gwen gathered a few small bottles from the spice cupboard.

"Add a heaping teaspoon of each of these to the milk," she instructed, setting the ingredients down beside me on the countertop.

Their labels were handwritten, and their contents a mystery to me even after I'd managed to decipher the fancy script.

"What is valerian root?" I asked, popping the cork off the bottle. Immediately, a stench similar to opening a laundry bag of old, smelly socks assaulted my nose. "Please don't tell me you expect me to ingest this."

"You'll hardly notice it," she answered with a chuckle, "once the rest of the ingredients are mixed in."

I sniffed it again and made a face before dumping a spoonful into the pot and putting the cork back in as quickly as I could. I doubted there was any magic in the world powerful enough to make that stuff taste good, but I was so desperate for sleep that I was willing to hold my nose and hope for the best. The next three bottles, labeled passionflower, magnolia bark, and lemon balm, were far less odiferous, though I still eyed them suspiciously as I measured out their contents and stirred them into the milky brew.

Aunt Gwen handed me a coffee mug and a silver tea strainer. After I'd poured the concoction into the mug, she picked up the plastic honey bottle from beside the stove, the one shaped like a teddy bear, squeezed a few squirts into the mug for good measure, and gave my work a satisfied nod. "That should do it.

Just stir it thoroughly and make sure it's cooled down enough so you don't burn your tongue."

"That's it? No incantations? No adding a vial of magical owl tears?"

"Owl's tears? Goodness no. That would keep you up all night."

I blinked, taking the mug from her without response. I'd been trying to make a joke, but I should have guessed magical owl tears were really a thing. I gave the contents a sniff, relieved to discover that it didn't smell like dirty socks at all. "So, I just drink it now and hope for the best?"

"Take it upstairs, drink it slowly, and maybe do some meditation, if you'd like."

Meditation? That was still a hard no, right up there with a downward-facing dog pose, on my list of things I never wanted to try doing. As for the rest of her instructions, I headed to my room and did as I was told. When I touched my tongue tentatively to the steaming liquid, I was surprised to find it tasted pleasant, like a sweet hot cocoa but without the chocolaty flavor. However, it was still too hot to drink, so I set it on the nightstand to let it cool. Since meditation was out, I opted for the next best sleep-inducing thing I could think of and grabbed the box of Strong Corp. financial records from my desk. I fluffed the pillows behind my back and snuggled into the covers, then spread several years' worth of bank statements out across my grandmother's quilt.

If you've never had the experience of sorting through piles of financial records at midnight, I'll spare you the trouble by saying right off, yes, it's exactly as boring as it sounds. I know that, as an accountant, I probably should've found it fascinating, but here's a little secret. I never wanted to be an accountant. That was my father's idea, one hundred percent.

My father was as practical as my mother was a dreamer. How they ever ended up together long enough for me to come along, I'll never comprehend. With my red hair, pale skin, and bright blue eyes, I looked exactly like my mother, so if my father had ever questioned whether I was really his, I wouldn't have blamed him. Sometimes I wondered myself, but he always seemed satisfied on that account, so I didn't ask too many questions. When I was sent to live with him, after my mother...well, after she was gone, I think I reminded him of her a little too much. From day one, as soon as I'd been enrolled in the same preparatory school my father had attended as a boy, I was told I was going to be an accountant just like him.

Though it might not have been my first choice in careers, I turned out to be surprisingly good at it—not counting being fired, which really wasn't my fault. I had a talent for seeing patterns, and for catching on quickly when things weren't adding up. I was halfway through my sleepy-time potion and about the same way through a box of records when it hit me. Those Strong Corp. bank statements? They weren't adding up. Not at all. I couldn't put my finger on how or where, but money was missing. A lot of it.

I pushed the records aside and rose from my bed, downing the last of the tepid contents of my mug in one big gulp. Outside my bedroom window, the full moon shone almost as brightly as the sun, reflecting off the black, rippling water of Pinecroft Cove. In the distance, the roofline of Cliffside Manor was dark and imposing. There was a flash of light from the lighthouse, and the image of Douglas Strong standing on the lawn, dripping with rain, was so vivid in my memory that, for a moment, I thought I saw him peeking out at me from the trees.

While that might have been an illusion, the fat black crow that landed on the lawn was not. Was it the same one I'd seen at Cliffside Manor before the funeral? There was no way to be sure, but I was jarred by its appearance. I shivered and stepped away from the window, pulling the curtains shut, but even though I could no longer see his house, his company's paperwork covered my bed. There was no escaping the man, almost as if he were haunting me.

I began to pace back and forth across my bedroom floor. This was my favorite activity when working through something puzzling. What I'd found in the Strong Corp. records was quite the brainteaser. By any measurement, Douglas Strong was a wealthy and successful man. But even though he'd hidden his tracks cleverly, there was no doubt in my mind that he had been skimming money from his own business, going back at least a year. Why? And could the reason have anything to do with his death?

I rifled through the rest of the documents in the box, hoping for something that would shed more light on my discovery. I came across an envelope near the bottom whose flap had been torn open, leaving a ragged edge. The return address on the front would make even the most innocent person's heart beat faster. The Internal Revenue Service. Inside was a notice that the Strong Corp. accounts were being audited. If I'd caught onto the accounting discrepancies, a trained auditor surely would have, too. According to those who knew him, Douglas Strong had been in good spirits and in sound mental health, but would the threat of getting caught embezzling money from his company have been a powerful enough reason for him to have crashed his plane into the bay?

My pacing slowed as my limbs and eyelids grew heavy, and I scooped the documents back into their box so I could stretch myself out on the bed. But even with the papers out of sight, I couldn't get the implications of their contents out of my head. Which was more likely that Larry Sloane had sabotaged the plane out of revenge or that Douglas Strong had crashed on purpose out of fear of the scandal that was about to unravel around him. Or maybe both theories were wrong, and the whole thing had been an accident after all.

I switched off my bedside light and drifted into a fitful sleep, filled with disjointed dreams of airplanes and rain. I woke some hours later, disoriented, to the sound of scratching at my bedroom door. I stood in the dark and shuffled to the door. When I opened it, Gus came bounding in, meowing at me incessantly as he jumped onto the bed and spun himself in circles.

"Seriously?" I muttered as he settled into the nest he'd created and curled into a ball with his bushy tail tucked beneath his nose. "You woke me up in the middle of the night so you could steal my bed?" He didn't bother so much as to open an eye in response. Why my aunt kept him around, I couldn't imagine.

With a sigh, I started down the stairs. My throat was dry, and while I didn't relish the thought of making any more sleeping potions, a glass of cold water was tempting. As I reached the second-floor landing, I paused. The house should have been silent, but the faint sound of music coming from the direction of the living room tickled my ear. I turned away from the back stairs and crept down the main staircase instead. The music grew louder, a classic jazz song, and I detected a tinny quality to the sound like it was a very old recording playing over a static-filled radio station. I frowned, wondering if one of the guests had been unable to sleep and had come downstairs and turned on the old stereo.

I had no idea what time it was, except that it had to be early in the morning because a soft, gray light was filtering through the windows, making it possible for me to see the entirety of the living room as soon as my foot hit the bottom step.

The first thing I noticed was the absence of people, but this detail didn't matter much once I realized the room also looked nothing like the living room I'd expected to see. It was the same room, yes, but all the walls were covered in a floral paper I'd seen once before in a dream. This time, I was certain I was awake. I know, because I pinched myself so hard it made my eyes water. I blinked rapidly, and as I did, the walls returned to white, but my pulse continued to race. The music was still going strong.

The cherry cabinet, which I knew from memory was stamped with the brand name "Victrola" but had always held a modern stereo inside it for as long as I could recall, stood in its usual place near one of the windows. I could see it clearly. The music was defi-nitely coming from it, but as I walked closer, I realized the stereo I was expecting to see was gone. The lid was open, and a turntable sat inside, twirling rapidly while its heavy needle scratched its way across the black disc that spun on its surface.

I watched the spinning disc, mesmerized and breathless, until the song ended and the room filled with the sound of static. The needle reached the end of the record, and the arm raised itself and traveled back across the turntable until it came to rest on the other side. I was about to turn and leave when the large handle on its side began to crank all by itself. Then the needle lifted up from the cradle and started to play at the beginning of the record again. I gasped as something like an electrical current coursed through every nerve. I might not have known much about antique record players, but I knew enough to know they weren't supposed to do any of that. Not without help. Never mind that I had no idea where this one had come from, or why it was playing in an empty room before dawn. To be honest, I had no desire to find out.

I turned on my heel and raced upstairs. My empty mug sat on my nightstand, and I eyed it suspiciously. Whatever had just happened downstairs, I was almost certainly looking at the culprit. I should have known better than to drink a sleeping potion, no matter how harmless Aunt Gwen had promised it to be. She and I would be having a long talk about this once the sun was fully up.

I looked longingly at my bed, wanting nothing more than to sleep off whatever ill effects remained of the potion so I could wake up clearheaded in the morning, but Gus was sound asleep in the middle of it. I checked the time. It was just after five, and a cool breeze fluttered through my open bedroom window. With a sigh, I pulled on a pair of yoga pants and a lightweight sweater and slipped my bare feet into some old sneakers. If I couldn't sleep, perhaps a walk around the cove would be the next best option.

As I descended the main stairs for the second time that morning, the first thing I did was sneak a glimpse at the walls. I won't pretend I wasn't filled with relief to see the plain white-painted surfaces. The relief, however, was short-lived. I had only taken one step into the room when I froze in place. Every piece of furniture had been removed from its spot and piled, ever so carefully, one item on top of another to form a perfect pyramid in the middle of my grandmother's prized Persian rug. I didn't bother to inspect it closer or try to figure out the why or how of the situation. I simply unbolted the front door and ran.

My heart beat against the inside of my chest with such force I thought it might burst through. My breath came in short puffs that burned my lungs as my feet pounded against the crushed seashells that lined the driveway. The sun had just begun to turn the sky a pale shade of pink, but the air was still chilly from the night and instantly cooled the sweat that covered my body in a thin layer, whether from the exertion of running or from fear, I wasn't sure. All I knew was I was cold to my core.

I slowed as I reached the end of the driveway. As the initial shock of what I'd seen had started to wear off, I paused at the edge of the road and looked back at the house, trying to figure out exactly what had happened to send me running outside into the early morning light as if my life depended on it. I'd joked about being haunted before, but now I felt in my bones it was real. The giant black bird I spied perched on the ledge outside my bedroom window confirmed it. There was one ghost who I knew for sure had my number. Douglas Strong.

How can this possibly be my life?

I swayed back and forth in place, uncertain whether to return to the house or stay away. Either way, I doubted it would make a difference. My ghost would follow me wherever I went, until I'd figured out the truth of his death. I started to turn back toward the house, but as I did, a small furry beast darted onto the driveway and twined himself between my legs.

"Gus!" I scolded, but it was too late. I was already falling backward, away from the driveway and into the road, where the shining beams of a car's headlights blinded my eyes as it bore down on me at full speed.

CHAPTER TWELVE

The smell of burning rubber accompanied a piercing screech of tires as the car that had been hurtling toward me came to a stop just inches from my body. My eyes were still open—though why I hadn't closed them to at least avoid having to watch myself get flattened onto the road I'm not sure. Better yet, why hadn't I tried to use magic? Sure, I didn't know any spells for stopping cars in their tracks, and under the circumstances, it wasn't like I had time to bake a protective cake, if such a thing existed, but I could have improvised. Screamed out "alakazam," maybe? I don't know. Some pathetic excuse for a witch I was turning out to be. It was only by dumb luck that I hadn't ended up squished on the asphalt like a fly on the receiving end of a giant plastic swatter.

The driver scrambled out of the car and hurried

toward me. From my vantage point on the ground, all I could tell was he was male and wearing brown loafers.

"Tamsyn? Are you okay?"

I was panting heavily, unable to answer, but even before I shifted my eyes upward toward the source of the voice, I knew it was Noah. Because, of course, it was. If someone was going to almost run me over after I was sideswiped by a cat, it was going to be the handsome doctor who inexplicably reduced my brain to a pile of mush.

Before I'd caught my breath enough to assure him I was fine, Noah kneeled beside me, running his hands along my head and neck. I'm sure it was completely innocent, just a doctor assessing an accident victim for injuries, but that didn't make it any less distracting. I'm not proud to admit it, but I'd had a stressful morning, and his fingers felt so nice against my scalp I may have let out a most indelicate moan.

Noah's eyes grew wide. "Tell me where it hurts. Right here?"

"Uh, yeah. Yeah, there," I told him. I mean, I couldn't come right out and admit I'd made that sound because he was touching my hair, now could I? A girl has to be allowed some pride. I rolled to one side, attempting to get up, and groaned. I didn't think the damage was serious, but I was sore in places I hadn't known existed before.

Noah pressed a hand against my shoulder, urging

me back down. "Don't get up until I make sure noth-ing's broken."

"I'm fine," I argued. "I should go back inside."

"I'd feel better if you'd come with me to the clinic, just to be safe."

I opened my mouth to argue some more, but as I raised myself to a sitting position, the edges of my vision grew fuzzy. I nodded, cautiously, so as not to black out by moving my head too quickly. "I suppose. If it will make you feel better."

Noah helped me up, supporting my weight with one arm as he opened the passenger door with his other. I climbed into the car—which was a Nissan of some sort, as I'd had the chance to discover when my head was a few inches from the logo on the front grill —and sank into the soft leather seat. We were both quiet as he started the ignition and inched along the road at a snail's pace, as if he was now afraid some other crazy person would launch herself in front of his car from the next driveway.

"What were you doing out so early in the morn-ing?" he asked once he'd made it to the end of the neighborhood without further incident.

"Going for a walk," I replied, leaving out one or two details, like how I had also been running from the ghost of his dead uncle before being attacked by my aunt's twenty-pound monster of a cat. "What are you doing up?"

"Heading to work."

"At six in the morning? I didn't think the clinic opened until nine."

"Wednesday is biscuits and gravy day at the Dockside Diner," he confessed with a sheepish grin. "I like to stop in for breakfast before work."

"Every week? But you're a doctor," I teased. "Or does the Dockside serve special gravy that doesn't clog your arteries and send your cholesterol sky high?"

"Afraid not. But like I always tell Uncle Doug, we've all gotta die somehow."

At first there was laughter, but the shift in mood was palpable as Noah's use of the present tense somewhat belatedly caused the memory of Noah's recent loss sank in. I shifted awkwardly in my seat. "Any new developments in the investigation?" I asked.

"Actually, yes. I heard from the lead investigator at the NTSB, and they've pretty much ruled out mechanical failure."

"Really?" I chewed on my lower lip. If the plane wasn't to blame, that meant no matter how perfect a suspect he might be, Larry Sloane was off the hook. Which also meant I could take my car to be fixed, so that was good. "So that means what, then?"

"It means it was pilot error, whether accidental or...not."

"Oh, Noah. I'm really sorry." His hand was resting on the gear shift, and I placed mine over it, giving it a squeeze before quickly pulling away. "How are you and your family dealing with the news?"

"I've told Curtis I think we need to be prepared for whichever way they decide. He refuses to hear it." Noah's jaw had hardened, and I could tell it was tearing him up much more than he wanted to admit.

We were nearing the turnoff for the clinic, and I pointed out the window in the other direction, toward the docks. "Why don't we skip the checkup and go to the Dockside for some coffee?"

"Are you sure? You fell pretty hard. You could have a concussion."

"I feel fine. I promise. Besides, you can keep an eye on me there just as well as in the clinic. Come on, my trea—" As soon as the words hit my lips, I remembered that when I'd fled the house in terror, I hadn't exactly stopped to grab my purse.

"What is it?" Noah asked, picking up on my not-so-smooth delivery.

"I left my wallet at the house." Right next to my dignity and poise, apparently.

"That's okay. Breakfast is on me."

"No, I couldn't."

"The least I can do after almost running you over is buy you some biscuits and gravy."

"Trying to kill me the slow way this time, huh?" I laughed. "Fine. Let's go."

The Dockside Diner was a hole-in-the-wall kind of a place on the waterfront that had been in business for decades. It shared an entrance with a shop called the Fisherman's Friend, where they sold everything from live bait to that head-to-toe yellow rain gear like the guy on the fish sticks box wears. Behind the diner was the stretch of dock where the lobstermen stored their traps, rows of cage-like boxes stacked ten high and stretching all the way to the seawall. The sign on the window announced that the diner was open for breakfast at three o'clock every morning. Though I shuddered at the thought of such an early start to the day, I knew that was half the secret to the diner's success. Lobstering was the lifeblood of the island in the off-season, with long hours that started before dawn and hard work that built up a healthy appetite.

We sat ourselves at a booth near the kitchen. It was one of several that were available, arriving as we were after the boats had headed out to sea but before most tourists had opened their eyes. The menu was posted on a chalkboard on the wall, next to a corkboard filled with community news. A flyer announced a missing cat, but as the picture bore absolutely no resemblance at all to Gus, my hope of pawning off my aunt's murderous beast to some unsuspecting family was quickly dashed.

The waitress came over, a woman in her mid-fifties with blonde hair pulled into a tight bun on top of her head and black liner applied thickly around her eyes. She had a coffeepot already in hand, which endeared her to me immediately. There was a mug sitting upside down beside the paper place mat in front of me, and as soon as I flipped it over, she filled it to the brim.

"Morning, Noah," she said. "The usual?"

"Good morning, Sheila. Yes, please, with extra gravy."

She rested a hand on her hip, where I could see the elaborate designs on her manicured fingers. "Have I ever forgotten the extra gravy?"

"Uh, no," Noah mumbled.

Sheila laughed. "And what'll you have, hon?"

"The same for me, but you can just go ahead and give me however much gravy you'd like," I told her, shooting a teasing look at Noah. "I'm not picky."

"Oh, I know that. Not if you're hanging out with Nerdy Noah here."

The waitress laughed even more, and the tips of Noah's ears turned pink. "I think I'm outnumbered this morning," he said.

"Sure, he may be a handsome doctor now, but I'm old enough to remember when. Thickest glasses I've ever seen and, oh Lord, that hair. You know, he used to write poetry. He was scribbling all the time in that notebook he'd carry around." The waitress ruffled his hair, the type of affectionate gesture that suggested she'd known him forever and had probably changed his diapers a time or two. "Why'd you ever stop, Noah? Some of it wasn't bad."

"I…uh…" The poor guy was staring at his place mat in agony.

"Probably 'cause of a girl, am I right?" Mercifully, she didn't wait for an answer but was still chuckling as she returned to the kitchen with our orders. My stomach twisted and my cheeks blazed. Sheila was definitely right on the mark about that one, even if she seemed oblivious to the fact that the girl in question was sitting right in front of her.

It was my turn to stare at my place mat, which was printed with advertisements for local businesses. I studied each one carefully. Sadly, there wasn't anyone on the island who specialized in smoothing over embarrassing memories, as I would've been willing to pay pretty much anything at that moment for their services.

"I'm sorry about the teasing," I said when the silence between us had stretched on long enough to be even more uncomfortable than speaking.

He shrugged. "Not your fault. If a guy's going to go around writing poetry in a place like this, he should know what he's getting himself into."

I felt my shoulders hunch as my head attempted to retract, turtle-like, deep inside my torso. "I meant about the biscuits and gravy. I shouldn't have given you a hard time about your order in front of the waitress, since you did invite me to breakfast."

"No worries." He brushed away the whole incident with a wave of his hand. "Sheila's harmless, and it's all in good fun with her."

He sure had become the cool and collected one.

Was all of his childhood sensitivity gone now, or had he just learned to hide it? Even more puzzling to me, perhaps, was to try to pinpoint when I had lost those traits. There'd been a time when nothing had rattled me, but the recent upheavals in my life had left me floundering and doubting myself constantly. All things considered, I was fortunate he was so willing to put the awkwardness of our past and be my friend. "I really do appreciate...everything."

His eyes flickered to his place mat, and the lopsided half smile on his lips hinted that the sensitive poet side of him wasn't completely gone, after all. "Between nearly running you over and saddling you with all those financial reports, breakfast was the least I could do."

I sucked in my breath at the mention of the reports. With everything else that had happened, I'd forgotten about my discovery from the night before. "Speaking of that, I think I found something."

"In the financials?" Frown lines creased Noah's brow.

"Did your uncle have any money troubles you knew of, or maybe a gambling problem or something?"

"Not that I was aware of, no." The lines grew deeper. "What did you find?"

I bit my lip, not wanting to tell him but knowing it was the right thing to do. "As I was reconciling the bank statements, I came across some irregularities. I have reason to believe your uncle was skimming money from the business and moving it to shell accounts."

"You think Uncle Doug was stealing from Strong Corp."

"It's not the only explanation, but it's a real possibility." My heart dropped at the sadness in Noah's eyes. "There's something else. Strong Corp. had just received notice they were being audited. I have no doubt a trained auditor would have picked up on the clues I found in a heartbeat."

"Most of Strong Corp.'s major investors have ties to the island. If a rumor started that he was stealing money, his reputation would have been ruined."

"Rumors move like wildfire here. Not to bring up a sore subject, but weren't there already some whispers about your uncle's business practices?"

"You mean the Sloane property. That nearly ruined the business." Noah sighed heavily. "I'll have to mention the accounts to Curtis. He's not going to take it well."

Just then, Sheila returned to the table, setting a steaming plate of biscuits and gravy in front of each of us and plunking a bottle of hot sauce on the center of the table. "What's that nephew of mine not gonna like this time?"

"Nephew?" My tone conveyed as much surprise as I felt. "You're Curtis's aunt?"

"That's right," Sheila confirmed. "She might live in

that fancy house on the cliff now, but his mama's still my big sister."

"I had no idea," I said somewhat lamely. I'd only seen Curtis's mother, Audrey, in passing, but now that I looked more closely at the waitress, I could detect a resemblance. Sheila had a similar face, though etched more deeply with the type of lines that come not just with age but with a lifetime of worrying about how to make ends meet, and her light blue waitress uniform covered the same rail-thin figure that Audrey had shown off in her designer gown.

"Yeah, well, we don't keep in touch much." The way she said it suggested that they'd had a bigger falling out than she was letting on. "Say, you're working over at the Pinecroft Inn, right?"

"Yes, my aunt runs it, and I'm helping out."

"What luck! You're exactly the person I need to talk to, then. I heard from Kevin Young the other day that the Pinecroft Inn was moving into the pie-selling business."

Kevin Young? I thought for a moment then realized this must have been the man I spoke with at the airfield. Only, of course, that pie thing had been a ruse. "Oh, right. Well, we haven't quite—"

"I'd like to place an order for a dozen blueberry pies a week. You have no idea what a help that will be."

"I'll talk to Aunt Gwen about it," I assured her. She looked so relieved I didn't have the heart to say no.

"A dozen pies," Noah said after Sheila left our table. "That's a big order."

"I know," I said with a groan. "Especially considering I haven't even mentioned the idea to Aunt Gwen yet, let alone started taking orders."

Noah's face fell. "Does that mean I won't get a finder's fee?"

"What kind of fee were you hoping for?"

"A blueberry pie, for starters."

"I think I can hook you up, even if the order doesn't pan out." I was laughing as I said it, but that quickly faded as I remembered something else from my visit to the airfield that day. "Noah, I just thought of something. Does Curtis have any money troubles that you know of?"

"Curtis? I don't think so." Noah cocked his head to one side, looking troubled. "You're not asking just because you've discovered some of his family are locals, are you?"

"What? Of course not. I'm not a snob like that."

The sharpness of his expression softened. "No, I didn't think so, but unfortunately, I know how some of the summer people can be. It's the reason he doesn't talk about it much. Some of the investors can be awfully prejudiced against the year-round residents when it comes to money issues."

"No. The reason I asked is I only just remembered something I saw at the airfield the other day." I went on to recount how I'd witnessed his cousin arguing with the man in the suit and retrieving a briefcase. "I have no idea what was going on, but it seemed a little unusual, so I thought I'd mention it."

Noah took a deep breath and let it out slowly. "That's definitely odd, and I'm not sure what was going on, either. I do know Curtis has been getting into some heated exchanges with the insurance company. Maybe it had something to do with that."

"Insurance, like life insurance?" I asked, recalling a recurring payment from the bank records to Penobscot Life. Thinking back on it, the well-dressed man could have been an insurance executive, although something about him struck me as a little too glitzy for a small, regional company. Perhaps they were a subsidiary of a larger New York firm. "Would Curtis be the beneficiary?"

"No. Strong Corp. carried policies for both Uncle Doug and Curtis, payable to the company in the event that one of them died. Not to sound coldhearted, but obviously my uncle's death has disrupted business, and I think the insurance was intended to help with that."

My brain kicked into high gear as a new possibility occurred to me. "Did that policy have a suicide clause?"

"I have no idea. I've been helping out because my mom's on the board, but I don't really get involved in that level of detail. Sadly, though, I had a patient a few years ago who died by suicide, and I know for a fact that his family was able to collect on his policy. In fact, I kind of thought suicide clauses legally weren't allowed anymore."

"That could be, but I think there are still some loopholes. Like, insurers can have restrictions on paying out if the policyholder dies by suicide within a certain number of months after buying a new policy."

"I'm not sure when the coverage was obtained, but something like that would explain why Curtis has been so adamant that our uncle's death had to have been an accident."

After we finished our breakfast, Noah drove me back to the inn, but not before making me promise I would come to the clinic later in the day for a proper examination. I walked up the driveway to the porch and froze, unwilling to enter through the front door. I knew I needed to address the mysterious pyramid of furniture in the living room eventually, but I didn't think I could handle having it smack me in the face the second I walked inside. Instead, I went around the back and used the kitchen entrance.

It was still early in the morning, not yet seven-thirty, but even before I opened the door, I could hear the clatter of pots and pans coming from inside as the heavenly smell of cinnamon wafted through an open window. Aunt Gwen turned from the stove at the sound of the door latching shut, greeting my return with a look of mild surprise. "Tamsyn, you're up early. Would you like to help with the waffles?"

Her mood was so untroubled I immediately knew she hadn't been in the living room yet. "Aunt Gwen," I said as gently as I could, "I need to show you something."

She frowned. "What is it, dear?"

"Just follow me, through here," I said, my heart beating faster as I took her by the hand and led her into the dining room. I stopped abruptly as soon as the living room came into view. Everything was exactly where it was supposed to be, with not a single crocheted doily out of place. "I don't understand."

"What is it you wanted to show me?"

My insides buzzed like I'd had too much caffeine. "Did you notice anything strange in here this morning?"

She looked at me blankly. "Strange? No."

"You didn't move anything around or...?" My voice trailed off as I realized that, of course, she hadn't. Considering how the room had looked when I left, it would have taken hours of hard work for me to put it all back in place, let alone my elderly aunt. I swallowed hard as the concern in my aunt's expression deepened. "You know what? It's nothing. I think that sleeping potion hit me harder than I realized when I got up this morning."

But it hadn't been the sleeping potion. Of that I was certain. Something or someone had reached out to me the night before and again that morning, trying to get my attention. Well, it had it now, that was for sure.

What I didn't know was what it wanted, although I had an idea of who might help. Skirting around the edge of the living room, as I was too freaked out to walk through the center, I headed up to my room. I'd avoided it long enough. It was time to call my coven again.

CHAPTER THIRTEEN

"*I*'m being haunted by the ghost of Douglas Strong."

We'd gathered in Cassandra's house, or rather the house she shared with her mother and grandmother. It had been built at the height of the Queen Anne revival style of the late 1800s and was exactly the type of house you'd expect to find three generations of witches living in. It had brightly colored ornate gingerbread trim and a short wrought-iron fence surrounding the front garden.

A three-story tower in the center of the house rose above matching gables on each side, and it was in the small room at the top of the tower where we had gathered a few hours after I'd made the call. Unlike the cheerful Victorian tearoom I'd visited on Main Street, this space oozed otherworldly ambience. The deep-green walls sucked in most of the weak light produced by a single brass chandelier that hung from the embossed tin ceiling. Old wooden shelves sagged from the weight of books, crystals, and other magical ephemera, while a circular table in the middle of the room displayed a single, thick book. Its heavily ornamented leather binding was covered in mysterious symbols, and I sensed without asking that it was the Hollings family grimoire. As crazy as it still felt to think of myself as a witch, I would be lying if I said that finding myself in these surroundings didn't also give me a thrill.

"Haunted. You're sure?" Cass asked, but in a way that let me know she didn't doubt the possibility.

I nodded. "The pyramid of furniture in the living room was a dead giveaway."

"*Dead* giveaway." Sybil groaned. "Terrible joke."

My cheeks grew warm. "I didn't mean it like *that*."

"And you're sure it's Douglas Strong who's haunting you?" Cass asked.

"He's the only one who's died recently," I replied. "Who else would it be? The question now is what do I do about it?"

"I asked Mom and Gran about it," Cass said, reaching across the table for the book. She opened it and flipped through the yellowed pages. "Do you have anything that belonged to the deceased, like a piece of clothing, maybe?"

I shook my head. "I never even met the guy."

"Really?" Cass frowned. "I wonder why he's attached himself to you."

My facial expression mirrored Cass's as I pondered this. "I assumed it was because I'm a witch."

"Yes, but so are we," Sybil pointed out. "And we were both standing right next to you at Cliffside the first time it happened, yet neither one of us has caught so much as a glimpse of him."

"I..." My lips flopped open and closed like a gold-fish, but no words came out. I was stumped. "Isn't seeing ghosts a normal witchy kind of a thing?"

Cass and Sybil exchanged uncertain looks.

"Communicating with ghosts is something that every witch studies." Sybil said it cautiously, as if she had news that she needed to break gently. "It doesn't take a lot of training to operate a spirit board halfway decently. But actually seeing an apparition, fully formed the way you did, is much more unusual."

A hard lump formed in my throat, matching the one that was settling in the pit of my stomach. If seeing spirits wasn't something that every witch could do naturally, then why could I? Considering the mess I'd made of every spell Aunt Gwen had tried to teach me, I already knew I lacked a natural aptitude for magic. I was the worst kitchen witch ever, unless... Was it possible I was something else?

"It's true," Cass added. "When I was talking to Gran earlier, she showed me three different summoning spells but told me she'd never had much luck with any of them."

"That doesn't bode well for us," I said, a sinking feeling inside telling me I would never be rid of my ghost. Whatever variety of witch I was, I doubted I could do better than someone who had been studying and perfecting her magic for longer than I'd been alive.

"All we can do is try our best," Sybil said encouragingly. "Here. I brought a copy of a magazine that has an article about Doug in it. Without a personal possession, it's the next best thing."

She set the magazine carefully on the table beside the grimoire, folded back so his full-page photo was prominently displayed. Cass rummaged through the bookshelves and returned with a heavy brass candlestick, which she fitted with a fresh white candle before placing it beside the photo. Meanwhile, Sybil produced a glass vial from her pocket and outlined a circle on the surface of the table with some sort of gritty powder.

"What are we going to do?" I asked, my voice breathless as I took in the unfamiliar preparations. There was no spirit board in sight, and belatedly, I recalled Cass had used the word "summoning," as opposed to "communicating." Goose pimples covered my arms as I tried to work out what the difference between the two might be.

"We're going to attempt to bring Douglas Strong into our circle so we can find out how we can help him move on," Cass said. "Usually when a spirit appears the way he did, it's because some unfinished business is keeping them on this plane."

"The easiest way to rid yourself of a spirit," Sybil added, "is to help them complete their task."

I looked from one to the other in awe. "How do you both know so much?"

They looked at one another in confusion, and Sybil shrugged. "Probably because we've grown up around it from the start. You'll catch up soon enough."

My shoulders slumped with the weight of the work ahead. "But there's so much to learn. And I have to be honest. The whole seeing-an-apparition thing notwithstanding, so far I'm a terrible witch."

Cass cocked her head to one side. "Why do you say that?"

"The other day, I literally blew up a pie." I shut my eyes tightly, cringing at the memory.

"Oh, that's nothing," Cass said with a laugh. "You should see some of the potions I've concocted. Brown sludge is my specialty. And I've put cracks in not one but two crystal balls. Mom was livid."

"And I had to spend a week wearing a turban not too long ago," Sybil said, "because I tried a new spell to make my hair curly and, instead, it all disappeared."

A smile tickled the corners of my mouth. "Really? Or are you just saying this to make me feel better?"

"Cross my heart," Cass traced an X across her chest as she said it. "Crystal balls are wicked expensive. I'm still working off the cost with extra hours at the tea shop."

I chuckled at this and turned my attention to the leather book, which lay open in front of me to display a page of handwritten notes made in old, faded script. Mystical symbols filled the margins. I hate to admit it, but looking at that ancient tome, I experienced a serious case of grimoire envy. The Hollings book looked legit, unlike the tattered and stained cookbook that was the Bassett family legacy. Not that I'd mastered a single thing it contained, or even come close, and I doubted a better grimoire was what I needed. Assurances from my coven aside, I was pretty confident I knew who the weakest link in the witch chain would turn out to be. "So, where do we start?"

Sybil took another pinch of the white powder she'd used earlier, this time sprinkling it directly on top of Douglas's smiling face. "We'll join hands and repeat the incantation, and if it all goes right, this powder should rise up in a mist until we see the departed in physical form."

"Or, at least his head," Cass added.

Oh, was that all? Simple. I drew a deep breath and clasped hands with the other women, hoping they didn't notice how sweaty my palms had become. "Let's give it a shot."

At first, the incantation sounded like a string of utter nonsense, but after pronouncing the foreign phrases haltingly a few times, the words flowed freely from my tongue and joined with the other women's in a steady cadence until it seemed I had lost track of how much time had passed, or of anything at all that stood outside the chalky circle on the table. Though the windows were closed and the heavy drapes were drawn against the midday sun, a warm breeze swept through the room, gliding across the back of my neck and making the stray hairs flutter. The small heap of powder on top of the photograph began to swirl, caught up in a miniature dust devil, but though it twisted and turned for what seemed like a very long time, nothing more distinct formed. Finally, the air grew still and the would-be apparition collapsed into a thin film of dust that coated the top of the table.

"Should we try again?" I asked in a low voice, though the exhaustion on my companions' faces was apparent and my own body felt as drained as if I had run a marathon.

"It's no use," Sybil replied, weariness reducing her voice to barely a whisper. "I think that's the best we can manage."

"Maybe if we can get something more personal of the deceased, though, like something he used to wear?" Cass added helpfully. She picked up the magazine, dusted off the powder, and handed it to me. "In the meantime, you might try taking this home and putting it under your pillow. Maybe that will help him communicate through a dream."

We parted with promises to reconvene soon and try

again, but as I walked down the hard granite steps that led away from the Hollings house, my heart was heavy. Even if I managed to find a piece of clothing or other possession that had belonged to Douglas, I didn't think it would be enough. I knew deep down what the problem with our spell had been, and it was me. So what if I could see spirits better than other witches? It was no use if I couldn't do anything about it. I was a weakling, as lacking in supernatural power as anyone who had become an accountant could be expected to be. No matter how hard I tried, I couldn't picture myself becoming any different. Aunt Gwen might have been the best kitchen witch in a generation, but there was just no way around it. I was a total dud.

BEFORE HEADING HOME, I STOPPED BY THE clinic, as I had promised Noah I would do. The pace of my steps slowed as I approached the front door. I didn't relish a repeat of the somewhat hostile greeting I'd received from the receptionist on my last visit. Then again, this wasn't a personal call, so perhaps she would be friendlier to me this time, at least until I annoyed her anew by revealing that I lacked a valid insurance card. Ah, unemployment. The gift that just kept giving.

As it turned out, I never got the chance to share my uninsured status with her, or much of anything else for that matter. I'd only made it halfway across the lobby when Noah came barreling down the hallway, his white lab coat billowing behind him as he talked loudly into his phone.

"Calm down, Audrey. I'll be right there. Just tell him... Audrey..." He held the phone to his ear with one hand while simultaneously shrugging the coat sleeve from his other arm. "Tell Curtis I'm on my way."

He tossed the lab coat onto the receptionist's desk with an apologetic shrug, though from the indulgent look on her face, I gathered she didn't hold it against him. After leaving the coat, he swiveled mid-step without warning, which landed him directly in my path. I only managed to avoid a complete collision by scampering backward, which when accompanied by the weird squeaking sound that came out of me must have made me look like a startled squirrel. Just one more missed opportunity on my part to display dignity and decorum, but to be honest, I was getting used to feeling like a complete fool in his presence. He had to have noticed it by now, and I wondered if each time it made him question why he'd ever had a crush on me all those years ago.

"We really must stop running into each other like this," I said, cringing at the blank stare I received as the lame joke I'd stolen from him fell flat. "I was just stopping by like you asked, but it looks like you're on your way out."

"Unfortunately, I am. There's been a little family emergency, so I'm on my way to my cousin's place."

"I'll come back another day," I assured him, following as he continued toward the door.

"No, don't do that," he said, pushing the door open but then stepping aside to let me pass through first. My heart fluttered at the effortless display of chivalry. He'd been nothing but nice to me since I'd arrived in Summerhaven, but as far as I could tell, Noah was nice to everyone. I reminded myself that I wasn't special, and whatever feelings he'd had for me were far in the past. "Would you mind taking a ride out to Cliffside?"

"Tag along for your family emergency?" I scoffed, assuming he wasn't serious.

"I know it's weird, but I could use some backup," he admitted bashfully. "My cousin can be a handful. Do you think you could come with me?"

"Sure," I replied in a steady tone. Truthfully, I was ready to jump at the offer. What better way could there be to find something that had belonged to Douglas Strong to strengthen my summoning spell than to check his house? I decided not to let the fact that I was seriously contemplating stealing from a dead man bother me. It was for his own good after all.

When we reached Noah's car in the clinic lot, he walked to the passenger's side and opened the door. I followed him gladly, taking my seat quickly before he could change his mind. And yes, that was two doors opened for me in under two minutes. The man was positively a knight. It was kind of a shame that grown-up me was such a walking disaster that he'd never give me a second glance.

When we arrived at Cliffside, Curtis was pacing the massive front room in a rage, screaming into the phone while his mostly unintelligible words ricocheted off the marble walls. Audrey hovered near the front door, nearly pouncing on Noah the moment we entered.

"Thank God you're here," she said, clutching Noah's arm. "Maybe you can get through to him."

"How long has he been like this?" Noah asked.

"He got a call about an hour ago. The next thing I knew, he was screaming and throwing things around the room."

I hung back with Audrey, holding my breath as Noah approached his cousin, anticipating the possibility that Curtis would respond violently. To my relief, he appeared to calm somewhat as Noah spoke to him in a hushed tone.

Audrey stood beside me, dressed in the stylishly casual clothing that was popular with the island's summer ladies, and if I hadn't known better, I would have assumed she was on her way to or from the country club. She appeared older than she had the night of the party, distress contorting her facial features and deepening the lines around her eyes and mouth. Her hands were clenched together so tightly her knuckles had turned pale white.

"You have no idea what started it?" I asked.

"It had to be related to the accident. That's the only thing that would make him behave like this." The concern for her son was evident, and sympathy for her flooded me, even as I somewhat unexpectedly experienced a sharp stab of loss for my own mother, a pain which was usually little more than a dull ache now that fifteen years had passed. "Doug was like a father to him, ever since my husband died." Her lips pressed into a thin line. "I can't believe they're both gone."

"I'm really sorry," I replied, not knowing what else to say.

By now, Curtis had collapsed onto one of the leather sofas that was grouped around an oriental rug near the massive fireplace. His head was cradled in his hands while Noah stood beside him resting a supporting hand on his cousin's shoulder. Noah glanced over and motioned for us to come closer.

"Uncle Doug's bloodwork came in this morning," he explained in a low voice after stepping several feet away from Curtis. "It showed a significant concentration of zolpidem tartrate."

Audrey's hand flew to cover her mouth as she inhaled sharply, but I just stared blankly at Noah. "I don't know what that is."

"It's a sleeping pill," he replied. "It appears my uncle had taken about twice the usual dose, maybe fifteen or twenty minutes before takeoff."

"So, he died from an overdose?" I asked.

"Two pills aren't enough to kill someone, but it's fast acting. Taken that close to flying, he would have been seriously impaired or even unconscious by the time he was halfway across the bay and lost control of the plane."

Beside me, Audrey's face had gone pale and unshed tears glistened in her eyes. "Oh God."

"I know. It's terrible." Noah put his arm around her shoulder, pulling her close for a hug. "I don't know what he was thinking, taking those pills in the middle of the day."

Audrey pulled away from Noah's embrace, her lower lip trembling as she looked at her son. She had every appearance of being about to speak but instead turned and walked quickly toward the grand staircase. When she was about halfway up the stairs, she let out a loud sob, and my own eyes stung in empathy.

"He wasn't trying to kill himself," Curtis growled from the couch. Where his mother's grief had taken the form of crying, Curtis appeared to be channeling his into rage.

"I'm sure no one would think that," I said awkwardly, mostly because I couldn't think of anything better to say. I felt every bit the outsider I was and regretted accepting Noah's invitation.

"That's exactly what they're saying," Curtis snapped, his eyes narrowing as he glared at his cousin. "Tell her, Noah."

"At this point," Noah said, addressing Curtis with a

tone that was both firm and soothing, "the medical examiner has declined to determine the cause of death…"

"Yeah, well that hasn't stopped Penobscot Life from delaying the check. Again." Curtis's reply was as bitter as it was passionate, but it struck me as I took in his words that this wasn't grief for his uncle. This was about money, pure and simple, and the well of sympathy I'd felt toward him quickly ran dry.

"I need to use the restroom," I announced, wanting at that moment to put as much distance as I could between myself and Noah's loathsome cousin. Besides, I'd come to Cliffside with the intent of finding one of Doug's personal belongings to strengthen the summoning spell, and I couldn't exactly swipe something with both his nephews watching.

"Down the hall," Noah said.

I walked briskly in the direction he had pointed, my eyes gliding from side to side to check out each open door as I passed. I doubted I would find anything useful in a main floor guest bathroom, but it was the first excuse that had popped into my head, and it afforded me the opportunity to scope out the first floor for something suitably personal but small enough to slip into my handbag undetected. To my great delight, the door directly across from the bathroom appeared to lead to Douglas Strong's home office. I took a step toward it, but a sound on the other end of the hall stopped me short, and I popped into the guest bath to avoid being caught somewhere I wasn't supposed to be.

For a room whose main purpose was to hold a toilet and sink, the space was opulent to the extreme. The walls sparkled with what I suspected was not just paint but actual gold leaf. The white enamel sink sat in a heavily carved mahogany cabinet with intricate gold fixtures. I drew closer to examine the workmanship, but my attention was caught by a tooled leather container, oval in shape, that stood to the right side of the sink. I thought it might be a box that held something important, but a more thorough inspection revealed it to be nothing more than a waste basket. It had been emptied recently, but there were a few crumpled tissues in the bottom, along with a plastic bottle that was the distinctive amber shade of a pharmacy bottle. The label had mostly been torn away, but a strip of it remained.

Curious, I reached in and plucked it out, using a few sheets of toilet paper to shield it from my fingerprints, just in case it turned out to be important. My pulse ticked faster as I read the label, and I was thankful for my foresight. In the twinkling light of the bathroom's crystal sconces, I could just make out the words "zolpi" and "rate" along with the last name "Strong" and a partial address for what I assumed was a pharmacy on the mainland. I struggled to remember the name of the drug Noah had mentioned from the bloodwork, but I was willing to bet money this was it.

I wasn't sure exactly where it would lead, but this had to be a clue.

Wrapping the bottle carefully in layers of tissue, I buried it in the bottom of my purse before leaving the bathroom. I'd made it three steps in the direction of Douglas Strong's office when once again I heard a sound, this time Noah's voice as he came closer down the hall.

"Tamsyn?" he called. "Are you ready to go?"

"Yes, I'm ready." Frustrated, I turned my back on the office door. I'd missed my opportunity to steal something belonging to Douglas Strong, but as I returned to the main room, I tried to look on the bright side. I'd uncovered what could very well be the bottle of pills that had led to Douglas Strong's death. That had to be worth something. As for finding the item I needed for my spell, I would just have to come back soon and search some more.

CHAPTER FOURTEEN

The next morning, well before any of the inn's guests had risen, I found Aunt Gwen standing silently at the stove, slowly stirring the largest of the cauldrons with her wooden spoon. There was no mistaking the fact that the steam rising from the pot was glowing a bright and mystical blue, but by now I'd gotten used to this type of thing, and it hardly fazed me. I cleared my throat loudly to announce my presence, but my aunt continued the rhythmic circles while staring blankly at the wall. Finally, after at least a minute had passed, she turned her head toward me, her eyes blinking rapidly as if coming out of a trance.

"Good morning, my dear," she said with a smile.

"Good morning, Aunt Gwen." I craned my head to see into the pot. I'm not sure what I had expected to see in there—a large batch of oatmeal, perhaps?

Instead, I was surprised to find a dark liquid topped with soap suds. "What are you up to?"

"Cleaning the house," she replied, tapping her spoon against the pot to shake off the water droplets. A single bubble that had clung to the spoon popped as she slipped it into the pocket of her apron.

"What is that, a magical cleaning solution?" I expected the next step involved handing me some rags and the contents of the cauldron and telling me to get to work. I was, after all, the summer intern. "Just tell me where to start."

"No need. The cleaning's done."

"Are you...?" But as I looked around, I realized she was right. The kitchen was immaculately clean, every surface shining. I poked my head into the dining room and saw that it was the same. "The whole house?"

She nodded. "My grandmother's cleaning spell. It takes some practice to perfect, but once it's done, you can get all three stories sparkling clean in the time it takes to boil the water. I wouldn't be able to run the inn without it."

"That's amazing," I said, then frowned as I recalled the hours I'd spent helping her prepare the rooms for our latest arrivals. "If that's the case, why did you have me changing the sheets on all the beds the other day?"

"Nothing beats the sunny smell of line-dried sheets," she replied. "Besides, I've never been able to perfect the spell so that it produces a sharp hospital corner. Even the best witches need to know their limitations."

"Speaking of limitations," I said, suddenly remembering my breakfast with Noah, "I may have gotten myself into a little bit of trouble over some pies."

Her shoulders slumped. "You didn't blow them up again, did you? Because the cleaning potion doesn't do very well on burnt blueberries. I'll have to find the scrub brush."

"No, nothing like that," I assured her. "It's just, I was talking to Sheila at the Dockside Diner, and she heard a rumor that we were expanding the pie business and wanted to place an order."

"Where did she hear a rumor like that?"

"It's a long story," I mumbled. "Anyway, she looked so happy about it that I didn't have the heart to say no. So I was, uh, sorta hoping you would consider it."

"Oh, I don't know. It's not such a bad idea. I already do the occasional special order. And with you here to help—"

"Me, help?" I shook my head so vigorously something in my neck popped. "Remember the part about how hard carbonized blueberries are to clean off the ceiling?"

"This is the perfect opportunity for you to really master the techniques. We'll start tomorrow."

My mouth was wide open but nothing was coming out, and it didn't really matter because Aunt Gwen had turned her attention to emptying the cauldron's dark suds into the kitchen sink. I set out fresh fruit and muffins for any of the early risers among our guests who wanted to get a head start on breakfast, then swiped a blueberry muffin for myself and returned to my room. Sure enough, it was cleaner than when I'd left it. While my bedcovers were still rumpled and in need of smoothing, this fact was more than made up for by the neatly folded pile of laundry sitting on top of the dresser. I'd been aware I was a witch for nearly a month, but realizing that someday I might perfect a cleaning potion myself was perhaps the first moment I truly appreciated it.

There was a clicking noise as something fell onto the floor. Turning toward the sound, I discovered Gus tiptoeing across the surface of my desk. He'd knocked over a container, which, thanks to Aunt Gwen's spell, had magically refilled itself with all the pens I'd left scattered around the room. One pen was on the floor, and soon there was another click as a second pen followed, and then a third.

"Gus..."

A fourth and fifth pen joined the growing pile. Without so much as looking me in the eye, he swiped the container with his huge, furry paw and sent it rolling off the desktop. Then he stood and moved toward my laptop, which sat open on the desk. Using a single claw on his massive front paw, he popped off a key with surgical precision.

"Hey!"

Ignoring me, he dispatched three additional keys to the floor in record time while I stood frozen in horror. My laptop didn't work all that great as it was, but without keys it would pretty much be useless.

"Gus!"

This time he looked up at the sound of his name and stared me down. I stomped my foot at him, and he jumped to the chair where he proceeded to dig through the large straw handbag I'd carried the previous day. Before I knew it, he was buried head deep into the bag, and I heard the distinctive crunching noise of cat teeth on a plastic wrapper. A moment later, the sound was joined by that of paper being shredded and torn.

"All right, buddy," I growled. "I have *had* it with you."

I lunged toward the chair, but he used my handbag as a springboard to launch himself midair toward the windowsill. My handbag tumbled from the chair with the open end facedown, and even as I kneeled to inspect the damage, I already knew there would be no way to retrieve it without all the contents dumping out onto the floor. Gus sat in the open window, his tail twitching in a silent taunt. His eyes sparkled in the light, mocking me.

A hot wave of anger overcame me, and although I was nowhere close enough to reach, I lashed out at him with my arm. Before I could process what was happening, he jumped vertically several inches into the air. I screamed and shut my eyes as he disappeared over the sill.

My regret was immediate as the heat that had filled me dissipated, replaced by cold dread. The drop from my third-floor window was precipitous, with nothing on the way down to break a fall. Common wisdom was that cats always land on their feet, but from a distance of more than twenty feet? I wasn't convinced. How could I have forgotten the window had no screen?

My knees cracked as I rose to creep close enough to see down, but it took every ounce of effort I could muster to overcome my guilt and force my eyes to look at the ground. When I did, I saw nothing. The flowerbed below my window was undisturbed. There was no sign of an impact. No footprints leading away. Gus had simply vanished. I backed away from the window, the weight of blame replaced by dizzying confusion. Where could he be?

I massaged my temples, looking from the window to the open bedroom door. In the split second in which my eyes had been closed, could he have actually fallen inward and scampered out of the room? Though it felt unlikely, it was the only explanation, unless Gus could fly. My eyes widened. *Gus can't fly, can he?* Then again, maybe he could. *No, he can't,* I reprimanded myself, forcing the craziness out of my mind with every ounce of my will. He was just a flesh-and-blood cat, albeit one whose naughtiness approached the level of a superpower, and he was probably hiding in the attic and laughing at me. *Not actually laughing,* I corrected. Laughing out loud wasn't something a normal cat could do, but I felt certain he could do it in his head and frequently did. I made a mental note to ask Sybil and Cass next time I saw them if they'd ever encountered flying cats, just to be sure.

My conscience somewhat assuaged and sanity minimally restored, I turned my attention back to the mess the cat had made on the floor before he disappeared. I lifted my overturned bag carefully, leaving the contents in a pile. The source of the shredded paper was immediately clear. Gus had ripped and clawed through the first several pages of the magazine we'd used for the summoning spell, the one containing the article about Strong Corp. I plucked the magazine from the pile and leafed through the pages, dislodging thin ribbons of torn paper that fluttered to the floor. When I came to the first page that had not been shredded, I gasped. On it was a full-page photo of Douglas and Curtis standing beside a man I'd seen once before. The name in the caption identified him as Marcus Levine, CEO of the Papagayo Development Initiative. I knew him better as the man in the fancy suit at Cabot Memorial Airfield.

"Not a claims adjuster after all," I muttered. And another letter L associated with an airplane. Perhaps he would turn out to be the right one.

I turned to my laptop to look up more about him and was confronted by the sight of five gaping holes where keys used to be. Not just any keys, mind you, but the shift, return, and delete keys, plus the space bar. In addition to these, Gus had managed to remove the letter L. No matter how hard I looked on the surrounding floor, not a single one of the missing keys was visible. They'd vanished just as thoroughly as had Gus. If I wanted to know everything I could about Marcus Levine and whatever Papagayo was, I had only one option. I grabbed my backpack, hopped on my bike, and headed for the library.

It was midmorning when I arrived, and as I pedaled into the parking lot, I saw Sybil standing in front of the door with a cup of coffee in each hand, shifting her weight as if trying to figure out whether it would be possible to grasp the handle with an elbow or her foot. I stowed my bike and hurried over.

"Here, let me get it," I said, pulling the door open. A rush of cold air flowed out, pushing back the humid warmth of outside.

"Thanks, Tamsyn," she said with a bright smile. "I'm bringing my gran her favorite latte. What brings you here?"

"A little bit of research," I replied. "I need to borrow a computer."

"Internet troubles at the inn?"

"Not exactly. Say, have you ever heard of a cat being able to fly?"

"What?" She shot me a thoroughly confused look. "Is this what you're researching?"

"No. Never mind. I was just curious." It was obvious by her response that flying felines were not the norm in the world of witchcraft.

As Sybil turned toward the archives desk to deliver the coffee, I made me way to an empty computer to begin my search. As it turned out, having a functioning L key wasn't the only barrier to me finding the information I needed. Although I searched everywhere I could think of for any mention of either Marcus Levine or the Papagayo Development Initiative, the only thing I had to show for my trouble was a stiff neck. After what felt like an eternity of fruitless searching, which in reality was probably closer to twenty minutes, I inched my way to the back of the library and, with some reluctance, approached the archives desk. Auntie Sue was in her usual spot, sipping her latte and chatting quietly with Sybil, who was leaning against the desk.

"Good morning, Tamsyn," Auntie Sue greeted me warmly. "How nice to see you this morning. Sybil mentioned she'd run into you on the way in. Did you change your mind about those articles on your mom I mentioned?"

The news coverage of my mother's disappearance and presumed drowning at sea fifteen years ago? My stomach churned at the thought of them. No, I had not had a change of heart and didn't expect to. I shook my head fervently. "Actually, I have a favor to ask. I'm trying to find out more about someone I saw on the island recently. I know his name and the company he works for, but I've spent all morning on the internet and have come up empty-handed.

"You think I might have something in the archive?"

As a matter of fact, I didn't think that at all, which is perhaps why I was having so much trouble making my request. "Actually, I was wondering if you might have some more…uh, unorthodox means of finding information. You know, by like…"

I looked to Sybil, hoping she would jump in with the right term for whatever it was I was wanting, but when she didn't, I put a finger on the tip of my nose and wiggled it back and forth. It was, I assumed, the universal symbol for using your witchy powers to put your nose where it didn't belong, though I'm not sure why since as far as I had been able to work out, a talent for nose twitching wasn't an automatic part of every new witch's tool kit, no matter what the television wanted you to think. At least, it hadn't been for me. Then again, maybe that's why I was turning out to be such a disaster at it.

"Oh, I see." Auntie Sue winked at Sybil, who was covering her mouth with one hand in a not so subtle attempt to hide her smirk. Then Auntie Sue sat quietly behind her desk for several moments, so deep in thought I was certain what I'd asked must be well outside the realm of what was possible, or at least what was allowed. But when she spoke, it wasn't the difficulty of the task that had been weighing on her. "Are you certain you shouldn't ask your Aunt Gwen for help? It would be a wonderful learning opportunity for you to figure out how to use your abilities to get what you need on your own."

I sighed. Finding information that didn't seem to exist was right up there with making a soufflé. Sure, I should probably learn how to make one someday but perhaps not when my greatest culinary triumph to date was managing not to turn a pot of blueberries into miniature incendiary devices. Baby steps. "I would, Auntie Sue, but I'm a little pressed for time."

"Okay, I guess I can help just this once," she said, and my heart leaped.

She opened the top drawer of her desk, pulled out a clunky, black laptop, and set it with a thud on the work surface in front of her. When she opened the lid, the machine whirred to life with all the creaks and groans of an old woman being woken up early from her nap.

"What's his name?"

"Marcus Levine of the Papagayo Development Initiative."

The elation I'd felt moments before fizzled as Auntie Sue's fingers hunted and pecked their way across the keyboard. "Mar...cus. Levi was it?"

"Levine," I replied, sounding more impatient than I had a right to be considering I'd brought this on myself. "But I've already checked the internet."

Her lips twitched into a half smile, though she

didn't look up from the screen as her fingers continued to poke at the keys. "I'm not checking the internet, dear."

"No, she isn't," Sybil said with a shake of her head, confirming her grandmother's assertion.

"Uh, right. Of course." I had no idea what that meant, having zero frame of reference for what might constitute the magical equivalent of the world wide web for witches. I gestured vaguely toward the nearby bookcases. "I'm just gonna..."

I took a step back from the archives desk and wandered toward the stacks as nonchalantly as I could. The senior witch's monotonously slow clicking of keys felt like a bird pecking at my brain at half speed, and I moved deeper into the aisle of books to escape the sound. Whatever her sluggish efforts might produce, my expectations weren't overly high.

My eyes skimmed the titles along the book spines without much comprehension. I'd chosen the row for its convenience and to pass the time, not because I had any interest in the books it contained. This changed halfway along when I landed on an old hardcover copy containing a history of Pinecroft Cove. I pulled it from the shelf, its cover a cheap blue cloth that would usually be hidden under a dust jacket that was long since gone, and cracked it open to the copyright page. The publisher was a local operation I'd never heard of, and since the publication date was decades in the past, there was every chance they were no longer in business.

I thumbed idly through the pages, less for any specific information and more to pass the time, but when I reached a full page black-and-white photo a third of the way through the book, my fingers began to tingle. I knew the woman's face almost as well as I knew my own by now, and a glance at the caption confirmed that it was Lillian Bassett. The photograph was dated 1929.

I hadn't realized I'd made a sound until Sybil suddenly popped her head into the aisle. "Are you okay?" she asked. "I thought I heard you say something."

"Sybil, come take a look at this." I held out the book and tapped my finger on the photo. "This is the woman I told you about. The one from the dream."

Sybil studied the picture and let out a quiet whistle. "She looks just like you, all right. And did you see this?"

My eyes widened as I read the title of the chapter on the page opposite Lillian's photo, first silently to myself and then out loud. "Local Woman Lost at Sea?"

A deep line formed across Sybil's brow. "Isn't that what happened to your mom?"

Out of nowhere, I experienced a searing heat encircling my wrist. I looked down to see my silver bracelet glowing as if it had just been taken from a kiln, with a deep orange shine emanating from the center link, the one with the initials LB engraved in it. My pulse ticked like a stopwatch. LB. The bracelet from the attic had belonged to Lillian Bassett. My fingers flew open, and the history book dropped to the floor. Sybil gasped. "Tamsyn, what's wrong?"

"My bracelet!" I held out my arm for Sybil to see, but the fiery glow was gone. "It was glowing, and it felt like it was on fire."

Sybil ran the tips of her fingers along the links, finding nothing. "It feels perfectly normal. You're sure it wasn't just a pinched nerve or something?"

I rubbed my wrist with my other hand, but the pain had subsided. The silver links of the bracelet were cool to the touch, and there wasn't so much as a red mark on my skin. Had I imagined it? The way Sybil was looking at me, it seemed likely it was all in my head. Still rattled, I stooped to retrieve the book, dropping it twice in the process. As I straightened up, I heard Auntie Sue call my name. I tucked the book under my arm and headed out of the stacks with Sybil following behind.

"Here you are," she said, placing a thick folder on a small study desk in the archive area. "I hope it has what you're looking for."

I set the history book on the table and reached for the tattered, gray folder, which had the word *Confidential* stamped across the front in red ink. Even a quick flip through the pages was enough to reveal the sensitive nature of the documents inside, which included bank statements, real estate records, and more. "You couldn't possibly have had these in the library this whole time."

"Technically, they're not in the library now." When I frowned in confusion, she continued. "You've heard of glamor magic?"

"Yes, Sybil explained it. It's, like, making people look good, or feel good about things, or something, right?"

"Sort of," Sybil corrected, no doubt as much to prove to her grandmother that she understood the concept as to make certain I did. "What I tried to say was it's altering the perception of things."

"Exactly," her grandmother agreed. "In this case, I've altered your perception of a stack of blank pieces of paper so that when you look at them, you see the information you need."

"You mean, you can get any document from anywhere, at any time?"

Auntie Sue tilted her head slightly to one side. "Well, there are some limits. For one thing, the replicas have to be in close proximity, at all times, to the witch who cast the spell, which means they can't leave the archives room. And second, the spell only lasts about an hour, so you'll need to read them quickly."

"And after an hour?" I asked her.

"They go back to blank sheets of paper. And you'll have to jot down notes or commit what you need to memory because they can't be photocopied or photographed."

I flipped through the pages again and nodded. It would take every minute I had available to make it through them, but I was fairly confident I could do it. "Thank you."

"Good luck," Auntie Sue said.

"Yeah, good luck," Sybil chimed in as she gathered her things and prepared to leave. "I'll leave you to it."

I took a seat and eagerly dug into the files. Wherever the documents had come from, and whatever magic had temporarily allowed me to view them, reading them gave me important new insight on the altercation I had witnessed at the airfield. Curtis and Mr. Levine were business partners, with Curtis having invested nearly a million dollars in the Papagayo Development Initiative over the past two years. From what I had gleaned, their venture to turn a defunct coffee plantation in Costa Rica into a series of luxury vacation condos was seriously behind schedule and bleeding money.

Then it hit me. The value of Curtis's investment was almost to the penny the amount that was missing from the Strong Corp. accounts. Doug wasn't the embezzler. His favorite nephew was.

I would have liked to have done more digging, but time was almost up. The documents had already begun to fade a little at the corners, and soon the pages would be blank. I scooped them up and handed the folder back to Sue Ellen.

"Did you find what you needed?" she asked.

"I did. Thank you." I lingered at the desk a moment. "Can I ask you something?"

"Of course, dear."

"That magic you did, getting the documents to appear, is that really something I could learn to do?"

She nodded. "It might be different, mind you. Every witch's talent manifests differently, so a kitchen witch would have one way of going about it and a glamor witch would do it another way, but it would serve the same purpose in the end, if that makes sense."

"I think it does," I replied, though my heart felt heavy. I doubted I would ever master whatever recipe I needed to work magic like she had done, and I had no idea what other types of witchcraft there even were, let alone what might work for me.

"Did you want to check out your book before you go?" She pointed toward the history book I'd left abandoned on the study desk. I'd been so caught up in my sleuthing that I'd forgotten about it.

"I suppose I will." I went back to retrieve it, wondering if I would feel the burning on my wrist again when I touched it, but I didn't. It behaved just like any ordinary book, which is probably because it was. Sybil must have been right. I'd pinched a nerve, and my imagination had gotten the better of me. The only thing of importance was the new puzzle piece the book contained.

Lillian Bassett, whoever she was to me, had disappeared in 1929 from the waters surrounding Pinecroft Cove precisely as Mother would do nearly eight decades later. There had to be a connection, but what could it be? As much as I dreaded delving into the details I'd been shielded from for so long, it was getting harder for me to deny that I needed to know exactly what had happened to my mother fifteen years before.

Despite the intense summer sun outside, a chill remained with me as I got on my bike and began the ride home. It had nothing to do with the weather. The time was approaching when I would need to ask Auntie Sue to share those newspaper articles with me after all, though if I had my way, I was determined to ignore it for as long as possible. As I rounded the bend and the Pinecroft Inn sign came into view, a massive, black bird perched on top. He let out a loud caw, intensifying the cold I felt all the way to my bones. My mother's mystery could wait, I reminded myself. It's not like she was following me around and insisting I solve it, unlike another ghost I knew. From what I could tell, Douglas Strong's spirit didn't seem likely to let me forget that he had a job for me to finish.

CHAPTER FIFTEEN

When I returned to the inn later that day I checked immediately for signs of Gus, hoping the little guy had returned but was disappointed to find the foot of my bed empty. My elation over the discovery I'd made at the library soured at the memory of the role I'd played in whatever it was that had happened to him. In need of a head-clearing walk, and maybe a chance to scout the property for him, I went out the back door and strolled across the grass toward the water until I reached the path that circled the cove.

Although the area around the town square had been a hive of activity, the restaurants and public beaches overflowing with people, Pinecroft Cove remained tranquil in the late afternoon. Technically, the shore path and rocky beaches were open to the public, but if you didn't have a house that opened up to it, the cove was well hidden from view. The typical Summerhaven vacationer might spend a week on the island and never catch a glimpse of it. I counted two sailboats and a kayak navigating the calm waters. Beyond that, I was alone.

It was the time of day my mother had most enjoyed being out on the water, when the sun was low in the sky and the air still pleasantly warm. I'd sailed with her countless times, and though I'd only been a child, I could attest to her being an expert at it. How she'd fallen from her boat and drowned on an otherwise clear day had been the greatest mystery surrounding her disappearance and presumed death. A sudden squall that caught her unaware was the official story, but I knew better. Someone had told her to jump.

Shortly after we'd arrived on the island that final trip, right around the time my grandmother became ill, my mother started hearing things. Sometimes she'd come into the room where I was and ask me if I'd said something, only for me to tell her no. Sometimes she'd swear she heard a whisper when I was sure it was just the wind. I'd assumed at the time it was nothing, or maybe just the stress of Grandma being sick. Looking back, I wondered if it had been something else, something unseen from the magical realm, that had plagued her. But my mother had never told me we were witches, and I had no idea why. I turned my head away from the sparkling, still water, not wanting to remember any more.

The sun's brilliant reflections had left spots in my eyes, so when I first saw the shadowy figure creeping through the low-growing blueberry brambles, I assumed it was my vision playing tricks on me. I blinked and rubbed my eyes. At first, I thought it was gone, but then I saw a black, catlike tail flicking between the leaves a bit farther on. It was furry and familiar.

"Gus?" I said, clicking my tongue against the roof of my mouth to call him, not that he was the type of cat who responded to that type of thing. As expected, the tail slipped back into the brush. Convinced it was him, I followed the sound of rustling until I came to an outcropping of sand just before the start of a steep rock trail I'd never seen before. It looked impossible to access and even more treacherous to climb. I was about to move on without exploration when I heard the distinctive sound of Gus's meow. I turned my head in the direction it had come from and saw a sliver of gray that marked the opening in the rocks.

Scrambling up the rocky passage, I spotted the first stone step, almost completely obscured by fallen branches. I moved the largest one aside until there was room for me to pass. A pebble slipped into my sandal and lodged itself in my heel, but I shook my foot to dislodge it and continued to climb. I smelled the garden before I saw it, a strong whiff of wild roses that rode on the back of a light breeze. With just a few more steps I had reached it, a hidden garden at the edge of the woods with its circular gate built of stone, whose tall arch dripped in those small white blooms that produced the heady scent.

I approached the circle slowly, pausing in the center of the gate to run my fingertips across the rough, cold granite blocks. I could almost feel an energy emanating from them, buzzing through my fingertips and up my arm. I pulled away, but though it was unexpected, the sensation wasn't unpleasant. Beyond the gate was the most glorious garden I had ever seen. Flower beds full of delicate pink foxglove, radiant yellow zinnias, and dusky English lavender stretched along each side of an expanse of velvety green grass. I could just make out the outline of a house at the far end of the garden, a sturdy New England saltbox that lacked the pretension of the neighboring houses. Mindful that I was trespassing, I skirted closer to the tree line to avoid being seen.

Although the garden was warm and sunny, the chirping of crickets reminded me that dusk was approaching. I needed to get home, but as I turned to go, I caught sight of a cat's eye glimmering in the shadow of a tree, so I pressed on. Gus was well ahead of me, but he'd moved to walk along the center of the trail so I could see him clearly. I had no idea where I was headed, and the deeper I went into the woods, the more it dawned on me that following a cat I'd frightened out of a window only a few hours earlier might be a stupid move on my part. My aunt's cat seemed the type for revenge.

I walked for a good five minutes, maybe more. Despite trying numerous times to overtake him, the distance between me and my feline guide remained constant. Just as I'd become pretty sure I was doomed to follow Gus through the woods for eternity, the trees gave way to an expanse of perfectly manicured green lawn. The hulking house in front of me was all too familiar, even if the angle I was viewing it from was not the usual one. Somehow, I'd ended up at Cliffside Manor.

The path from the woods had deposited me behind the pool house. A few yards ahead of me was a row of shiny metal trash cans, and on top of the one on the far right side sat Gus. Normally the smug expression on his face would have filled me with annoyance, but at that moment I was so grateful he was alive and unharmed that my first impulse was to pick him up and kiss him between his fuzzy, black ears. I refrained. He was a cat after all. With claws.

Instead, I tiptoed toward him as slowly as I could manage, not wanting to frighten him again and end up chasing him all the way back through the woods. I was just inches away from him, arms extended to scoop him up, when he hopped to the next trash can, causing the one he'd been standing on to topple over and fall silently onto the grass. The lid popped off and went rolling toward the woods.

I chased after it, and as I dived to grab it, I was temporarily blinded by a bright light aimed at the woods. I froze, breathless and certain I was about to be discovered, until I realized the light was coming from an automatic motion sensor that was mounted on the side of the pool house. I let out my breath, grabbed the lid, and returned to the line of bins. Gus had remained on his perch the whole time, watching me with what I assumed was amusement.

As I straightened up the overturned can, something bright purple on the ground caught my eye. I picked it up and found that it was a small mailing box that had become partially buried in the soft, muddy ground. It had been hidden from view until Gus upset the trash can. Most of the address label had been torn off, but I could still make out a logo of two squiggly lines that looked a little like a ladder. More important, the return address was intact and bore the name Curtis Strong. I might not have known what was in the box, but whatever it was, there was no question I was taking it with me.

I turned to retrieve Gus, but he was nowhere in sight. Big surprise. "I swear, cat," I muttered, "you will be the death of me." At least he was unharmed, and I trusted he would find his way back to the inn when he got hungry. No one could resist Aunt Gwen's cooking, not even a mischievous cat.

I returned along the path I'd come, turning the little purple box over and over in my hands to study it as I went. I gave it a shake, but no sound came from inside. It wasn't heavy, either, which would have made me wonder if it was empty, except the edge had been carefully sealed with a strip of tape for mailing. How had it ended up half buried behind the pool-house trash?

I was so deep in thought I scarcely noticed when I reached the hidden garden again. I strolled across the center of the grassy path without bothering to look around me, until the shocking boom of a man's voice brought me to a sudden halt.

"Hey!" he called out, a shadowy figure emerging from the house. "What are you doing in my garden? Do I need to call the sher—oh, Tamsyn. It's you."

"Hi, Noah." Was there any doubt that of all the people in Pinecroft Cove whose garden I could have chosen to trespass through, it would be his? I struggled to speak calmly, wishing I could sink into the nearest flower box and disappear. "This is your garden? It's beautiful."

"It's my mother's. I take care of it for her while she's away." The melancholy tone beneath his words reminded me his mother was in poor health, and I knew he must be more worried than he let on.

"I'm sure she appreciates it," I told him, lacking the words to express the sympathy I felt.

"It's her favorite place in the world." The softness of his smile as he spoke of her made his eyes twinkle and my heart flutter. "Look, I'm sorry for yelling earlier."

"It's okay. I shouldn't have been cutting across your grass like I own the place."

"It's just that ever since a botanical garden opened not too far from here, I've had lost tourists traipsing through right and left, thinking this was it." He paused, his expression betraying confusion as he looked in the direction from which I had come. "Although they usually come from the opposite way."

"Oh, yeah. Um…" I fidgeted with the box I was holding, searching for an explanation that would go over better than *I was just on my way back from rummaging in your cousin's trash.*

"What's that you're holding?" Noah's eyes narrowed, and he reached out as if to take the package. "Is that from My Family Tree?"

"Is it?" I had no idea what that was, but I held the box out to get another look. Before I realized what was happening, Noah plucked it from my hand.

"This has my cousin's name on it," he said with a hint of accusation.

"I can explain," I assured him, although I was no closer to coming up with a convincing story than I had been three seconds prior.

"Maybe we should go in the house. I have a feeling this might take a while."

I followed him along the path to the house without arguing because, let's face it, he wasn't wrong.

If the exterior of the dwelling was typical of a modest New England home, the interior was anything but ordinary. The walls were sheathed in a naturally warm wood paneling, and a large fireplace of faded, red bricks stood prominently against one wall. The ceilings soared to cathedral height with exposed beams, and at the top of the staircase an open landing revealed shelves packed with old books.

Two dark leather sofas were grouped on a worn woolen rug with a Native American design, and it was there that Noah led me. I chose a seat, and he took the one opposite me. As I crossed my legs, I could feel my foot beginning to twitch with nervous energy.

My throat had grown thick, and I cleared it more loudly than I had intended before I began to speak. "Noah, there's something I think you need to know. Remember the money I told you was missing from the Strong Corp. accounts?"

"The money you said Uncle Doug embezzled?" He shot me an incredulous look. "Yes, I think I remember that."

Right. Of course, he would remember me accusing his dearly departed relative of a crime. "I guess the good news is that I don't think he's the one who stole it. The bad news is I think it was Curtis."

"Curtis?" Noah's left eyebrow arched in a way that made his usually symmetrical face jarringly lopsided. "I assume that's why you—what, exactly—broke into Cliffside Manor and snooped around this evening?"

"Broke in?" My forehead scrunched as my eyes widened. Is that what he thought happened? "I would never do that."

"Right." It was clear he didn't believe me. "Then how do you explain the fact that you were traipsing through the woods from the direction of Cliffside, holding my cousin's DNA testing kit?"

My eyes shifted to the bright purple box, which he'd set beside him on the couch. "That's what was in the box?"

"Yes. Remember how I told you Uncle Doug had ordered these kits for everyone because he was trying to prove we were related to the Davenport family who built Cliffside Manor? I sent mine in before Uncle Doug died."

"Oh, that's right. I remember you saying that now, but I had no idea what it was when I grabbed it."

"What, you just rummaged around and took something without knowing what it was?"

"Look, it's true I was at Cliffside just now, but I swear I didn't go anywhere near the house. I found the box behind the pool-house trash." Yeah, that pretty much sounded as bad out loud as it had in my head. I knew bright red circles were forming on my chalk-white cheeks, making me look like a poorly painted china doll. Why could I never act like a normal human being when Noah was around?

"And you make a habit of stealing trash?" His delivery was so deadpan that it left it impossible to tell how much humor, if any, he found in the situation. My guess was not much.

"I was looking for my cat," I responded, bristling at whatever it was he was implying about my dumpster-diving habits while ignoring the fact that I had been doing exactly that. "You haven't even asked why I think Curtis was embezzling from Strong Corp., you know."

"Haven't I?" His tone had shifted from incredulity to bemusement, which under the circumstances was an improvement. "I guess I got distracted."

"Shall I fill you in?" When he nodded with a half-amused smile, I continued, feeling somewhat relieved that we'd moved past my garbage issues. "Two years ago, Curtis got involved with a condo timeshare development scheme in Costa Rica being run by a man named Marcus Levine."

"I've heard him mention Marcus, although I didn't know about the Costa Rica deal."

I nodded. "Marcus was the man I saw at Cabot Field that day, the one I told you about who was arguing and then tossed a briefcase at Curtis."

"I remember that. Any idea what was in the briefcase?"

I thought for a moment. "Money, I assume. Curtis invested over a million dollars with the Papagayo Development Initiative, and he hadn't seen any of the returns he'd been promised. When the life insurance got delayed, he may have demanded a payment."

"But what does this mean in terms of my uncle's death?" A deep furrow formed between Noah's brows. "Surely you don't think Curtis slipped Uncle Doug sleeping pills before the flight."

"I don't know." I chose my words carefully, not wanting to add to the pain that was evident on his face. "But I think it's worth considering if it's possible. Any crime show on TV will tell you that a killer needs means, motive, and opportunity. Curtis was a million dollars in the hole, and your uncle had a million-dollar life insurance policy. That's a pretty strong motive."

"But what about means? I happen to know that Curtis doesn't take sleeping pills."

"Maybe not, but someone in the house does, or did."

"How do you know that?"

"The other day when we went to Cliffside, I found an empty bottle of pills. The label had been torn, but I'm pretty sure it was the type of pill you said was found in your uncle's lab results, and I could read the last name Strong."

Noah gave me a long, searching look. "Where did you find these pills?"

I sucked in my breath, visibly cringing at the question I should have seen coming. "In the bathroom trash. Don't—" I held up my hand as he opened his mouth to point out the obvious. "I know how it sounds, okay? But it gives him the means, for sure."

To my surprise, Noah chuckled. "You know, you're not at all the way I remember you."

Was that a good thing or a bad thing? I waited for him to continue, but he didn't, so I was left to assume the worst. "Look, I'm sorry to lay this all on you, Noah. I just thought you should know. What you do with the information is entirely up to you."

"What I'm going to do is talk to Curtis. Right now." Noah's voice was firm, his expression filled with a steely determination that set my heart pounding. "And you're coming with me."

CHAPTER SIXTEEN

he darkness was palpable as we drove through Cliffside's iron gates, and the light from the waning moon hidden behind a thick layer of clouds provided the only illumination along the long driveway. The house itself was dark except for a single light that shone from a side window on the first floor. No one was expecting us, as Noah hadn't called ahead, preferring not to give his cousin time to prepare answers to our questions in advance. Or flee if he was so inclined, which was more what I expected of him.

The deep gong of the doorbell reverberated throughout the house, which was enough on its own to make me jittery, but the feeling intensified as the clouds parted and a beam of moonlight revealed a massive blackbird sitting still as a statue on the grass beside the house. The moment my eyes landed on him, the bird let out a loud, mournful croak that sent a shiver racing from the base of my neck all the way to my tailbone. Clearly the bird was a sign, but of what I wasn't sure.

An eternity passed before the door swung open, the creak of the hinges making nearly the same noise as the bird. Curtis stood in the doorway, appearing drained of life. Even in the darkness, I could make out the circles beneath his sunken eyes, and the expression he wore was devoid of all emotion.

"Noah. Polly. What are you doing here?" he asked.

Noah stiffened beside me. "You know that's not her name, Curtis."

Curtis stared blankly, almost confused, and it seemed he hadn't intended to tease. I doubted he was fully aware he'd used the wrong name. He blinked slowly, and the faintest spark of animation returned to his features. "Tamsyn. Sorry. Please, both of you, come in."

We entered the house and followed him past the opulent staircase and through the echoing front room, down the hall, and into a smaller room that appeared to be a study. There were oversized leather chairs and built-in shelves filled with books. Though it was the middle of summer, a fire crackled in the fireplace to ward off the chill that was common for evenings on the island.

"Have a seat." Curtis gestured toward the chairs as he crossed the room to a large globe, which he opened to reveal a hidden bar. "Can I get either of you a drink?"

"This isn't exactly a social call, Curt," Noah said. "Tamsyn's been helping me review the Strong Corp. financials for Mom, and I have some questions."

"Well, then we'll definitely need drinks." Curtis set out three cut-crystal glasses and a fancy soda bottle with a ceramic stopper instead of a cap. There was a quick hiss of pressure being relieved as he popped the top open and filled each glass until it was about two-thirds of the way to the top. Then he filled each one the rest of the way with a generous measure of rum. "Dark and stormy. Uncle Doug's favorite. Cheers."

As I raised the drink to my lips, I detected the strong, biting scent of ginger. Bubbles tickled my nose as I pretended to take a sip. The smell was inviting, and under normal circumstances I would've been happy to give it a try, but I had a healthy enough sense of self-preservation not to consume anything that had been offered to me by someone I suspected of murder. I noticed Noah, too, set his drink down untouched. Then he let out a long, slow sigh.

"I know about Costa Rica, Curt."

Curtis slumped in his chair at Noah's words, shutting his eyes and placing a hand to his temple. "Marcus swore it was a sure thing."

"Nothing's ever a sure thing," Noah chided.

There was a flash of fire in Curtis's eyes. "Quadruple my money in six months tops. Fast enough that no one would even notice it missing from the accounts. Until the tropical storm hit."

"Was it the life insurance you needed?" Noah's words were soft, nearly a whisper, but there was no mistaking the gravity of his meaning.

"Hold on there, bud." Curtis sat up straight, his shoulders and jawline equally stiff. "You think I killed Uncle Doug?"

"Look, I'm not saying you did," Noah soothed. "But I'm saying I can see how it sure would've made things easier for you. You'd have the insurance money to pay back what you owed the company, and Uncle Doug would never have to find out what you did."

"Nah, you don't get it." Curtis waved a hand, frustrated. "He already knew."

"Are you saying he was in on it?" I asked, unable to hide my surprise. "The real estate deal? The shell accounts?"

"No, not all that," Curtis said. "He only found out after the fact, when he discovered the money was missing."

"When did that happen?" Noah asked.

"Right after we got the notice from the IRS about the audit. He started reviewing the accounts, confronted me about the numbers not lining up, and I confessed everything."

"It was a million dollars, Curtis," I said, shaking my head in disbelief. "You're making it sound like your uncle just forgave you for it on the spot."

"He would do anything for blood," Curtis stated with utter firmness.

"It's true." Noah turned toward me. "I know the reputation our uncle had on the island, but when it came to family, that wouldn't be so far-fetched."

Curtis nodded. "Exactly. I mean, I don't want to make it sound like he was fine with what I'd done. He wasn't. But he didn't want me getting into trouble for it. He said he wanted to deal with the matter internally so it wouldn't hurt the family name."

"What did that mean, internally?" I asked.

"He was going to replenish the accounts with his own money, and I'd pay him back when I got the rest of what I was owed from Marcus. The day before the party, when he was leaving for the mainland, he told me he'd figured out how to move some stuff around so it wouldn't raise any red flags with the auditors."

"But he died before he could do it," I said, understanding sinking in. "Which means you're—"

"Up a creek," Curtis finished with a bitter laugh. "The money never got transferred, and what I got from Marcus won't make a dent. Without Uncle Doug to intervene, I'm ruined, and the company might be, too."

"I had no idea," Noah said, his face a mask of concern. "I'm really sorry."

"Yeah, well, at least now you know I didn't have anything to do with his death. I'm the last person in the world who would've wanted him dead." Curtis sniffed loudly, and I couldn't tell for sure, but I thought it might have been because he was holding back tears, though whether for his uncle or for himself I wasn't sure. He might not have been a murderer, but he was still Curtis Strong, instigator of Polly Parrot and tormentor of my youth, after all. "Can I get you another drink?"

"Still working on this one," I replied, raising my glass. This time, I took a real sip. Since Curtis most likely wasn't a murderer anymore, I could no longer see any harm. As I swallowed, I choked back a cough when the intense flavor of ginger hit the back of my throat. "Whoa. Powerful."

"The rum?" Noah asked.

"The ginger ale," I said.

"Ginger beer, you mean." Curtis chuckled. "Yeah, that was Uncle Doug's secret ingredient. He got it from a craft brewer on the mainland once a month. It's the spiciest ginger beer I've ever tasted, for sure. But he swore you couldn't make a proper dark and stormy without it. He'd have one every night before bed."

"Could I take a look at it?" I stretched out my arm as Curtis passed me the bottle. It was made of light-green glass and had a label on it that looked hand stenciled, with a blue anchor. Even empty, the gingery scent was intense enough to burn my nostrils. "Do you mind if I keep it? I wouldn't mind picking some up next time I'm off the island."

"Sure, be my guest," he replied, and I dropped the empty bottle into my bag.

It was an odd request, to be sure, but I had my reasons. You see, I hadn't forgotten my earlier mission of finding a personal item that belonged to Douglas Strong so the coven could attempt a second summoning spell. It wasn't an ideal choice, but let's face it, if I'd slipped out of the room and tried to smuggle one of Uncle Doug's bathrobes from the house, it would have been noticed. Plus, now that I'd accused Curtis of murder, there was a good chance that another invitation to Cliffside was not in my future.

"I haven't been off the island in a while, have you?" I directed this question at Curtis with as much nonchalance as I could manage. Sure, he'd given a solidly convincing motive for wanting his uncle alive, but it never hurt to double-check a suspect's alibi.

"Not since early June. Mom and I were up to our ears getting ready for Uncle Doug's party. We barely left the house. Then again, I rarely leave Summerhaven this time of year because so many investors are on the island."

That settled it. If Curtis hadn't left the island since well before the crash, there was no way he had slipped his uncle those sleeping pills.

After the final awkward pleasantries were exchanged, Noah and I found ourselves in his car, heading back down the driveway toward the main road. This time, Curtis had turned on the lights, so it was slightly less dark and foreboding than it had been upon our arrival. As a result, we were driving at a good clip when we reached the iron gates. The area around Cliffside was usually deserted late at night, but just as he began to turn onto the main road, Noah slammed on the brakes, pushing the seat belt deep into my flesh and causing a biting pain to rip through my shoulder. I gasped as a car careened toward us. It was an antique roadster, the convertible top folded back, and I could see a female driver with blonde hair frantically spinning the steering wheel. The car swerved toward the center of the road with a jerk, passing mere inches from Noah's front bumper.

"Schnookerdookies!" I exclaimed, thoroughly rattled.

His hands still gripping the wheel, Noah turned to me with a look that shifted rapidly from fright to confusion. "What did you say?"

"I...uh," I muttered, because I wasn't sure what to make of the revelation that the last thing I said on earth could have been "schnookerdookies," let alone how to explain that to another human being. "Any idea who that was?"

"Audrey." Noah's expression was grim. "One of these days her drinking is going to get her, or someone else, killed."

"Should we call the sheriff?"

"I hate to bring more trouble on the family than

there already is. She's home now, parked around the back entrance." He sighed deeply, clearly troubled. "Maybe I'll call Sheila and let her bring it up to Grady in an unofficial capacity."

"Sheila from the diner?" My brain whirred with half-remembered snippets of conversation from the ferry about the sheriff and his new lady friend. "Oh, she's *that* Sheila."

"Rumors spread like the plague on this island." His words were tinged with a bitterness that made me wonder just how miserable his teenage years had been thanks to his crush on me.

I watched as Noah inched the car the rest of the way out of the driveway and onto the road, but instead of seeing the handsome doctor, I saw the geeky kid he'd once been. "Can I ask you something?"

"Sure."

"It's just, well, your cousin was pretty awful to you when we were young." I tripped over the words just a little. It was the closest we'd come to discussing the unfortunate poetry incident, and I felt every bit as self-conscious about it as I was certain he must. "Why are you so quick to stand by him now?"

"You're right. He could be a real jerk sometimes. But he's family, and he's been through a lot. We all need someone in our corner, and I guess I like knowing I can be that person for him."

"Yeah," I scoffed, "but would he be there for you? Because if he thought you'd slipped those pills to your

uncle, he strikes me as the type to sell you out in a
heartbeat if it meant speeding up that insurance
money."

"I guess I don't place value on people the same way
you do."

Oh, schnookerdookies. My flippant observation on
human nature had not gone over the way I'd intended.
Not at all. But before I could figure out whether I'd
angered Noah by criticizing his family, or merely disappointed him with my cynicism, we'd reached the sign
for Pinecroft Inn. As soon as the car had made it to the
end of the driveway, I threw the door open and
hopped out.

"I'll walk you to the door," Noah said, pushing the
shifter into park.

"No need," I called over my shoulder as I all but
sprinted to the front steps. He waited to back away
until I'd opened the door and stepped inside, his sense
of chivalry outweighing whatever annoyance or anger
I'd provoked by criticizing his bully of a cousin. I
wasn't sure I'd ever understand what made Noah
Caldwell tick, or where I stood with him.

The stairs creaked beneath my feet as I headed up
to my room, the groaning sound echoing through the
otherwise silent house. It was late, and except for a
light on the second-floor landing, the house was dark,
and all had gone to bed. Wearily, I snapped on the
bedroom light, then stared, astounded, at the black
lump of purring fur on my quilt.

"Gus?" I broke into a broad grin when the little devil opened one eye as if he'd done nothing all day but nap in precisely that spot. "Oh, thank goodness. I thought...well, I don't know what I thought, but I'm glad you're back."

I rushed toward him with an arm outstretched to give his head a pat, almost unable to believe I'd just said so many nice words to a cat in one breath. He responded by plastering his ears back and fixing me with an icy stare, a sure sign this sudden rush of affection was not mutual. I retreated, and he readjusted his position on the bed so that his back was turned toward me, his gaze now fixed on the bedroom window. My eyes followed his to where the curtain billowed gently on a rose-scented breeze. I was certain I'd closed it before I'd left, and the sight of it standing wide open now sent a stab of unease through my gut. The last thing I needed after the day's upheaval was any repeat of feline defenestration.

With one eye on Gus to make sure he stayed put like the good kitty I knew he wasn't, I moved to the window and gave the pane a sharp downward tug. It didn't budge. The old wood had swelled in the humidity. I hit each side with my fist, sending the weights that were suspended by ropes inside the wall swinging and bumping. Still it didn't move. I stared out the gaping hole. In a patch of moonlight on the lawn, once again, stood a giant blackbird. Deep inside, I knew it was the same one I'd seen at Cliffside Manor. It was following me for a reason, but what message was it trying to send?

Unable to shut the window, I pulled the curtains across it as best as I could, not that the sheer fabric would stop a mischievous cat from going out, or a creepy bird from getting in, for that matter. Even so, I felt more secure once the view to outside was obscured. When I turned back around, Gus was watching me. "If you're actually a magical flying cat with the power to speak, this would definitely be the right time to speak up and give me a clue, mister. Just sayin'."

He did no such thing.

"Not a single word, really?" I chided. "Come on. You could at least tell me what's up with your birdie friend out there. Is he an omen? Is he the reincarnated spirit of Douglas Strong?"

Gus rolled onto his back with a little sigh as if to say "Stop talking, human. My belly needs scratching." I'm embarrassed to say I gave into his demands without arguing. He'd had a rough day.

"I just can't shake it, Gus," I said. "I can't get Douglas Strong's crash out of my mind. I was sure I'd figured it out with the embezzling. How could Curtis *not* be guilty?"

"Meow." It's not like I could understand what Gus was saying, but I sensed he was raising an objection, or perhaps it was just my own uncertainty coming to light.

"I know, his name doesn't start with an L, but I'm not sure it has to. Madame Alexandria never said for certain. Marcus Levine's name has an L, and he's the reason Curtis needed the money from the life insurance." I gasped as I made the connection. "Life insurance. Another L!"

Gus stretched, but the movement didn't give me any clue as to what he was thinking.

"The problem is, Curtis says he needed his uncle alive, and I believe him. Plus, he was definitely on the island the day the plane went down, so he wouldn't have had access to his uncle to slip him the sleeping pills anyway. Could it really have been an accident?"

Gus grabbed my hand with his front paws and gave the flesh below my thumb a sharp nip. Apparently, his belly had been scratched enough. I tried to pull my hand away, but he secured it with his hind legs in an iron grip.

"I wish I knew what was going on with the official investigation," I said, managing to shake my hand loose. "But it's not like Sheriff Grady is going to give me the time of day. If only there was someone else I could talk to."

"Meow," said Gus.

"Thanks, buddy. I know I can talk to you, but I was thinking more along the lines of a person. You know, someone who can talk back?"

"Meow."

"Someone who might know what was going on."

"Meow." Gus stood and spun himself in a circle. "Meow."

"You've been nothing but trouble, you know that? Ever since I saw you on the ferry."

The ferry. I'd seen that roadster before, the one that had nearly collided with the front end of Noah's car. It had been parked on the deck of the ferry the evening I'd made the crossing to Summerhaven. Curtis had said neither he nor his mother had made the trip to the mainland since well before the party, but that had to be a lie. Someone had taken that roadster to the mainland less than twenty-four hours before Douglas Strong plunged his airplane into the bay.

There was one person on Summerhaven Island who had personal ties both to someone on the crash investigation team and the two people who were most likely to have had a hand in the crash itself: Sheila Briggs. As the sheriff's girlfriend and Audrey's sister, I couldn't think of a better person to shed some light on what had really happened to Douglas Strong. All I needed was an excuse to drop by for a chat. Luckily for me, I owed her an order of a dozen of Pinecroft Inn's famous blueberry pies.

My heart pounded as a plan clicked into place. "First thing in the morning, Gus, I'm going to need to do some baking."

CHAPTER SEVENTEEN

I stared into Cassandra's brown eyes expectantly as she swallowed a spoonful of blueberry pie filling. "Tell me a lie."

"The queen of England is having tea at the shop tomorrow," she said blandly. "Mother's very excited."

I swiveled to watch Sybil, who was licking the last purple bits off her silver spoon. "How about you?"

"All of my dresses are hand sewn by enchanted mice."

"It's still not working." My shoulders slumped as I wiped a sticky hand across my sweaty brow. I pulled the recipe book closer and reread the directions. I'd followed them perfectly, including my great-grandmother's handwritten note that berries gathered from a particular set of bushes in Pinecroft Cove were especially valuable for their truth-telling properties. If I'd cooked up the spell successfully, it should have been impossible for either of my friends to lie. Clearly, I'd gotten something wrong. Again. "Maybe I'm not cut out to be a kitchen witch."

"Don't say that," Cass soothed. "You just need practice. That's what they keep telling me, anyway."

"But I don't have time," I whined. "I need Sheila to give me answers right now."

Sybil tapped an index finger against her chin. "What about adding a potion?"

"What do you mean?" I asked.

"Well, if the truth spell isn't working," Sybil replied, "maybe Cass could brew up a truth potion that you could sprinkle on the pie."

Cassandra's eyes grew wide. "Wait. Why me?"

"Because you're the potion maker," Sybil said. "Try as I might, I can't think of a glamour that would be of any help in this particular instance."

"Can you do it?" I gave Cass my most hopeful, pleading look.

She chewed on the edge of her fingernail for a minute, lost in thought. "Do you have any spicebush?"

I frowned. "I don't even know what that is."

"Check the pantry," Cass said. "Your aunt Gwen probably has some."

I crossed the kitchen and pulled open the door to the spice cabinet, inside of which were hundreds of glass bottles with handwritten labels. I plucked them out one by one until I found one that said spicebush. "Well, what do you know? I do have that."

"Perfect. How about angelica root, rose hips, and juniper?"

"Yes, yes, and yes," I replied, scooping up three more bottles.

Cass surveyed the ingredients as I placed them on the counter. "Good. I just need lemon juice, and we're all set."

"Lemon juice." I nibbled on my lower lip as I scanned the two-tiered silver fruit basket that Aunt Gwen kept near the windowsill. "I don't see any lemons."

"Check the fridge," Cass directed. "It doesn't have to be fresh. Even one of those little plastic bottles that's shaped like a lemon will be fine."

I scoured every nook and cranny of Aunt Gwen's industrial-sized refrigerator. Finally, I straightened up, my vertebrae popping in protest. "No luck. How could I have stuff like spicebush and angelica root and not have any lemon?"

"It's okay," Cass said. "I'll just run home and whip up a batch there, and you can pick it up on your way to the diner."

I spent the rest of the morning ladling my magically useless but surprisingly tasty blueberry filling into a dozen pie shells. I was just finishing weaving the final piece of lattice pie crust topping when Aunt Gwen poked her head into the kitchen.

"Look at you!" She surveyed my work, glowing with the pride of a mentor whose protégé has done her proud. "I knew if you practiced a little, you'd get the hang of it. Are those for the Dockside?"

My face grew warm as her praise sent the blood rushing to my cheeks. "I thought I'd bring them over today and see what Sheila thinks of them."

"I wouldn't be surprised if she doubles the order."

I nearly choked. Double the order? I was exhausted from making a dozen and wasn't at all convinced I could do it every week as I'd promised. Twice as many would put me in an early grave. Reluctantly, I loaded the boxes into Aunt Gwen's car and drove toward the docks, all the while hoping I hadn't done as good a job on the pies as I'd thought so that Sheila might rethink her order.

When I stopped at the Hollings' house, a note on the door informed me no one was at home but I would find the potion I needed on the kitchen counter. I took the note down and crumpled it into a ball, stuffing it into my pocket as I chuckled over the strangeness of living in a place where people not only left their doors unlocked but left messages on the door announcing to the whole world that no one was home. As soon as I stepped foot into the kitchen, I saw the clear glass bottle that must have been meant for me. The amber liquid inside sloshed against the cork stopper, but the seal was tight, so I shoved it into my pocket as I returned to the car.

The lunch hour rush was in full swing when I pulled into the parking lot in front of the Dockside.

The smell of burgers and bacon mixed with the salty sea air. Inside the diner, every table was full. I approached the counter carrying a single pie box. I spotted Sheila and raised the box for her to see. "I brought your pies."

"Oh, that's excellent news." She ran a hand across her forehead then tried in vain to smooth the hairs that had come loose from her bun. "Did you just bring one?"

"No. I helped Aunt Gwen by making up the batch, so this one's for you to try first. If you like it, the rest are in the car."

"I guess I can take a break just long enough to taste it," she said, eyeing the box greedily. "I'm sure it'll be fine."

"It would make me feel better if you at least took a few bites. I'm still in the apprentice stages when it comes to my baking skills."

Sheila placed two dessert plates on the counter, along with two forks and a long, sharp knife.

"Here, let me serve it," I offered, reaching for the knife. "I need to double-check the consistency of the filling." What I actually needed to do was sprinkle the top of her slice with the truth potion, which I did as soon as my hands were hidden from view by the open box lid. I'd considered dosing the entire pie, but since Cass hadn't left specific instructions on how much to use, I decided the safest thing was to dump the entire bottle onto a single piece and hope it was enough.

With the potion administered, I slid the slice onto the plate and slipped the empty bottle into my pocket.

Sheila took the pie from me and looked questioningly at the second plate. "Don't you want some?"

"Oh, no thank you," I said. "I've already gained five pounds with all of Aunt Gwen's good cooking. I'm going to have to learn to pace myself, but every time I smell food, I can't seem to resist."

"With your aunt's cooking, it's no wonder, although after thirty years in the diner, I have to say the very smell of fried food takes my appetite away, so there's hope for you." She laughed as she dished herself a generous slice. I held my breath as she dug in her fork and lifted the gooey bite of pie to her lips. "Delicious. If you hadn't told me, I wouldn't have had any idea Gwen didn't make these herself."

"Aw, thanks," I replied, genuinely pleased, as well as relieved the truth potion hadn't altered the taste.

"Did you leave your car unlocked? I'll send one of the girls out with a cart to bring in the rest."

"I didn't," I said, digging in my purse for the keys and handing them to her. "Here. I drove Aunt Gwen's car since I still need to find a mechanic for mine. You can send someone out for the rest of the boxes. I still can't get used to the way everyone just leaves everything unlocked around here."

Sheila took another generous bite of pie. "Oh, you'll get used to it eventually, although my boyfriend's constantly going on about people leaving their keys on the seat, but I just say, Joe, be grateful you're a small-town sheriff. You want crime, you need to move to the mainland." Something like confusion flickered in her eyes as though she wasn't quite certain why she'd shared so much with me, considering her relationship with the sheriff was technically a secret despite everyone on the island knowing about it. But I knew why her life was suddenly such an open book. The truth potion was kicking in. "You need a mechanic, you said?"

"Yeah. It started acting up on the ferry on the way here, and I haven't had the time to have it looked at yet."

"Well, if you need someone, Larry Sloane's the best. He's a regular here. I'd point him out, but he hasn't made it in yet today."

"I'll have to look him up," I assured her, then tried to shift the subject. "So, I saw your nephew and sister the other day…"

"Oh, Audrey." Sheila rolled her eyes. "How's Miss Perfect doing, anyway?"

I'd hoped that Sheila would take the bait and start dishing the dirt, and it looked like I would not be disappointed. "She seems to be taking Douglas's death hard. Has Noah talked to you?"

"You mean about her reckless driving?" Sheila snorted. "Yeah, he called this morning. Not sure what I'm supposed to do about it, though. It's not like my sister has ever listened to me. Not since she got it into her head to marry a Strong in the first place."

"Curtis's dad you mean?"

She snorted. "I guess you can call him that."

I frowned, trying to puzzle out her meaning. "Are you saying he wasn't a good father?"

"Oh, he was great with Curtis. Don't get me wrong. It's just..." Sheila's voice trailed off, her eyes shifting uncertainly.

"Have some more pie," I urged.

Sheila shoveled the last pile of the blueberry filling onto her fork and popped it into her mouth, licking her lips. "See, the thing is, that summer when Audrey got pregnant, Jeremy Strong wasn't the only guy my sister had her eye on. She dated at least two other boys that summer. I guess I've always wondered."

"Wondered what?"

Sheila cleared her throat, shifting uncomfortably. "I really should get back to work."

I took in the empty plate with dismay. Her slice of pie was gone, and the spell was fading rapidly. "Would you like some more?" I offered, reaching into the box for another slice, only to realize that it wouldn't matter anyway, as all the truth potion had already been used.

"Oh, I'd better not, but here comes Gracie with the pies. How much do I owe you? We'll make it a standing order going forward."

I waved the suggestion of payment away, noticing a

spot of blueberry on my finger as I did. "This was a test batch, no charge. You can work out the cost for the weekly order with Aunt Gwen." I popped my finger into my mouth and silently congratulated myself that even if the magic hadn't worked, the pie filling really did taste as good as Sheila had claimed.

"Well, that's real generous of you. Hey, everyone!" Sheila raised her voice several notches to be heard throughout the diner. "Blueberry pie all around, on the house."

There were murmurings of approval from the diners, mixed with a smattering of applause. As Sheila and Gracie set out plates on the counter and started to slice the pies, the door opened, and a man in blue coveralls walked in.

"Larry, there you are," Sheila called out. "Come on over and have some pie. Tamsyn here was just saying she needs her car looked at."

"Sure, I should have an opening coming up soon. Do you have a number I can text you at when I do?" I told him my number, and after he'd entered it into his phone, Larry leaned against the counter, turning his head to look at the heaping dessert plates. "Is this Miss Gwyneth's pie?"

"Uh, mm-hmm," I mumbled, frowning. I'd intended to say that it was, not wanting to invite another long conversation about my kitchen training, but for some reason the words had gotten tangled up on the tip of my tongue. Confused, I scurried out to the parking lot as quickly as I could and was surprised to find Cass standing, out of breath, by the car.

"Tamsyn," she called out as soon as she saw me, "why didn't you pick up the potion?"

I froze in place. "What?"

She held up a glass bottle that was identical to the one I'd grabbed from her house, but the liquid inside it was green. "The truth potion. I set it on the kitchen counter for you. Did you not stop by?"

I reached into my pocket and pulled out the empty bottle, holding it out to her. "If that's the potion, what is this?"

Cass took the bottle from my hand and removed the cork, lifting it to her nose. "Vanilla."

My eyes grew wide. "Seriously? Then why did Sheila just tell me all that stuff about Audrey?"

"Everyone loves to gossip," Cass said with a shrug.

Reeling from my latest magical screwup, I grabbed the last of the blueberry pies, the one I had set aside on the front seat, and headed to the clinic. After all, I'd promised Noah a pie, and the least I could do was deliver.

The receptionist barely looked up as I entered. She just reached for the phone. "The Bassett girl's here again." she said. "Fine, I'll send her back." She inclined her head in the direction of Noah's office, and I took that as my cue to proceed.

"Tamsyn, what brings you in today?" Noah asked

as I stepped into the exam room. "Your head's doing okay, right? No dizziness, blurry vision?"

"I'm fine. This isn't a medical visit," I assured him. "I remembered you said you liked blueberry pie, and I happened to be in the area…"

His face lit up as he noticed the box. "Your aunt made that for me?"

"Actually, I did, but it's her recipe."

"This is fantastic. I forgot my lunch, so I just might eat the whole thing."

"So, Noah…" I continued to clasp the pie awkwardly to my chest as I tried to decide how best to raise the topic that was weighing on my mind. "Do you remember that DNA kit I found the other day?"

"The one you swiped from my cousin's trash?" He said it jokingly, but I had to stop myself from cringing. "How could I forget?"

"Yeah. True." I cleared my throat. "I was wondering, how long does it take to run one of those tests?"

"They get it back to you in about nine to twelve weeks. Why? You interested in your family tree?"

My face fell. "That long? Wow, it never takes that long on television to run a DNA test."

"The test itself doesn't take long, and some labs can get results the same day, but those ancestry places don't exactly work with the same urgency as a state crime lab."

"I guess not." I took a breath, weighing whether to say more. "Can I ask you something?"

Noah cocked an eyebrow. "That sounds ominous."

"No, it's just…I was wondering if there have ever been any rumors about Curtis's father not being, well…"

A deep line creased Noah's brow. "Rumors about Uncle Jeremy?"

"Uh, you know…" I groaned inwardly. Why did this have to involve Noah's family? It was obvious he had no idea what I was hinting at, and I dreaded being the one to break it to him. Luckily for me, before I could get the rest of the words out, the phone on the exam room wall rang.

"Hold on just a minute." Noah pressed the receiver to his ear. "What is it? Wait, how many? I'll be right there." He snatched up his stethoscope, draped it around his neck, and raced toward the door.

"What was that?" I asked, hurrying to keep pace with him down the hall.

"Half a dozen people or more just walked in the door with injuries."

"Car accident?"

"Brawl."

My mouth dropped open as I surveyed the waiting area, which had been deserted when I arrived but was now packed with people. Some held bloody cloths to their noses while others pressed hands to heads or shoulders. The receptionist had begun triage, sorting those with minor injuries to the chairs while those who were actively bleeding formed a line next to her desk. I recognized Larry Sloane, second from the end, along with at least three other people I was certain had been in the Dockside just minutes before.

"How dare you say that about my wife?" yelled a man who was sitting in one of the chairs, shaking a fist at another man who stood in the line.

"It's the truth!" the man in the line bellowed. At first, I thought the napkin he clutched to his mouth was covered in blood, but upon closer inspection I realized it was blueberry pie filling.

The truth? The lid of the pie box I still held rattled as a terrible thought made my hands start to shake. Surely, my pies couldn't have been responsible for this. But in every corner of the waiting room, folks were bickering over secrets that had been spilled and other hurtful truths. Then it hit me. I'd licked a little of the filling off my fingers. Was that why I'd stumbled over that little white lie I'd tried to tell Larry? I doubled my pace toward the exit, in desperate need of fresh air.

"Tamsyn!"

I spun my head as Noah called my name, slowing down but not stopping.

"My pie!"

I gulped. "You know what, I'll bring it another time, when it's less busy." I hurried out the door before he could argue, knowing there was no way I could explain just how big a magical screwup I'd managed to make this time.

CHAPTER EIGHTEEN

*S*ybil stared at me in disbelief. "The entire diner was under the truth spell?"

"Don't remind me," I said with a groan, wishing I could sink into the overstuffed cushions of Sybil's love seat and disappear forever. Our coven had gathered at Sybil's home, a modern but cozy ranch-style house with a giant picture window in the living room that overlooked the cove, to discuss my latest magical predicament. "It took hours for the last remnants of it to wear off everyone."

"What did your aunt say about it?" Cass asked.

"Nothing, because I haven't had the heart to tell her what happened." I nestled a little deeper into the couch. "She was so proud of me for finally getting the pie filling right, I think I'd die if she knew about the mess I made."

"Then what are you going to do?" Sybil leaned

closer, not willing to let me escape into her furniture without answering. "None of us knows what went wrong with your spell, why it didn't work one minute and then the next it did. We need to get to the bottom of this, and I think we're going to need help."

I sighed in defeat. "I know. Just give me tonight to figure out how to approach it before you mention it to anyone at home, okay?"

With some reluctance they both agreed, and as soon as I'd returned to the inn and locked myself in my bedroom, I began pacing the floor, trying to come up with the least humiliating solution I could. Gus sat on his spot at the foot of the bed and did absolutely nothing to help, as was his usual routine. In fact, as he began to gnaw on his hind toenails, I started to suspect that he was actively working to drive me stark raving mad with the monotonous cracking sound of his teeth colliding with his claws. Finally, I'd had enough.

"Will you stop that?" I glared at him, and he did pause momentarily, but only, as it turned out, to maneuver himself into a better position to reach his other paw. Quickly, my approach shifted from anger to whining. "Seriously, Gus. Please?"

As if by magic, the cat stopped his chewing. He blinked once, then stood up, stretched, and hopped off the bed. It was then that I noticed he'd been resting directly on top of what looked like a tarot card but which I recognized as the business card the older witch had given me at the start of the summer. Madame Alexandria. I shook my head, laughing. I was almost getting used to that fluffy feline having all the answers.

I held the card in my hand and studied the address. She'd made me promise to call. Well, I wasn't big on phone calls, but when it came to asking for advice, I had to admit it was time. I added the card to my bag and resolved to make a trip to the mainland on the first ferry in the morning.

It was my first crossing back to the mainland since my move, and the first thing I noticed was how much quieter it was than when I'd arrived. Tourists were always eager to get to Summerhaven, at any time of the day, but would hold off leaving until the very last ferry if they could. The passenger cabin was nearly empty, and as I grabbed a book from my bag, I was almost disappointed not to have the distraction of juicy, local gossip to entertain me on the journey. Gossip? Me? It was nothing less than shocking to realize the degree to which I'd started to assimilate to my new home, and how much like a native islander I seemed to have become. If the trend continued, it would be no time at all before I left all my doors unlocked or parked with the keys still in the ignition of my car.

The ferry docked at the terminal in Rockland a little past nine o'clock, and from there, it was a quick walk to the address on the card. The main street was already bustling with tourists and shoppers in even greater numbers than I'd grown accustomed to seeing on Summerhaven, and the sense of claustrophobia that overcame me as I pushed past them to reach the front door of Madame Alexandria's shop drove home how thoroughly I had adjusted to the slower pace of island life.

My destination turned out to be a bookstore with bright yellow stars, moons, and suns painted on a display window filled with all manner of New Age and occult offerings. The pungent scent of incense assaulted me the moment I stepped inside. A young man looked up from behind the cash register while two shoppers browsed a rack of crystals with a *Buy One Get One Free* sign on it.

"Can I help you?" the man asked.

"I'm looking for Madame Alexandria," I replied.

"Through the curtain," he said, inclining his head toward a doorway filled with strands of multicolored, iridescent beads. "She's expecting you."

"No, you have the wrong person. I don't have an appointment," I explained. "I was just hoping she could fit me in."

The young man greeted my words with a half smile. "She blocked off this morning on her calendar a month ago, told me not to make any appointments because someone would come in looking for her, and when they did, I was to send them back."

"Oh. I guess that would be me." No matter how

many times I was given proof that magic was real, I didn't know if I would ever get used to it.

"Yes," he assured me, his patience seemingly limitless. "Right through there."

The cool, heavy beads clacked against my arms as I parted the curtain and stepped through into a small, square room. To my left was a massive slab of amethyst, nearly as tall and wide as the wall, which sparkled in the dim light of a row of votive candles that flickered on a shelf against the opposite wall. In the middle of the room was a table, slightly smaller than a card table and made of thick pieces of gleaming dark wood. The same silver-haired woman I'd met at the inn sat behind the table, shuffling a deck of cards in her hand. She faced the beaded doorway but paid it no attention. A chair sat empty across from her, pushed slightly back from the table as if waiting for my arrival.

"Welcome, Tamsyn." Madame Alexandria's voice was low and soothing as she continued to fan through the cards without so much as an upward glance. "Come sit down."

"How did you know—?" I swallowed the rest of the question as I realized that whatever the answer, I wouldn't really understand. "Never mind."

She chuckled knowingly as she held out the tarot deck. "Cut the cards."

I did as I was told, then watched her shuffle them a final time before dealing them face up into a configuration I didn't recognize but that clearly held some sort of meaning. She set the rest of the deck down and studied the upturned cards in silence, with the exception of the occasional wordless murmur.

"Tell me about the man in the rain," she said.

I breathed in sharply. I hadn't expected her to know anything about that. "The man was Douglas Strong. I believe his ghost appeared to me right after he died, and I've been trying to solve the mystery of the plane crash that killed him ever since."

"Dark and stormy."

"Yes. There was a freak thunderstorm the night he died. When I saw his ghost, he was standing, drenched, in the rain."

She nodded slowly, her eyes closed, and I wasn't certain whether she was acknowledging what I'd said or was responding to some otherworldly entity I could neither see nor hear. "Ravens?"

A lump formed in my throat, and I had to swallow before I could speak. "The next time I visited Cliffside, a big blackbird landed on the spot where his ghost had been, and I saw one later in my backyard. I thought it was a crow, but it might have been a raven. I don't really know the difference."

"Ravens are harbingers of misfortune and death, tricky shape-shifters that transform from man to bird and back again."

"Do you mean to say that blackbird that's been following me is actually Douglas Strong in the flesh?"

"More like in the spirit, but yes, it might very well be."

"But why?"

"He needs your help."

"But I'm just a kitchen witch," I argued. "And a bad one at that."

"No." She shook her head vigorously from side to side. "You're something else."

"Something else?" My heart raced. I'd already considered the possibility that I might not be a kitchen witch at all, but hearing it from someone else's lips still sent a frisson of nervous anticipation through me.

"Yes. You're something different, something more. I'm not certain what. It's cloudy, unclear. May I see your hands?"

I stretched them out in front of me, trying to keep them from shaking as I rested them on the table. Madame Alexandria held them in hers, running her thumb over the links of the silver bracelet I'd nearly forgotten I was wearing.

"Have you found her yet?" Her thumb had come to rest on the link that was engraved with the initials LB.

I gave a tentative nod. "Lillian. Lillian Bassett. At least, I think that's who it belonged to. She seems to be tied to the house in some way. I think she might've lived there back in the nineteen twenties."

She nodded. "The letter L and an airplane."

I stared at Madame Alexandria, dumbstruck. "That

was her the whole time? You mean, what you told me had nothing to do with Douglas Strong's crash at all?"

"Apparently not." She said it in such a matter-of-fact way that I nearly yelled at her for misleading me, but she continued speaking, not giving me the chance. "Her spirit is twined with yours, two sides of a coin. Salvation or destruction, you understand?"

"No. I don't understand." Anger waned as fear gripped my heart, squeezing my chest as I gulped at the air like a fish who suddenly found itself outside the safety of its tank. Whatever this Lillian Bassett had to do with me, I didn't care to know.

"You will. Soon." Still clutching my hands, Madame Alexandria closed her eyes and took several slow, deep breaths before opening her eyes and releasing my hands so she could point to one of the cards in front of her. "The seven of cups. It means searching for purpose. Three of pentacles—collaboration and team-work. And finally, the world card. It points to harmony and completion."

"So, that's good, then?" Though my fear had abated, I found myself more confused and uncertain than I'd been when I first sat down. "I mean, it sounds good."

"It can be. It all depends on you, and how you manage your journey. You'll need to branch away from the simple kitchen magic your aunt Gwen is teaching you."

I gnawed my lower lip, lost in thought, until a

sharp sting and the taste of blood against my tongue brought me back to the present. I quickly shared with her the story of my ill-fated truth pies. "If I'm truly not a kitchen witch, why did the truth spell work at all?"

"I don't know for certain, but if I had to guess, I'd say it worked because, and only precisely when, you required it to. It was your need that made the magic work." She clasped my hands again and looked into my eyes with the type of solemn intensity that seemed to bring the world around us to a halt. I couldn't have looked away if I'd tried. "There's more to your magic than you, or anyone around you, might know. It's hidden deep, but it's powerful. I can help point you in the right direction, but traveling that path of discovery will be up to you. Are you up for the challenge?"

"I...I think so." As answers went, it wasn't the most convincing or inspiring. The truth was, I barely understood what the old witch was telling me, and what I did comprehend filled me with apprehension. Yet her words stirred something deep within my belly, a longing to figure out who I was and what I was capable of doing. As timidly as it had been uttered, this was the first time I had truly accepted myself as a witch, embracing whatever destiny the future held.

I left the shop an hour after I'd arrived with two plastic bags looped around my wrist. One was filled with books, the other with candles, fortune-telling cards, crystals, and other magical accessories. Since Madame Alexandria had been unable to determine the exact nature and source of my powers, her advice had been to cast a wide net and see what came of it. I'd had no idea until I perused her shop just how many facets of magic there were beyond the realm of kitchen witchery that my aunt had introduced me to, but now that my eyes had been opened, I realized with some trepidation that it could take a lifetime to absorb all of what I didn't know.

It was on my walk back to the ferry terminal that a familiar logo caught my eye, a blue anchor on a sign for a craft brewery half a mile outside downtown. On an impulse, I followed the signs until I reached a warehouse on the water's edge, near the shipping docks. A sign above a nondescript glass door marked the entrance to what they called the company store. It was a space about the size of a large walk-in closet and was filled with bottled soft drinks and beers in a variety of flavors.

"Good morning," said the man who was stocking the shelves as I entered. He was in his early thirties and sported a bushy, black beard and a T-shirt with the company logo. "Have you tried Blue Anchor before?"

"The ginger beer," I replied. "I had it at Cliffside Manor recently."

The cheer seeped from the man's face, replaced by somberness. "Douglas Strong was one of our best customers. He and Audrey were not only fans of the products, they were among our earliest investors."

Investors? Curtis hadn't mentioned that part. "I hadn't realized they were so involved."

"Yeah, they'd both come in all the time, see how things were going." He shook his head sadly. "I can't believe I'll never see Doug again, and Audrey hasn't been in since the morning of the crash. Not that I blame her for keeping to herself. That had to have been such a shock."

"She was here that morning?"

"Sure was. She'd stopped in the night before to pick up several cases of our handcrafted sodas for the party then came back in the morning for a bottle of ginger beer. I remember because we weren't open yet. She came around to the warehouse door around six, and I gave her the bottle myself, on the house."

"Just one bottle?"

"Yeah. I guess she was planning to drink it herself on the trip back."

I frowned. "Six in the morning. Do the ferries run that early?"

"The ferries don't, but she was on her way to the airfield."

I'd seen her myself, taking the ferry to the island the night before. Or at least I'd seen her car. Either she hadn't been the one riding in it, or she'd flown back to the mainland in the middle of the night. But why? My pulse pounded. Curtis may have had the airtight alibi of not having left the island in the weeks leading up to the crash, but with this new information, the same could definitely no longer be said of Audrey. I had no idea why the woman might have wanted to slip those sleeping pills to Douglas, but as I studied the neat line of ginger beer bottles lined up on the store shelf, how she could have done it and when were clicking into place.

I made one final stop on my way back to catch the ferry: Rockland Family Pharmacy. It was the same establishment I'd seen on the partially torn label of prescription sleeping pills in the trash at Cliffside Manor, and I had a few questions swirling around in my head that I hoped the pharmacist could answer.

A woman in a white coat was working behind the counter when I entered, counting out pills as she placed them into a plastic bottle. I waited quietly until she was done, at which point she turned to greet me with a smile. "Are you dropping off a prescription?" she asked.

"No," I replied. "But I do have a question about a medication that my, er, mother was prescribed recently." I'd almost said aunt but caught myself at the last moment as I remembered that even on the mainland, my aunt Gwen was well-known, and my telltale red hair linked us immediately.

"Happy to help. What's the medication?"

"Zol...zolpi...oh dear. I can't remember the name, but it's to help her sleep."

"Yes, I know the one you mean," she said, sparing

me the misery of trying to remember how to pronounce it. "What would you like to know?"

"You see, she doesn't like swallowing the pills, so I was wondering, could she crush them up and put them in her favorite cocktail before bed?"

The pharmacist's eyes doubled in size. "Heavens, no. That could be very dangerous."

"Oh dear," I answered as innocently as I possibly could, hiding my excitement at getting the answer I'd been expecting. "Why?"

"Well, for one thing, if your mother is taking a time-release version of the medication, the pills are designed to break down slowly over the course of the night. If you crush them up, she'd get a very strong dose all at once. Plus, you said cocktail."

"Yes, is that a problem?"

"Absolutely. You don't want to mix sleeping pills with alcohol, crushed up or otherwise."

I nodded. "What if they aren't time release, and I just crushed up one and put it in some soda? Like maybe ginger ale?"

The pharmacist's mouth puckered a bit as she thought. "I suppose you could do that."

"It wouldn't taste bad?"

"I doubt she'd notice it. That type of pill dissolves quickly and doesn't have much of a flavor. Still, though, I'd feel better if we checked with her doctor. If you give me the name, I can give the office a call right now."

"We're just in town for vacation," I said quickly. "You know what? I'll just tell her not to try it. Thanks for your help."

Audrey'd had access to the sleeping pills, a drink to conceal them in, and had been on her way to the airfield the morning of the crash. There was no doubt in my mind that she *could* have killed Douglas Strong. But just because she could have done it didn't mean she did. What I still needed to figure out was why she might have wanted her brother-in-law dead.

CHAPTER NINETEEN

I returned by the late afternoon ferry, settling onto my bed at the inn and surrounding myself with the purchases I'd made that morning. The cynical side of me suspected Madame Alexandria's mystical mumbo jumbo was all an act, a way to sell more books and crystals to a doubting witch. But deep down, much of what she'd said resonated, and I knew on some level that she'd spoken the truth. Kitchen witchery was not my calling. Before I could decide whether I wanted to fully embrace my witch heritage and dedicate myself to the study of magic, I needed to explore a broader path than what Aunt Gwen had presented to me.

My head swam as I ran my hand over the glossy covers of half a dozen new books on astrology, numerology, divination, crystals, runes, and moon magic. Until my visit to Madame Alexandria's shop, I'd had no idea just how many paths there actually were. The options were overwhelming. Finding the one that would work best for me could take a lifetime. Meanwhile, I had a restless ghost who had taken on the form of a raven and was hanging out on my back lawn when not disturbing my sleep. I needed to know how to send him into the light, or whatever it was spirits were supposed to do, like, yesterday.

One thing I gleaned quickly as I thumbed through the pages of my new purchases was that there was no shortage of methods that witches used to communicate with the dead. It seemed each system of magic had a suggested way of doing it, whether it was the use of sacred geometry to summon my ghost or dangling a pendulum to ask him yes or no questions.

I picked up what I thought was an empty plastic shopping bag and was surprised when a dark purple crystal tumbled out onto the bed. I pinched its silver chain and held it up so the pointed tip of the crystal was suspended in the air. Immediately, it swayed gently from side to side, just as the book on divination with crystals had said it would. *Ask a yes or no question, huh?*

"Spirit of Douglas Strong, do you hear me?" I spoke the words out loud, speaking clearly and with as much volume and authority as I could muster. The crystal continued on its same path, but a warm tingling of energy traveled down my arm and into my fingertips. I'd expected to feel stupid, talking to nothing like this, but instead I felt empowered. I tried again, even louder. "Douglas Strong, are you here?"

"Caw!" The raven's cry sent an electric current along my spine. The next moment, there was a flapping of wings, then a sudden thud as the raven alighted upon the windowsill. "Caw!"

My scream pierced the air as I flung the crystal from me and dashed out of the room, not stopping until I was safely on the first floor. Aunt Gwen was in the kitchen, her back to me as she stirred an iron cauldron brimming with neon pink foam. I made a beeline for the front door before she could notice my presence and ask for my help. Between the mysterious concoction brewing on the stove and whatever the heck had just happened in my bedroom with that raven, I was in desperate need of a respite from all things bewitched, enchanted, or otherwise otherworldly.

My phone buzzed, and as I pulled it from my pocket, the sight of an incoming text from Larry Sloane's garage brought my thoughts safely back to the mundane realm of real-world problems. The message said if I brought my car around at seven o'clock that evening, he could make time to look at it first thing in the morning. With a glance at the clock, I fired up Miss Josephine for the first time since I'd arrived on the island. Thick black smoke billowed out her backside, and I prayed it wouldn't mean the end of her. I still had about an hour to go before Larry was expecting me, but I needed to make one very important stop on my way.

The truth was, when it came to figuring out who or what had caused Douglas Strong's plane to crash, I had exhausted the limited resources of both my sleuthing and magical abilities and wasn't sure where to turn. Without help from Doug's spirit, I had no idea what to do with the clues I'd gathered on the mainland. As much as I hated the idea, there was only one thing I could do with my new information. It was time for me to pay another visit to the sheriff's office.

Miss Josephine survived the drive, but barely. As I walked into the lobby, I could still smell the remnants of exhaust that clung to my clothing. The first thing I saw inside was Sheila Briggs standing at the main desk, filling out forms. When I heard her utter the words *pie* and *brawl* to the deputy who was assisting her, I nearly turned around on the spot. I wasn't sure if anyone had connected the dots between my blueberry pie and the anger that had been provoked by excessive truth telling, but if they hadn't, the last thing I wanted was to give them a reason to. Before I could sneak away, Sheriff Grady entered the room and immediately caught sight of me. "Miss Bassett, you were at the diner yesterday, right?"

"I was, but—"

"Here to make a statement?"

"No, I actually had something else I was hoping to speak to you about. Privately."

He gave me a bland look then shrugged. "Come on back."

I followed the sheriff to the same office where Noah and I had met with him several weeks ago. That encounter had not gone well, and without Noah to intervene, I expected this one to go even worse. Still, it was the only option I had left. After we'd both taken seats, I drew a deep breath and began. "Sheriff, I've come across some information about the Douglas Strong crash that I think you should be aware of."

"Not the crash again." He rolled his eyes, not bothering to conceal the action, or his disdain, from me in the slightest. "Look, Nancy Drew, you may not be aware of this since you're new here, but law enforcement on the island works pretty much the way it does on the mainland. My department doesn't need you, Bess, and George gathering clues for us so we can solve the case."

"I assume that means you're already aware that Audrey Strong was on the mainland right before the crash?"

Sheriff Grady fixed me with a condescending stare. "Of course. We got alibis from everyone who might've been connected. She was on the mainland the day before the accident, picking up last-minute supplies for the party. If I remember correctly, she said she came back on the last ferry that night. Corroborated by several witnesses who saw her drive on and off."

"Yep. I saw her myself, or her car, anyway." I bristled as he'd recalled the details of her alibi from memory. I couldn't help hoping what I said next would pop that little pride bubble he had going on. "Did you know she was on the mainland again early the next morning, before the first ferry?"

The sheriff's eyebrows bunched to form a bushy caterpillar in the middle of his face. "The next morning?"

I resisted the urge to grin. "One of the workers at the Blue Anchor Craft Brewery recalls her dropping by before they opened, around six o'clock. She wanted a bottle of their ginger beer, and he gave it to her, on the house."

"Six o'clock, you're positive?"

"He sounded very certain of it and said she was headed to the airfield. So, either she found another way from the island to the mainland on her own in the dead of night, or she wasn't on the evening ferry after all."

"You said you saw her yourself, Miss Bassett. Now you say she wasn't on it. Make up your mind."

"I only saw her car, that antique roadster. It's distinctive. But I never actually saw Audrey herself. I just assumed, as I'm sure most of your witnesses did. The top was up, and the truth is I have no idea who the driver was."

"If she returned to the mainland, I'm sure Audrey had her reasons. Maybe she needed to fill a prescription."

"Funny you should say that, because someone at Cliffside had a prescription for the same sleeping pills that were found in Doug Strong's blood. But I'm sure you knew that."

The sheriff's mouth twitched as if he was trying to decide whether or not to tell me something. "Audrey had a prescription on file at the mainland pharmacy."

"They're very helpful there," I told him, watching with amusement as the war between wanting to know what I had discovered and not wanting me to know what he didn't know played out on the sheriff's features. "Did you know that if you crush them, that type of pill has hardly any taste? You could dissolve several in some soda, like ginger beer, and no one would ever notice. Of course, if they happen to be time release instead of the normal capsules, they'd kick in after just a matter of minutes and completely incapacitate the person. I don't suppose you know what type Audrey used?"

"I'm afraid I can't comment on an official police investigation." That was sheriff-speak for he hadn't bothered to find out and didn't enjoy being shown up by an amateur female detective. "Look, between you and me, the lead investigator at the NTSB is leaning toward declaring it an accident and closing the case any day now. The crash really rattled this little community, and I think what we could all use right now is some closure."

"I'm sure you're right." As I studied the sheriff's

face, I couldn't decide if he was ignoring the evidence I'd brought him because he was a coward who didn't want to send his secret girlfriend's sister to jail, or just because he was lazy. If it was the former, I hoped what I was about to say would make him think twice. "On the off chance Audrey *did* murder Douglas, it's not like anyone could ever say you have ties to the Strong family that might have influenced your part in the investigation in any way."

"If Audrey murdered Douglas Strong, she had to have a reason. You've given me means and opportunity but no motive, Miss Bassett."

"Isn't that your department's job, Sheriff Grady? I could've sworn you said you didn't need Nancy, George, and Bess to solve your cases for you."

On that note, I left the sheriff's office without much satisfaction but with the vague hope that maybe Sheriff Grady would be inspired to do his job, overlook his disdain for my Nancy Drew-like interference, and at least mention my concerns to the lead investigator, or even just to his girlfriend that night at dinner. Hey, a girl can dream.

It was still about fifteen minutes before seven o'clock when I coaxed Miss Josephine to within sight of Larry Sloane's shop on the far side of the docks. The knocking of her engine warned me she'd given me all she had, so I pulled to the side of the road and shut off the engine, traveling the last quarter of a mile or so on foot. Though I was earlier than he'd said to arrive, the front of the shop was already dark.

I grabbed my phone and pulled up a web browser, searching to see if there was a listing for the garage that would show the hours. As luck would have it, I was in one of the island's many dead zones where the service was, at best, as slow as molasses. With the sinking suspicion they were already closed, I made my way around the back in hopes of finding Larry still on site so I could tell him where I'd left the car.

I found a door along the side, and when I twisted the knob, it turned in my hand. Not a single light was on inside, and the air was pungent with the acrid smell of rubber tires and engine fuel. I called out for Larry, and my voice echoed in the empty space. I pulled my phone out again and frowned at the screen. The website I'd been trying to load had finally come up, and on it was a photo of Larry Sloane, captured in profile in a way that highlighted his distinctive jawline. My breath caught in my throat. I'd never noticed it before, but now that I was looking at him from this particular angle, the resemblance he bore to Curtis Strong was undeniable.

My heart thudded against my rib cage as I recalled that Sheila had said her sister dated at least two other men the summer she'd gotten pregnant. If Larry Sloane had been one of them, well, let's just say I suddenly had some insight into what Sheila had always wondered about.

Noah. His name echoed in my head as strongly as if I'd spoken it aloud. I needed to talk to Noah and get to the bottom of things once and for all.

I spun to leave, which was when I felt a sharp pain in the back of my head, and the already dim garage went completely black.

CHAPTER TWENTY

The first thing I became aware of was the sound of two voices somewhere in the distance, though how far away they were from me or who was speaking were both impossible questions to answer. I could only make out that one belonged to a man and the other to a woman before I became aware of something else: a wave of dizziness and nausea which threatened to send me tumbling back into the blackness.

My pulse throbbed against the back of my skull, the pain expanding with each beat until I became convinced my head was blowing up like a helium balloon. I tried to touch my hand to the spot where the aching seemed the worst, which is when I made my next unfortunate discovery of the evening: my hands were secured firmly around a metal pole behind my back with some type of thick plastic tie.

The odor of gasoline and rubber that surrounded me hinted I was still inside the garage. As my eyes adjusted to the dim light, I saw two shadowy figures standing perhaps ten feet away, one appearing to be male and the other female, matching the voices I'd heard as I first came to.

"Are you out of your mind?" the man's voice boomed. "You can't crush up an entire bottle of pills. If that high of a dose doesn't kill her, she'll fall into the bay and drown. Either way, it's murder."

Pills? I would've done almost anything for a couple of ibuprofen to dull the pounding in my head, but even in my groggy state, I doubted those were the kind of pills the man meant. I focused every ounce of concentration on my captors as if my life depended on hearing every word they said. Maybe it did.

"It's not murder. We just have to get her in the boat and let nature do the rest. People have accidents in the water all the time." A chill ran through me as I recognized Audrey Strong's voice. What exactly did she have planned for me? As panic clawed at my insides, my first instinct was to cry out, but fear had welded my throat shut, trapping the sound inside. "I don't like it any more than you do, but she's asking questions all over town. How long do you think it's going to be before people start listening? And then we're done for."

"I don't want any part of this."

"Then you shouldn't have worked so late," Audrey

snapped. "When I sent her the text from the garage phone, I specifically said to come by after hours so you wouldn't be here, and I could take care of this myself."

"If I'd known what you were planning to do to Doug, I never would've taken your car over on the ferry that night and given you an alibi." Though I wouldn't have recognized his voice from our brief encounter at the diner, I surmised from Audrey's mention of the garage that her accomplice was Larry Sloane. "I'm not a murderer."

"Neither am I! Please, sweetheart, you know that." Her pleading tone may have swayed Larry, but the fact I'd just overheard her plotting to give me an overdose of pills and launch my body out to sea left me less convinced. "I didn't mean for Doug to drink that ginger beer on the plane. I just wanted him to mix it into his cocktail that night, like he always did, so he would sleep long enough for me to sneak into his room and find that stupid DNA kit he had Curtis take before he had a chance to mail it in and expose us all."

"I know that. I do." Despite his assertion, I detected a layer of doubt beneath Larry's words that gave me hope. "It's just I guess I still don't get why you thought slipping the spiked soda into the cockpit of his plane would work. What if he'd left it there? Or didn't drink it for weeks? Or, well, decided to drink it before takeoff, like he obviously did?"

"I don't know!" Audrey roared with all the ferocity

of a woman who was incensed at someone questioning her lies. She took a few panting breaths, and when she spoke again, all traces of anger were gone, replaced by a connivingly girlish tone. "I wasn't thinking, okay? I was panicked. You know how Doug was about bloodlines and genealogy. If he'd found out Curtis wasn't really his nephew, he'd have been cut out of the will on the spot and probably would've fired him from Strong Corp., too. Is that the kind of life you'd want for your son?"

Had Audrey just admitted that Curtis was Larry's son? That meant my observation about the resemblance had been just as shrewd as I'd thought. Despite the immediate jeopardy I was in, my lips twitched upward in triumph. As Sheriff Grady had so annoyingly pointed out earlier, up until that moment, I'd only had the means and opportunity for Audrey to kill Douglas. But now I had the motive, too. There was no doubt in my mind Audrey had known when she put the spiked bottle of soda in Doug's cockpit that he'd drink it right then and there and would be sound asleep halfway across the bay. Killing him was the easiest way out, just like killing me would be.

Oh, Fudgsicles, I thought, *they're actually going to kill me!* My muscles tightened, ready to spring into action. I'd been so intent on catching Audrey's confession that I'd momentarily forgotten the peril I was in. As silently as possible, so that neither Larry nor Audrey would realize I was awake, I began to work my hands free of the plastic tie that bound me to the pole. I needed to get out of that garage, and fast.

"I don't know," Larry said, after a pause that lasted just long enough that I suspected his own doubts about Audrey's story were mounting. "Seems like you coulda asked me what I wanted for our son thirty-two years ago, when it might've mattered. I woulda provided for you if I'd known, but all you wanted was to marry that rich boyfriend of yours."

"You don't really think that's true, do you, sweetheart? If only I'd realized back then that Jeremy couldn't have children, I would've known you were his father, and it all would've been different. You know that, right?"

The desperation behind Audrey's words pushed her volume louder, and I used the opportunity to twist my body, tugging at my restraints unnoticed. As I shifted, the slightest flash of red and blue lights, like from a police car, caught my eye through a mostly dark window on the far side of the garage. My heart fluttered with sudden hope. I held my breath, waiting for Audrey or Larry to see it, too, but it was out of the line of sight from where they stood, and they continued their heated conversation unaware.

"Even back then, you knew it was possible." Larry's tone was sharp and bitter, though I doubted Audrey's feelings were hurt by it. A woman who could carry out one murder and plot another while her intended victim was tied up nearby probably had pretty thick skin. Larry, on the other hand, was becoming more worked up with each passing moment. "Maybe not for certain, but you knew he wasn't the only one you'd been with. Still, you went ahead and married the guy you *wanted* Curtis's father to be, the one from the rich summer family, the one who went to college and could afford to buy you fancy dinners and cars."

All of a sudden, the staccato rap of knuckles against a steel door echoed through the garage. It was enough to snap me back to my senses and provide the incentive I needed to give my right arm a good yank. The plastic band on my wrist snapped. I was free but still sat frozen in place on the floor, uncertain what to do next.

"Larry?" a man's voice called from outside. "It's Joe Grady. You in there?"

"Don't answer!" Audrey hissed.

"He'll come in guns blazin' if I don't," Larry spat back.

Wait, guns? I jumped to my feet and scrambled toward the tiny sliver of light on the floor that marked the location of the back door. As delighted as I was that law enforcement had shown up, my confidence in the local sheriff's department wasn't strong enough to remain on the floor like a sitting duck.

"She's getting away!" Audrey screeched.

"Is somebody in there?" the sheriff bellowed.

A deafening bang shook the walls of the building. I tumbled against the solid surface of the wall, feeling around frantically for the doorknob. My eyes squeezed shut against the terrible pain that radiated from the back of my skull. Another boom followed, and I couldn't tell if it was the sound of the door crashing open or a gun going off. I didn't care. All I knew was I had to get outside where I would be safe.

As if by a miracle, my hand brushed against the cold metal surface of the knob. I wrenched the door open and started to run even though every inch of me cried out in agony, and I had to keep my eyes closed so I didn't pass out from dizziness. The air was filled with angry shouting coming from inside the garage. A thundering crack rang out, and there was no doubt this time that it was caused by a firearm being discharged. I willed my feet to move. I went as fast as I could, running blindly until I thought my lungs would burst. Then I plowed right into a firm, warm wall.

"My God, Tamsyn, are you all right?"

I gulped in air, unable to answer. My body trembled. Though this was at least the third time I'd nearly tackled him to the ground since arriving in Summerhaven, the sound of Noah's voice didn't fill me with soul-crushing embarrassment. Instead, I was flooded with the sweet relief of knowing I wasn't alone. If

Noah was here, there was a chance I was going to make it out alive.

"Audrey," I finally managed to squeak out. "Audrey and Larry..."

"It's going to be okay," he soothed, resting his broad hands on my shoulders. "What happened? Tell me everything."

"There's no time. They're coming after me." The edges of my vision darkened, and for a moment, I thought I was going to faint. I turned my head, and out of the corner of my eye, I saw a dark, bird-like shape in a grouping of trees at the edge of the property.

Noah pulled me nearer, the heat that radiated from his body helping to thaw my chilled bones. "Sheriff Grady and his deputy have it under control. They burst in on them just as you came running out. They're not coming after you anymore."

I relaxed my head against his shoulder, my body going limp as an uncontrollable laugh burst from my mouth. "You know, we've really got to stop running into each other like this." Whether out of pity for my recent ordeal or because he'd actually started to find me a tiny bit amusing, Noah laughed at my dumb joke. Then he wrapped his arms tightly around me as I started to shake from head to toe. It was several minutes before I could speak. "Noah, it was Audrey. Audrey killed your uncle, and Larry helped her."

"I know."

"But how? And why did the sheriff...?" My voice

trailed away, my brain too tired to continue. I was steady enough now to stand unsupported, but Noah kept one arm around my shoulder, and I was grateful for the warmth.

"I was heading home from the clinic, and I saw your car pulled off at a strange angle on the side of the road. Considering what I'd found out from that DNA test you dug up, I was worried, so I called Joe. Turns out he'd had a little talk with Sheila about her sister's romantic history; he shared my concerns enough to come out and take a look."

"You ran a test on the DNA kit? Then you know Curtis isn't your cousin. I heard Audrey and Larry talking about it as they plotted how best to kill me and dispose of my body."

"They did what?" Noah's eyes went wide.

"It's a long story. The important part is that I know Larry Sloane is Curtis's father. I heard Audrey say so herself."

"That's the interesting thing," Noah replied. "The DNA test was conclusive. Curtis is definitely my cousin."

"What? But that kit was the whole reason she decided to kill Doug." I stared at Noah, my mouth hanging open as I tried to process this news. "Audrey was certain Larry was the father, and since blood was thicker than water with your uncle, if he found out Curtis wasn't really a Strong, he'd cut him out of the will for good."

"I think she underestimated my uncle," he said, his jaw clenched.

"That means Audrey was wrong about her husband being unable to have children?"

"No, but she'd forgotten there was another possibility for who Curtis's father could be."

"Who was it?"

"The DNA test showed a ninety-nine point nine eight percent paternity match for Douglas Strong."

I gasped. "You mean your uncle Doug was Curtis's father? But how? I thought you said they'd never been romantically involved."

"They weren't, but Audrey did a lot of partying that summer. They both did. It's probably why my uncle was always on her case if she so much as started to drink, because he knew how she got. Very...affectionate, for one thing."

I nodded in understanding. "You mean, the two of them..."

"I don't even know if they knew it. They both were probably too drunk to remember the encounter, but when a young Sheila stumbled in on her older sister and Doug in the guest bedroom...let's just say *her* memory of the event is crystal clear."

"Wow." I shook my head slowly as this revelation sank in. "I don't get it, though. As soon as I saw the profile photo of Larry on his website, I saw the resemblance immediately, even before I heard Audrey confess. Clearly she'd seen it, too, and I'm sure that's why she assumed Larry was the father."

"It turns out the Sloanes and the Strongs are related. I saw it when I accessed my uncle's genealogy files. Third cousins. He found the connection several years back."

"Really? But what about all those rumors of your uncle cheating Minnie Sloane out of a fair price for her house by making up a chemical spill?"

"Oh, that contaminated soil was very real. Curtis has the documentation from the cleanup. It would have cost Minnie a fortune, but by then Uncle Doug had found the family connection, and, well, Audrey was right about one thing. Blood was definitely thicker than water with him."

"Did Larry know?"

"About the contamination being real, yes. But the family connection, I'm not really sure. None of us knew." Noah shrugged. "Look, my uncle wasn't perfect. He wouldn't let a relative, even a distant one, go broke, but finding out we were related to a local lobstering family didn't exactly fit in with his being descended from the great and powerful Davenports narrative. It's not the type of thing he was likely to share."

The sound of a booming voice coming over a police radio shattered the stillness of the evening, and Noah and I watched as the sheriff and his deputy led Audrey and Larry from the garage in handcuffs toward the police cruiser that waited at the edge of the road. As the car pulled away, lights flashing, a rustling in the trees drew my attention. With one loud caw, a massive black raven emerged, spread its wings, and took flight. Douglas Strong's spirit was at peace.

CHAPTER TWENTY-ONE

$\mathcal{I}$t was the night of the new moon, the last day of July, and the start of the ancient feast of Lughnasadh, which marks the traditional beginning of the harvest season. From my arrival on the island at the summer solstice, one-eighth of the witch's year had passed. Though the summer was only half gone, there was a briskness to the air as salty breezes swept across the island and continued out to sea. It had been nearly a week since the incident at the garage, and my life had at last settled into a normal routine at Pinecroft Inn, or at least as normal as life can ever be when you're a bona fide witch.

With Aunt Gwen's help, I was learning the basics of running a bed and breakfast, and I'd finally mastered a perfect blueberry pie, both filling and crust. I'd even handled my magical wooden spoon several times without anything blowing up. Though I hadn't yet been brave enough to raise the issue with her that I wasn't, in fact, a kitchen witch as she'd presumed, but something else entirely, and should be studying other branches of magic instead, I was nevertheless pleased with the progress I'd made. After so much upheaval, it felt strange to feel at ease.

I had just sprawled out on my grandmother's quilt, closing my eyes for a moment to enjoy the gentle chirp of crickets that came through my open window, along with the ever-present scent of wild rose. There was no sign of Gus this evening. Hunting was especially tricky during the new moon, and from what I'd come to know of him, I suspected he would be prowling through the woods most of the night, keen on the added challenge posed by the dark. He was that kind of cat.

Eyes still closed, I stretched my arm toward the nightstand and rummaged around until my hand closed in on a book, but when I opened my eyes, I frowned. The volume I'd grasped wasn't the best-selling beach read I'd been hoping for, but the history of Pinecroft Cove I'd checked out nearly two weeks before. As I opened the book, my stomach tightened—not at the prospect of an overdue fine for keeping the book longer than a week, which I was fairly certain Auntie Sue would waive, but at the sight of a folded slip of paper that slipped from the middle of the book and fluttered to my lap. Unfolding it, I saw it was a photocopy of a newspaper article from fifteen summers before, with the headline reading: *Local Woman Lost at Sea.*

Tears pricked the corners of my eyes. No matter how much time had passed, a part of me would never give up the belief that it had all been a dream, that my mother—excellent sailor that she was—had gone out that day and returned just fine in the night. Somehow, my time at Pinecroft Cove had served both to impress her absence on me in a hundred different ways each day, and also to make that dream of her return more real to me than I'd allowed it to be in years. I stared at the headline, my vision blurred, until a knock at my bedroom door snapped me back to the present.

"Tamsyn, the others are all here," Aunt Gwen told me as I opened the door. "Are you coming down?"

"In a minute," I said, resisting the urge to sniffle loudly and confirm the crying my pink eyes must certainly have hinted at. Without commenting on my appearance, Aunt Gwen held out a shimmering gold scrap of fabric. "What's this?"

"The dress you brought over to Sybil's shop for her to look at. She brought it back this evening. Do hurry down. The new-moon celebration starts promptly at sunset."

"I'll be right there." I took the dress and glanced at the clock. It was nearly eight, and I'd been informed at least half a dozen times that day that sundown was at 8:01. I draped the dress over the chair in the corner. As I did so, a sparkle of purple caught my eye from an object that was tucked into the corner mostly out of sight. I bent down and retrieved the crystal I'd tossed from my hands when I'd been startled by the raven. I watched for a moment as it swung back and forth in my hands. Then I set it carefully on top of the dress and headed down the stairs.

"Tamsyn!" my aunt bellowed from the first floor, just as my foot hit the landing halfway down the final staircase.

"I told you I was coming!" I'll admit my tone was less respectful than it should have been, but she had kept reminding me about the time. Only this time, she hadn't been nagging. When I made it to the bottom step, I saw Noah Caldwell standing in the open doorway.

"You have a visitor, dear," my aunt said blandly before skirting around him to join the rest of the witches on the front lawn. "I've given him some lemonade while he waited."

"Hi, Noah. How's you're...? How are you?" I'd nearly asked how his family was. Talk about putting my foot in my mouth. Did I expect him to start with how his aunt was going to prison for murder, or maybe tell me all about the investigation into his cousin's possibly criminal handling of the Strong Corp.

finances? Rumors had been zinging around the island that Curtis was cooperating with investigators and likely would avoid jail time but had decided to leave Summerhaven for good. Considering what he'd gone through, I couldn't really blame him. Bad memories could be as haunting as actual ghosts.

"I'm hanging in there. I'll be spending the next few weeks closing up Cliffside since it won't be occupied for a while. I'm sorry, am I interrupting?" Noah asked with a glance outside. "It looks like you're having a party."

"No, just an informal gathering," I said, deciding not to mention that we would be casting a circle and setting intentions for the coming month to celebrate the rebirth of the moon and the start of the harvest season in precisely eight minutes, if my watch was correct. Considering his own family troubles, that really wasn't a detail about my life he needed to know. "What brings you around?"

He took a sip from the glass tumbler he held in his hand. "I was on my way home, and I thought I'd stop in and ask—"

"About my head?" I completed, raising a hand to the bruised spot on the back of my head. "No dizziness, ringing of the ears, or nausea. I think the danger has passed."

"Actually, there was something else." Noah scuffed one loafer-clad foot against the threshold.

I sighed. "Headaches, I know. I didn't mention them at first because I do still have a little bit of—"

"No, Tamsyn, I meant I didn't stop by to ask you about your symptoms. It's not a professional call."

"It's not? Then why are you here?" My mind had gone blank, unable for the life of me to puzzle out why he'd bothered to stop by if not to check on my head. Only when I saw the expression of crushing defeat flit across his face did it occur to me that he might have had a social purpose in mind. It was at this point that I wondered exactly how much damage that blow to my head had really caused. "I'm sorry. What I meant to say was how nice to see you."

He studied me for a moment in total silence, until I thought I would burst out of my skin. Then his lips twitched into the ghost of a smile. "Look, with all the strange things going on the past few weeks, we haven't really had any time to catch up since you got here. I was wondering if you wanted to have dinner with me next week."

"Dinner?" I swallowed and nearly choked on my sandpaper tongue. I glanced sharply at the yellow contents of his glass. I never had raised my love potion concerns with Aunt Gwen, and I wondered if it might not be high time.

"Just a friendly meal," he hastened to add, perhaps panicking at my less than suave reaction. "Over at Salt and Sea."

Right. On the one hand, it was just a friendly meal. On the other hand, he'd suggested taking me to the most expensive restaurant on the island. Talk about sending a girl mixed signals. "Well, maybe. I'm not, uh…"

Now I was the one shuffling my feet, kicking my toe against the edge of the door as I contemplated what to do or say next. I can't be certain, but I think if he'd asked me on a date when we were teenagers, it would have felt exactly this awkward. After fifteen years, I had apparently not added a single ounce of smoothness where my ability to interact with the opposite sex was concerned. Fortunately, as the first of eight deep chimes rang out from the grandfather clock on the first-floor landing, I was spared spending additional time ruminating on this fact.

"I'm afraid I have to go join Aunt Gwen and the others," I said. "She's warned me not to be late."

"Oh, of course." Disappointment etched his face. He turned rapidly toward the porch, and I sensed an eagerness on his part to extricate himself from this bumbling encounter.

"Hold on!" I called, suddenly remembering the day of baking I'd just completed.

"Oh, sorry," he said, holding out the nearly empty lemonade glass. "I almost stole this."

"No, it wasn't that. I have a pie for you." Glass in hand, I ran to the kitchen and was back in a matter of seconds with a freshly boxed blueberry pie. "Here you go. I wanted to say thank you for coming to my rescue last week at the garage. If you hadn't shown up when you did with Sheriff Grady, well, I'm not sure what might've happened."

He took the pie with a boyish grin. "I do get to keep it this time, right?"

"Of course," I assured him. There was a heavy ache in my chest as he turned to go, and I called out to him as his foot hit the bottom porch step. "Noah, about dinner. Just let me know the night." The grin that was his response made my heart flutter.

Despite my best intentions not to be tardy, I arrived in the front yard at three minutes past eight and was greeted by the sight of six witches gathered around a small table set out on the grass. Sue Ellen Wolcott was there with Sybil, and Bess Hollings stood with her daughter, Phoebe, on one side and her granddaughter Cassandra on her other. Aunt Gwen looked at her watch with a sigh. "We've already cast the circle without you," she said. She stretched out her arms as if to push aside an invisible curtain. "You may enter."

"Um, okay." Feeling like a fool, I scurried through the imaginary opening. To my utter astonishment, I immediately felt the hum of a soft, protective energy closing around me as Aunt Gwen lowered her arms to close the circle once more. "Sorry I was late. What else have I missed?"

"Normally, we wouldn't hold up the new moon

ceremony for a latecomer," she scolded, "but since this is your first official ritual, we've made an exception."

"Thank you," I mumbled, feeling completely embarrassed. But it wasn't my fault Noah had chosen this of all times to drop by, and it wasn't like I could've shooed him away empty-handed after he'd saved my life. Deep down, I knew Aunt Gwen would've been horrified if I had, and she was just enjoying giving me a hard time.

I stood with Sybil on my left side, and soon Cassandra had shifted her position so that she stood on my right. There were seven of us in total, with six in the circle and Aunt Gwen standing at the table in the middle, which I knew by the candles on it was meant to be an altar. There were seven of them, pure white to symbolize the moon, and they were taken from the altar and quickly passed around until we each held one. Aunt Gwen held hers high above her head. The wick sparked and produced a bright yellow flame the moment her arms were fully extended.

"Welcome, new moon!" she called out, her head tilted skyward. "We rejoice to see you, our goddess, as another cycle has passed, and we move forward on our path."

Aunt Sue Ellen moved to stand beside Aunt Gwen, repeating the upward motion with her candle, which also ignited on its own. "We greet the new day," she called out with every bit as much volume as Aunt Gwen had done. "Today a new month begins, the moon rises, the tides flow. We are thankful our goddess returns and rejoice in her light."

Aunt Bess entered the center of the circle and took her position on the other side of Aunt Gwen, raising her candle as the flame sprang to life. "We ask for wisdom and guidance and for your protection in the coming harvest season. Stand behind us with each step we take, watching and guiding."

The three old witches shifted into a tight circle, standing with their backs to one another and facing out with their candles at chest height. Phoebe walked toward them and took a spot directly in front of Auntie Bess. Cassandra followed and stood between her mother and grandmother. Sybil headed into the circle next, stopping in front of Auntie Bess. Sensing the pattern, I followed suit, coming to a stop in front of Aunt Gwen. There was a gentle rush of air like the tickle of a hummingbird's wings, and suddenly the darkness dissolved as all of our candle wicks simultaneously burst into brightly glowing flames.

"Well done, my dear," Aunt Gwen said to me as my candle flickered brightly.

"I didn't really do anything," I countered, staring breathlessly as a droplet of white wax trickled toward my clutched fingers. "I didn't even light my own candle. I wouldn't know how to make it burst to life on its own like you did if I tried."

"You'll learn. You're doing well." Aunt Gwen

placed her weathered hand on mine. "Tell me, are you glad you came to Pinecroft Cove?"

Was I glad I'd come? The truth was, I couldn't say for sure. It had been a strange six weeks, that much I knew, and nothing like I'd expected it to be. Had I known what I was getting into, witchcraft and spirits, I might have stayed in Cleveland. On the other hand, with no job and no boyfriend, there was nothing left for me there. Maybe this had been the right move for me after all. Though doubt swirled inside me, I gave a tentative nod. "I'm settling in."

"You have a lot of memories here, not all of them good. I know it can't be easy sometimes." Aunt Gwen gave my hand a squeeze and looked earnestly at my face with blue eyes that sparkled with a hint of tears. "But we're counting on you, Tamsyn. On you, Sybil, and Cass. After what happened with your mother, and then Sybil's mother deciding to live in Manhattan, we lost a whole generation. You're the last hope to keep magic alive in Pinecroft Cove."

So, no pressure, then. I looked around the circle, at the women who had become so much a part of my life in such a short time, and my stomach twisted at the prospect of letting them down.

Aunt Gwen's lips twitched in a hopeful smile. "Will you stay?"

Would I stay? I didn't have to. When I'd checked my bank account recently, not only had a paycheck gone in from the inn, but it had been much more generous than I'd expected. I could afford to leave if I wanted. Plus, thanks to the island's second-best mechanic, a man named Rick who had stepped up to help as soon as word got out what had happened to me at the number one mechanic's shop, Miss Josephine was back in tip-top shape and ready to drive anywhere I needed her to go. The question was, did I want to leave?

"Yes," I whispered, my head bobbing with a slight nod. I cleared my throat and repeated my answer more loudly so the rest could hear. "Yes, Aunt Gwen, I think I'll stay."

Even I hadn't been sure what my answer would be until the words had left my lips, but once they were out I knew that leaving had never been an option. As strange a world as my new home had turned out to be, with its bubbling cauldrons and spooky ravens and things that go bump in the night, something told me it was where I needed to be. I still had no idea where I was going or what I would do when I finally arrived, but at least I could find comfort in knowing that I would be surrounded by three generations of women who would protect me and guide me on my path. It was more than I was likely to find anywhere else.

Besides, even if the rest of the whole kitchen witch thing fell through, at least I could now bake a decent blueberry pie.

It was a peaceful night as we sat out on the lawn and celebrated the start of a new cycle together. We watched fireflies flickering in the grass and drank sparkling lemonade as, in the distance, green and purple wisps of light danced beneath the stars. It was one of the rare evenings when the aurora borealis could be seen in the sky, and I soaked it up like magic, which I truly believe it was.

"Have you had any disturbances, Tamsyn?" Sybil asked as she plopped onto the ground beside me, criss-crossing her legs. "Any sightings of ravens, or Doug's face in your dreams?"

"Not a one," I answered. "Everything's been back to normal since the truth came out. I think he's finally at peace."

"That's good news," she said.

"I have a confession," Aunt Gwen announced as she came to join us, pulling up a tattered lawn chair. The expression on her face was almost sheepish, and I could hardly wait to hear what she had to confess. "Those visions you were having of Douglas Strong? I may have been partially to blame. You see, during the solstice celebration last month, the visiting witches and I may have gotten a little carried away and tried some spells that were, well, a little beyond my comfort zone."

My eyes widened. "What exactly do you mean? Aunt Gwen, what did you do?"

"Oh, nothing harmful, child. We just tried a summoning spell or two. They didn't work, or at least, I didn't think they did. Only now that I look back, I wonder if that wasn't the reason you started seeing what you did."

"Will I always see them?" I asked.

"No, I don't think so," she assured me, much to my relief. "It isn't in the nature of kitchen witches to see ghosts."

Some of the relief I'd felt subsided at this news because I, unlike Aunt Gwen, was fairly certain I was not a kitchen witch. And though I wasn't sure, I was starting to suspect my mother might not have been one, either. The more I thought about it, the more convinced I was that my mother had heard spirits. Perhaps she'd seen them, too, though I guessed I would never know for certain. Still, I hoped Aunt Gwen's prediction was correct. I could happily live the rest of my life apparition free.

It was nearly midnight when we closed the circle, and the others left for home. I followed Aunt Gwen into the house, piling our used glasses in the sink. "Should I wash them tonight?" I asked.

"No, they'll keep until morning. You should head up to bed and get some rest."

"I think I will," I said as I reached the back staircase and placed my foot on the first step. "I hope I remembered to turn the quilt down before I left the room, or Gus will be terribly upset."

"Okay, good night, dear," Aunt Gwen said, her fatigue making her sound more absentminded than usual. I was halfway up the stairs when I heard her ask, "Who is Gus?"

I chuckled, shaking my head as I continued on. Old age was getting to her, that was for sure, if she couldn't remember the name of her own darned cat.

The first thing I noticed as I entered my room, aside from the stifling scent of roses, which I'd mostly grown accustomed to by now, was that while the quilt had indeed been turned down, Gus was not on it. Still mindful of that time he'd flown out the window, my eyes darted around the room. They got exactly as far as the chair in the corner before my swiveling neck came to a sudden halt, to the popping and snapping of several unhappy tendons. My whole body began to hum with an energy I couldn't explain, except that it was almost definitely tied to the woman who was sitting in the chair, one hand stroking the massive, furry black cat who sat on her lap like a happy princeling.

"Gus! Who is this?" I demanded, too shocked to know what else to say.

"Hiya, Tamsyn," the woman said. "How's tricks?"

Time stopped as I studied every inch of her, this mysterious woman who was sitting in my bedroom, dressed in the sleeveless, gold 1920s' party dress. Her brilliant red hair was perfectly coiffed in classic finger waves, a narrow band of jewels encircling her forehead while the plume of a black ostrich feather framed the back of her head. From the hand that wasn't busy petting Gus, I glimpsed my purple crystal dangling hypnotically on its silver chain. To look at her face was like looking in a mirror. I swallowed hard, my throat threatening to trap my voice inside. "Lillian?" I managed to say.

"That's me. Nice to meet you. Oh, and thanks for taking care of my cat."

"Oh, uh..." I stammered, staring at the furry beast whose presence had tormented me since the day of my arrival. "What do you mean *your* cat?"

Lillian laughed, a girlishly lilting giggle that did absolutely nothing to answer the questions that swirled in my head. Though she appeared in every way to be solid, as she shifted in the chair, I detected a shimmer that let me know my guest wasn't quite flesh and blood after all. At the same time, the silver bracelet I'd grown so accustomed to wearing, which I'd nearly forgotten about, began to emit a radiating warmth that encircled my wrist. I was as close to certain as I could be that my late-night visitor was a ghost, but if that were true, what did that make the cat? As if sensing I was thinking of him, Gus jumped from her lap and landed on the bed, promptly curling up as if nothing out of the ordinary was going on.

"Pardon me for asking," I said, not really sure how to address a spirit who was neither in a dream nor a foot tall and covered in feathers, "but how did you get here?"

"You know," Lillian rolled her shoulders and gave

them a saucy shake, "I'm not quite sure. One minute I was out on the water, next it was dark, and then, all of a sudden, boom. Here I am."

My mind was reeling. "Not to be blunt, but you're dead, right?"

"Don't know." The apparition shrugged. "I guess so. I seem to be togged to the bricks and hitting on all sixes now, though."

I had absolutely no idea what any of that meant, but frankly, Lillian's slang was about the least confusing thing going on at that moment. I glanced longingly at the stack of books from Madame Alexandria that I had yet to read, wishing I had been a bit more studious the past week. "So, now what—I help you cross into the light or something? The last spirit I met was a bird, and he just sort of flew away." I flapped my arms too mimic a bird in flight.

"The light? Oh, heavens no. You and I have way too much to do to waste any time looking for a light." Lillian laughed, clapping her hands together like a delighted child on Christmas morning.

I watched in dumbfounded silence as my new spirit friend twirled around the room.

"Meow," said Gus.

I turned to him and glared. "Don't you start with me, too."

A dizzy and breathless Lillian collapsed into her chair with another outburst of infectious giggles. "Oh, Tamsyn. This is going to be so much fun!"

Fun? As far as I could tell, I'd just landed myself in a world full of trouble.

This story is over, but the adventure has only just begun! Don't miss Tamsyn's next magical mystery in *Covens, Cakes, and Big Mistakes,* coming soon.

A NOTE FROM NICOLE

It was nearly twenty-five years ago when the first spark
of the idea that would eventually become this book lit
up my brain. I'd been invited to stay with friends at
their house in Northeast Harbor, a cute little village on
Mount Desert Island, Maine. Having grown up on the
west coast, this was only the second time I'd visited
Maine, and I found the whole experience magical, but
what really caught my imagination was the thought
that, in only a few weeks' time, the summer folks like
me would return home, and who knew what kind of
interesting things could happen then?

Ghosts. That's where my mind went straight away,
naturally. Ghosts.

Over the years, I've thought about that cedar-shin-
gled house a lot. During all that time, my imaginary
island grew more remote, the mysteries that took
place there more magical. Slowly, a whole cast of char-

acters took shape, until finally the time was right to put the words on paper, (or laptop, as the case may be, since it isn't 1996 anymore).

So that's how the Witches of Pinecroft Cove came to be. I hope you enjoyed this first adventure with Tamsyn, Gus, Lillian, Aunt Gwen, Sybil, Cassandra, Noah, and the rest of the residents of Summerhaven Island. It was a joy to bring them to life, and I look forward to sharing many more of their stories with you.

Special appreciation goes to my beta readers: Tabitha, Vicky, Patti, and Eva. Thank you also to Em, Paula, and Kelly for editing my manuscript until it shone. Also, a big shout out to Victoria for the amazing cover art, and Stephanie for the audio narration.

The next book in the series, *Covens, Cakes, and Big Mistakes*, will be coming soon. Be sure to sign up for my newsletter to be notified of new releases, subscriber-only giveaways of signed paperbacks, ebooks, and audio, plus special behind-the-scenes articles, and more.

Subscribers also receive a free PDF replica of the Bassett family grimoire, filled with all the recipes featured in the series, plus fun hints about the Bassett family and the enchanted island of Summerhaven, Maine.

Visit me at NicoleStClaire.com

ABOUT THE AUTHOR

Nicole St Claire lives in Massachusetts where she writes paranormal cozy mysteries when not at the beck and call of her three fluffy feline fur balls. You can often find her dressed in vintage costume on her way to a ball, or perusing antique cookbooks for the perfect recipe to make when hosting her next Victorian afternoon tea. Yes, her hobbies are a little odd.

Made in the USA
Monee, IL
23 June 2021

72177167R00178